A Murder for Master Wat

A Murder for Master Wat

The interminable

Chronicles of Brother Hermitage

by

Howard of Warwick

From the Scriptorium of
The Funny Book Company

The Funny Book Company

Published by The Funny Book Company
Crown House 27 Old Gloucester Street
London WC1N 3AX
www.funnybookcompany.com

Copyright © 2021 Howard Matthews
All rights reserved. No part of this publication may be reproduced, copied, or distributed by any means whatsoever without the express permission of the copyright owner. The author's moral rights have been asserted.

Cover design by Double Dagger.

ISBN 978-1-913383-26-8

Scriptorial appreciation is due to:
Mary
Susan Fanning
Karen Nevard-Downs
Lydia Reed
Claire Ward

by Howard of Warwick.

The First Chronicles of Brother Hermitage
The Heretics of De'Ath
The Garderobe of Death
The Tapestry of Death

Continuing Chronicles of Brother Hermitage
Hermitage, Wat and Some Murder or Other
Hermitage, Wat and Some Druids
Hermitage, Wat and Some Nuns

Yet More Chronicles of Brother Hermitage
The Case of the Clerical Cadaver
The Case of the Curious Corpse
The Case of the Cantankerous Carcass

Interminable Chronicles of Brother Hermitage
A Murder for Mistress Cwen
A Murder for Master Wat
A Murder for Brother Hermitage

The Umpteenth Chronicles of Brother Hermitage
The Bayeux Embroidery
The Chester Chasuble
The Hermes Parchment

The Superfluous Chronicles of Brother Hermitage
The 1066 from Normandy
The 1066 to Hastings
The 1066 via Derby

The Unnecessary Chronicles of Brother Hermitage
The King's Investigator
The King's Investigator Part II

The Meandering Chronicles of Brother Hermitage
A Mayhem of Murderous Monks
A Murder of Convenience
Murder Most Murderous

Brother Hermitage Diversions
Brother Hermitage in Shorts (Free!)
Brother Hermitage's Christmas Gift

Audio
Hermitage and the Hostelry

Howard of Warwick's Middle Ages crisis: History-ish.
The Domesday Book (No, Not That One.)
The Domesday Book (Still Not That One.)
The Magna Carta (Or Is It?)

Explore the whole sorry business and join the mailing list
at
Howardofwarwick.com

Another funny book from The Funny Book Company
Greedy by Ainsworth Pennington

A Murder for Master Wat

Caput I	We're Not Going	1
Caput II	We Are Going Then	17
Caput III	Moot	31
Caput IV	Malicious In Tent	42
Caput V	The Element in The Loom	55
Caput VI	The Grey Guild	67
Caput VII	The Moot Money Motive	80
Caput VIII	Wat the Wonderful	92
Caput IX	Funny Shades of Grey	104
Caput X	The Sheriff of Nottingham	114
Caput XI	Osbert the Expert	126
Caput XII	Escape, Please	138
Caput XIII	Where do Dead Weavers Go?	149
Caput XIV	Room with a Loom	159
Caput XV	I Know Who Did It. No, I Do	169
Caput XVI	All Together Now	180
Caput XVII	The Taking of Wat	192
Caput XVIII	Before the Killers Strike Again	205
Caput XIX	The Chase is Moot	216
Caput XX	A Very Grand Murder	228
Caput XXI	Follow That Guild	240
Caput XXII	The Grey Guild Confesses	252
Caput XXIII	What a Rotten Lot	264
Caput XXIV	What's the Expression?	277

A Murder For Brother Hermitage   283

Caput I: We're Not Going

'Upon the rise of Monday next,
All gather and take heed.
For weavers far and wide will meet,
And so it is agreed.
Take up your warp, take up your weft,
Make haste, a lot's in hand.
And travel far across the land,
To the moot in Nottingham.'

'𝕳onestly,' Wat the Weaver threw the parchment down on the floor in front of him. 'Lot's in hand - Nottingham? I ask you. Anyone would think it's a guild for bad poets and not weavers at all.'

'Shouldn't it be Snotingeham, anyway?' Brother Hermitage frowned his familiar irritation at linguistic improprieties niggling at him. 'They haven't even got the word right. I'm sure the great Saxon chieftain, Snot, would be very disappointed to hear that the place's name was being changed already.' He shook his head at this sad abuse of language. 'In years to come, the people of England may even forget that there was a great Snot here at all.'

He snatched the document from the floor and brushed the poor thing down, sympathising with it at such shocking treatment. He examined it and saw that although it was a reasonable piece of work, there was a certain carelessness about the script. The majuscules in particular displayed a haphazard quality. It was probably produced by one of those wandering scribes of loose quill, the sort who would write anything for money. He couldn't resist letting a low "tut" pass his lips.

'I hear the Normans are building a castle there,' Cwen observed with a snort. 'Place will probably be called Normaningham before long anyway.'

Hermitage, Wat and Cwen were sitting in Wat's private chamber on the ground floor of his workshop enjoying the end of their noonday meal, freshly delivered by Ern from the tavern in town. The workshop apprentices were enduring the products of Wat's kitchen, summoned into existence by his cook, Mrs Grod. Summoned like demons from the nether regions of culinary hell where they had probably been thoroughly festered.

'The whole thing's ghastly.' Wat spoke through a mouthful of bread. 'Who in the world would want to go to a moot with that lot?'

'I'm going,' Cwen said as if there was no question about it.

Wat looked more surprised than disappointed, but then he looked disappointed as well. He shook his head at this ridiculous suggestion. 'Obviously, you're not.'

Cwen looked at him as if he'd said nothing at all.

'You can't,' the elder weaver explained. Not elder by much and certainly not enough to tell Cwen what to do. Hermitage wondered if anyone would be old enough for that.

Even Cwen's own father, Stigand, didn't dare tread that path. They had only recently discovered one another, poor Stigand never having been told that he even had a daughter. On his side, the discovery was quickly accompanied by the realisation that he was to do what he was told. The idea that being a father gave him any sort of authority was soon stamped upon. Hermitage found him a charming fellow full

A Murder for Master Wat

of conversation and anecdote. Granted, a lot of the conversations were about hawks, with which he seemed a little obsessed. Still, there was no reason for Cwen to send him on his way just for asking when she was going to settle down.

She was now casting her thoughtful glance to the ceiling. 'Let's think. Nottingham eh? And we're in Derby. That would make it, oh, just down the road, through the forest. Yes, that's right. It's just down the road. There we are. I can go.' She sounded surprised by her own argument. 'I even know the way and can do it all by myself.'

Wat sighed and ran his hand through his curly black hair, usually a sign that he was preparing for a difficult and possibly never-ending conversation.

Hermitage imagined that Wat's concern was not that Cwen, a slight young woman of only seventeen years (or twenty, depending who you spoke to), would come to harm on the road.[1] She was very capable of looking after herself. It would be more charitable to send warning to the robbers hiding in the Nottingham forest that Cwen was coming.

No, Wat's concern was obviously something about this weavers' moot and Cwen's presence at it.

She folded her arms. 'You're not going to go on about women weavers again, are you?' This sounded more like an instruction than a question.

'I'm not, no. I know better than to even mention the question anymore. The point is that most other weavers, no, beg your pardon, all other weavers have strong views on the subject. No, I correct myself again, they only have one view. There are no women weavers.'

---

[1] A Murder for Mistress Cwen explains what this is all about. (It doesn't explain much else.)

'But they're wrong.'

'So you keep telling us. We get constantly reminded. The weavers at the moot haven't had the benefit of you being around all day.' Wat didn't sound like he was enjoying this particular benefit. 'They will not take kindly to you turning up saying "hello, I'm a weaver as well, can I join in?" There's probably several of them quite capable of producing the Tapestry of Death to show you the error of your ways.[2] I don't think even you would argue that women can still be weavers when they're dead.'

Hermitage needed to step in before the conversation started getting too lively for his comfort. He was between them in age and had to step between them quite frequently as well. He knew that they harboured respect and affection for one another but not usually in the same harbour. 'There's a weavers' moot then?'

'There is,' Wat seemed grateful for the change of subject, even if it was only slight. 'Every few years weavers gather for the Grand Moot. They come from all over and talk weaving for days on end. And try to sell as much as they can get away with, of course. According to the guild, the last moot was a great success. What I heard from the local folk was a different picture.' Wat shook his head, sadly. 'A lot of them had rented out rooms to travelling weavers.'

'Probably good for the local population then.' Even Hermitage, whose total understanding of commerce comprised how to spell it, could see that this would be a boon.

'Not if you've got a gathering of rowdy weavers away from home in your house with you. There was a lot of rebuilding to be done, and most people found they'd bought large

---

[2] The Tapestry of Death eh? There's a book called that…

A Murder for Master Wat

numbers of tapestries they didn't want.' Wat shrugged and waved towards the parchment. 'Looks like this one is in Nottingham. The last one was about five years ago, in Antwerp. All I can say is God help the people of Nottingham.'

'Saint Eligius.' Hermitage nodded.

'Eh?' Wat shook his head, wondering what this had to do with anything.

'Antwerp,' Hermitage pointed out.

'Probably,' Wat said, with some resignation. He seemed torn between succumbing to a lecture on the role of women in weaving or a recitation of the hagiography of Saint Eligius.

'Patron saint of goldsmiths,' Hermitage explained. 'He was asked to make one throne of gold for the king of the Franks and actually made two from the same amount of gold.'

'Remarkable,' Wat sighed.

'Of course, he gave away all his own gold and jewellery and went dressed as a pauper.'

'Hm, sounds just like a saint. So. The Grand Moot. They met in Antwerp and now they're meeting in Nottingham.'

'And you've been to this moot?'

'Yes, I was in Antwerp. It's a good place for business, catch up with other weavers and find out what the latest news is. At least I behaved decently.' Wat was clearly engaged in some internal reminiscence. And not a comfortable one, by the look of him.

'But you're not going to Nottingham?' Hermitage thought it odd that a weaver of Wat's reputation would not attend such a gathering.

'Oh no,' Wat held up his hands as if warding off some horror. 'Not me. One moot in a lifetime is enough for anyone.'

'But if it's the Grand Moot for weavers?'

'The Grand Moot probably being organised by the most boring weaver in Christendom, old Hemlock.' Wat sighed as if the thought of this fellow alone was enough to induce torpor.

'Hemlock?' Hermitage asked. 'Funny name for a weaver.'

'It's not his real name. It's just what we call him because most people would rather take hemlock than spend an hour in his company.'

'What's his real name then?'

Wat frowned and thought hard. 'No idea,' he shrugged. 'Even if I could avoid him there's the rest of the weavers' guild. I think you know their opinion of me.'

Hermitage did know. And he knew why they thought as they did. And he knew that they were largely correct. 'But you have changed. The tapestry you produce now is wholesome and uplifting.'

'Yes, it is now.'

'But it didn't use to be.' Hermitage had to accept that it didn't use to be. It didn't use to be wholesome and uplifting in the same way that dung gathering is not wholesome or uplifting. In Wat's case it was making tapestry that revealed the most intimate secrets of men and women; mostly both together. As Hermitage thought about it he considered that dung gathering probably was quite wholesome and uplifting in comparison. 'So why did you go to Antwerp?'

'Much more broad-minded folk in Antwerp. They positively encouraged the very widest range of subject matter.'

Hermitage coughed at that thought.

'The Saxon Weavers' Guild is a gathering of old men who don't want anything to change.'

A Murder for Master Wat

'Like accepting women weavers,' Cwen pointed out.

Now Wat coughed. 'The point is, I was welcome in Antwerp, I will not be welcome in Nottingham.'

'All the more reason for me to go,' Cwen said. 'Got to be a useful place to find out what's going on in the world. I could come back and tell you.'

'And what makes you think the Grand Moot will tell you anything? They're bad enough at giving away secrets to one another, never mind a strange woman wandering about the place.'

Cwen did give this some thought. And then came up with a fine idea. 'I might be a customer. A tapestry collector come to look for the latest thing.'

Wat looked her up and down. 'I don't think so.'

'Well, I'm going anyway so you'll just have to get used to it.'

Wat looked resigned and exasperated at the same time. 'Please yourself. Just don't blame me if they throw you out without speaking to you. And don't come back here in a foul mood and take it out on us.'

Cwen glared.

'And for God's sake don't tell anyone you work here. That'll be the final straw. They'll be coming up the road with flaming torches before you can thread your needle.'

Cwen said nothing at this, and Hermitage hoped that she would exercise discretion. Cwen's discretion needed all the exercise it could get as it was in very poor condition. He did have a thought which might be helpful though. Then again, maybe not. So few of his thoughts were helpful at the end of the day.

'What if I went as well?'

'A monk at a weavers' moot. What would you be doing there?'

'Oh, I don't know. Considering new works for my monastery?'

'From what you've told us, none of your monasteries would have anything as luxurious as a tapestry.'

'But this moot wouldn't know that. I could just be browsing around. Cwen could be my sister. We're not that far apart in age.' As he said this he thought it sounded rather exciting. He immediately realised it was deceitful and frowned at his own thinking.

'She doesn't look like a nun.'

'Not that sort of sister. A real sister. Like a brother, only a girl.'

Wat simply sat and looked at both of them, gently shaking his head. 'I can assure you that it won't be worth the bother. I don't know what sort of thing you think this moot is, but whatever you're thinking, it's not like that. This is organised by the guild. The Saxon guild in the hands of Hemlock. The man who thinks a four-day lecture on wool is rushing things a bit.'

'Ah,' Hermitage recalled their previous encounter with the weavers' guild. 'Is that Hoofhorn fellow likely to be there, the guild's keeper of ritual? After that other business with the guild, I'm not sure I'd care to meet him again.'[3]

'That's a good thought.' Wat seized on the idea. 'You know what the guild is like for its ritual. That and atrocious rhyme. There's probably a six-hour opening ceremony to be endured. I doubt if The Hoofhorn would officiate himself, a bit too public for him to pop up, but even so. You could be recognised.'

'Excellent.' Cwen scooped the last crumbs from her

---

[3] The Tapestry of Death again. (No more footnotes about it for a while now.)

A Murder for Master Wat

wooden plate and dropped them into her mouth. 'Once they recognise me I can tell them I'm a weaver now and ask to join the guild.'

'Ha! Do that and you won't have to worry about finding your way back from Nottingham. They'll probably put your body on display as a warning.'

'Oh Wat, really,' Hermitage chided. 'It's only weaving. It can't do any harm just to go and see what's happening. After all, as Cwen says, Nottingham is just down the road and if these things happen so seldom it would seem a waste to let this one go by.'

Wat finished his own plate now and stood to take it away and get back to work.

'Surely the workshop needs to know something of this moot? After all, you do still make tapestry. What if there is some great innovation that you miss through not attending?'

'Great innovation? In weaving? If they have come up with something, it'll be a miracle and I can always get it from someone. There are still weavers who talk to me you know.' Wat seemed to have given up on the idea of stopping Cwen from going but was showing no more interest himself. He turned back to Hermitage. 'What if there was an investigators' moot, would you go to that?'

'A what?' Hermitage asked, the very acting of putting the words together sending a shiver down his habit.

'Yes,' Wat warmed to the idea. 'For all you know King William has appointed quite a few investigators as well as you. You could all get together and discuss the latest innovations in murder.'

'Please, don't.'

'It's a really good idea.' He winked at Cwen. 'Perhaps the king could even come and address you all. You know,

11

encourage you by pointing out how if you don't do what he tells you he'll burn you all to the ground.'

'This is not funny.'

'What do you call a moot of investigators anyway? A pry? A nose?'

'You know very well that I do not want to be the King's Investigator and never have. The thought of spending my time discussing the topic is quite revolting.'

'There you are then. You know how I feel about the weavers' guild.'

As Wat turned again and reached out to lift the wooden latch on the door it was opened from the other side.

Hartle, the old weaving instructor, was coming in, a small piece of bread clutched in his own hand.

'Mrs Grod's?' Wat nodded to it with some surprise.

'God, no,' Hartle almost choked on a crumb. 'Stole it from your delivery.'

'Really?'

'Of course.' The grey-haired Hartle considered the food he was holding. 'I didn't spend years learning my trade to eat the swill you give the apprentices.'

Wat looked confused. 'Do you get from Ern as well then?'

Hartle tutted, looked at Wat and gave a bemused chuckle. 'You really don't have a clue most of the time, do you? I've been eating your meals from Ern for years.'

'What?'

'Come on, Wat,' Cwen joined in. 'Did you really think he's been eating Mrs Grod's horrors?'

'You knew about this?'

'Everyone knows about this.' Hermitage said with a shrug.

Wat simply shook his head. 'The things you find out.'

'The things you find out when you bother to pay

A Murder for Master Wat

attention,' Cwen scoffed.

'I pay for that food,' Wat protested.

'Never mind the food,' Hartle produced his own parchment. 'Have you seen this?' He held it up for Wat's appraisal.

'Oh, not you too? The moot in Nottingham, yes, I know.'

'I'll be taking a couple of the senior apprentices. Just checking that you don't want to go as well.'

'No, he doesn't,' Cwen spoke up quickly. 'But Hermitage and I are going.'

'Ah, right. We can all go together then.'

Hermitage thought that this was probably sensible. Travelling was always a trial, better to do it in company. Particularly if that company included the apprentice Gunnlaug who was spectacularly large and would deter any robbers not already scared away by Cwen.

He also thought that Hartle attending was wise as well. If there were things to be learned from this great moot of weavers, the workshop would need someone there. He recalled his own experience of the great church conclave of 1066 and how he had hoped to learn more about the role of footwear in the New Testament. That experience wound up with him being accused of murder and then appointed King's Investigator, so was perhaps not a good example.[4] He was puzzled though, which was never a good thing. Puzzles had to be solved; no matter how much trouble they got him in.

'Why would Hartle be going with apprentices but you won't? Is it just because you fear the guild won't let you in?' Hermitage knew that Wat deserved his reputation, but he had changed now. Perhaps this was the moment to come forward as the new Wat.

---

[4] The Heretics of De'Ath, in case you were wondering.

'This moot may be your chance to announce your abandonment of the old works. You could let the world of weaving know that the workshop now produces devout and decorative works fit for the whole family. They may even accept you back into the fold.'

Wat gave a small cough indicating that that was the last thing he wanted.

'It's not that,' Hartle said, sounding as if everyone should know this.

'Not what?'

'It's not that they won't let him in because of the old Wat the Weaver. They won't let him in because he's not allowed.' Hartle looked from Cwen to Hermitage to see that they knew what he was talking about. They obviously didn't.

'So you haven't mentioned that then?' he asked Wat.

Wat looked out of the window, showing very little interest in the conversation.

'Mentioned what?' Cwen asked, suspiciously.

'I'm sure I have,' Wat said in an offhand manner.

Hartle folded his arms. 'Wat's not allowed into the weavers' moot because he's not a weaver.'

Now Hermitage's confusion was of an altogether different order. He did wish that people wouldn't put words together that simply made no sense. It was bad enough when the words on their own made sense but he just didn't understand them, which happened quite a lot. 'Wat the Weaver is not a weaver?' No. They still didn't make sense even when he said them.

'Not a master,' Hartle explained. 'Wat has never become a master weaver.'

'Ah,' Hermitage nodded. 'Yes, I did know that. He mentioned it when we first met. Bad relations with his own master and the necessary steps never completed. Then he was making his way with his own, may I say disreputable trade, and the need never arose.' He cast a glance at Cwen and saw that she did not know this. He also saw that she seemed to be having trouble taking the concept in. He then noticed the change that came over her face when she did. She broke into a broad smile. 'Not a master weaver, eh?'

'Never wanted to be,' Wat shrugged as if this really didn't matter. 'I've made more than most master weavers put together and I wouldn't join that guild if you tied me to them.'

'But not a master,' Cwen repeated the words and she looked like she was tasting them as well.

'Thought everyone knew that.' Hartle didn't seem concerned.

A further thought bothered Hermitage. 'Then the apprentices?' He knew very little of trade practises, but he did know that an apprentice needed a master.

'They're mine,' Hartle said. 'I'm the master weaver and the apprentices are mine, not Wat's.'

'It's better for them this way,' Wat said as if it was all a carefully planned scheme. 'When they want to set out on their own they can say that their apprenticeship was under Master Hartle. Better prospects than if you mention Wat the Weaver.'

'Wat the Not Weaver,' Cwen snorted. 'Or even better, Wat Not the Weaver, ha ha.'

'Yes, thank you,' Wat sounded rather bored with the topic now.

'But if you are the master weaver?' Hermitage addressed Hartle, 'why is this not the workshop of Hartle the Weaver?' He realised as he said this that it sounded very disloyal to

Wat.

Hartle didn't seem bothered about this either. 'Wat's ten times the weaver I am. I may be a master in the guild's eyes, but I could never have made the works Wat produced; just haven't got the skill.'

'I see.'

'None of the apprentices have either. Two or three are a long way off, the rest, not a hope. So what would you do? Spend your life in your own workshop producing mediocre tapestry because it's the best you're capable of, or work with a real master?'

Wat gave a modest nod of acknowledgement at this.

'Who isn't a real master,' Cwen put in.

'Isn't an official master,' Hartle corrected with a glance at Cwen. He spoke to Hermitage again. 'If anyone is even close to Wat's skill I'd say it was Cwen.'

Cwen beamed her satisfaction at this.

'Give her a few more years and she might get there. With a bit of hard work.'

The smile moved over to Wat's face now.

'This is remarkable,' Hermitage was having to take a lot in all at once. 'But, Hartle, the tapestries Wat was making were disgraceful.'

'I know. No way I'd have made so much money without him,' Hartle smiled. 'Now I get to run a workshop, make a good living and work with an artisan of the highest quality.'

'I'm not sure I want to go to this moot at all now,' Hermitage sighed. 'If they only let masters in, a monk and a woman have no chance.'

'Only masters, journeymen and apprentices are allowed into the formal moot,' Hartle explained. 'But there's lots else going on. Tradesmen, exhibits, entertainers, stalls of all sorts.

A Murder for Master Wat

It's a big event. All sorts of people go.'

'But then?' Hermitage cast a frown at Wat as it seemed there was more to it than long lectures on wool. He folded his arms waiting for some clarification.

'Alright,' Wat slapped his hands to his sides and faced the room. 'I just don't want to go. I hate the guild, I hate their moot, I'm not going, and you can't make me.'

Caput II: We are Going Then

The road to Nottingham was gloomy with the sulks of Wat the Weaver. He should have known that as soon as he told Cwen that she couldn't make him go, that's exactly what she would do.

'Look on the bright side,' Hermitage encouraged.

'That being?' Wat asked.

'Ah.' Hermitage wasn't really expecting an interrogation. It was just a polite thing to say. 'I rather thought you might be able to come up with one yourself.'

Wat's face dropped even further into his wallow of self-pity and resignation.

Hermitage thought that this was actually quite a jolly occasion. The three of them were accompanied by Hartle and three apprentices, including Gunnaug, who towered over them all and must be frightening off any robbers who were spying them from a distance. Travel was usually trouble but with this many together, the journey could be enjoyed.

The moot in Nottingham was clearly quite an event as the road was full of people, all heading in the same direction. Hermitage had no idea how many usually went this way, but there did seem to be a lot just at the moment. Many of them carried large packs and even bore the marks of the weaving trade: fine jerkins and coats, embroidered with decoration. It was also a reasonable conclusion that they were familiar with the craft as several of them pointed at Wat and sniggered as they passed.

As one particular group came up behind them at a fast pace and moved to pass them by, a singular fellow turned his head and spoke out.

'Well, well, well, if it isn't my old friend, Wat the Weaver.'

A Murder for Master Wat

Hermitage considered this greeting and the greeter and couldn't quite reconcile the two. The speaker had the look of a man who was a friend to no one. His clothes were rather dirty and while his face was clean his hands looked like they'd been somewhere very nasty. His clothes were dishevelled and had certainly seen better days; or perhaps a single better day, after which they abandoned all hope.

The man had the slight stoop of someone trying to go unnoticed, and while he was in the company of a larger group it didn't look as if he was really one of them. In fact, when he spoke, one member of the group seemed to notice he was there and shooed him away. And it didn't look like this was the first time.

'Stinky,' Wat said, with a heavy sigh.

'That's Master Stinley to you,' the rather wretched figure corrected as he drew close.

Hermitage caught a whiff of the very clear justification for why people had changed his given name.

'But not to anyone else,' Wat pointed out. 'And I'm not old, and I'm not your friend.'

'Now then, Watty.'

'In fact, no one is your friend.'

Hermitage's assumption had been correct, then. He was quite pleased about that. Until his natural sympathy for his fellow man took over.

'What do you want, Stinky?'

Master Stinley sighed heavily but seemed resigned to his name. 'Just a fellow traveller on the way to the moot, greeting his brother in trade.'

'There you go again. Not a friend and not a brother either.'

'Ah, of course not.' Master Stinley nodded his acknowledgement of this. 'Still not attained the status of a master weaver then?'

Wat shook his head with resignation. 'And you wonder why no one likes you.'

'Clear off, Stinky.' Hartle had joined them now. 'We don't want to be seen on the road with the likes of you.'

'Me?' Master Stinley sounded outraged that he was being slighted like this. 'I'm happy enough to be seen with the likes of Wat the Weaver, there's not many would do that.'

Cwen had sidled up to Wat's side now to see what was going on.

'Hello,' Master Stinley said, in what can only be described as a very unpleasant manner. 'What have we here then?'

'We'll have one broken nose and one bruised fist if you look at me like that,' Cwen replied. 'And my fists don't bruise easily.'

Stinley held his hands up in mock surrender and backed away. 'Looks like we'll have plenty to talk about at the moot,' he commented.

'It's going to be different this year then?' Wat enquired, sounding mildly surprised. 'People are going to talk to you? After Antwerp?'

'That was a complete misunderstanding.' Stinley sounded very defensive.

'I think everyone understood only too well,' Wat replied. 'That was the problem.'

'Antwerp was years ago. This is Nottingham and there is change afoot.' Stinley did his best to sound knowing and mysterious.

'Perhaps he's going to wash before he gets there,' Hartle suggested.

'You may mock,' Stinley pointed a grimy finger at them all.

'I think we just have,' Wat snorted.

A Murder for Master Wat

'You will see, you will see. Change is coming, you will see.' And with that Stinley backed off down the road in front of them, only bumping into two or three people who moved quickly away when they saw who it was.

'What an extraordinary fellow,' Hermitage observed.

'He certainly is,' Wat confirmed. 'None of the other weavers like me because of what I do. None of them likes Stinley for a whole host of reasons. What he does, how he does it, the way he talks, the way he tries to touch you when he talks, and the smell, of course.'

Hermitage gazed after Master Stinley who was now trying to talk to some other people further down the road; people who were actually shouting at him to make him go away. Seemingly safe from any further contact, the party continued their journey towards the moot.

'But if he is a master weaver?' Hermitage couldn't reconcile the contradictions.

'Yes,' Wat spoke slowly. 'No one's quite sure how that happened. Could be corruption and dishonesty but more likely a mistake. The guild probably meant to do Stanley of Cherchebi and got the name wrong.'

'So he's not a good weaver?'

'Oh, competent enough, I suppose.'

'It's what he uses,' Hartle spoke up.

'What he uses?'

'The things he makes tapestry from.'

'What?' Hermitage was roundly puzzled. 'The wool and such?'

'Wool?' Hartle sounded surprised. 'No one really knows what it is but it certainly came from no sheep. Or anything wholesome, come to that.'

'I don't understand.' Hermitage glanced to Cwen for some

help but she looked just as lost.

'That's probably for the best.' Hartle nodded as if it was wise not to enquire further.

'What does he do tapestries of?' Hermitage couldn't let it go but had a horrible feeling that this Stinley was perhaps a follower of Wat the Weaver. Wat the Weaver of old, the one who produced images that followed the viewer round the room, long after they'd shut their eyes.

'No one knows, really,' Hartle said.

'No one has seen them?'

'Oh no, lots of people have seen them. They just don't know what they're supposed to be.'

'Whatever they are,' Wat shivered slightly, 'they're not nice.'

'Stinley says he's pushing the boundaries of tapestry and that no one understands him,' Hartle explained.

'I think we understand perfectly,' Wat grunted.

This was not helping Hermitage at all, but he was starting to think that he didn't want any more help now.

'And he says he uses authentic material,' Hartle continued.

'What does that mean?' Hermitage tried to think what an inauthentic material would be but couldn't come up with one.

'Well, when a weaver wants to create a scene of bloodshed, a battle, something like that, he'd use the madder plant.'

'Really?' Hermitage was intrigued by this piece of information.

'The roots,' Cwen explained. 'They've got huge roots and they make a good red.'

'I see.'

'Of course, Stinley says that's not authentic so he uses real blood.'

A Murder for Master Wat

Hermitage gaped.

'And no one knows where he gets it,' Hartle concluded with a knowing nod.

'And as for his brown,' Wat added. 'Well, he had to get the name Stinky from somewhere.'

Now it was Hermitage's turn to shiver. 'It's no wonder he has no fellows.'

'There are a few others he loiters with. But no one likes them either.'

'How does he make a living?' Hermitage couldn't imagine how money would change hands for the works described.

'Yet another mystery,' Hartle said. 'And not one we want solved.' He gave Hermitage a warning glance at this.

This rather disturbing conversation had brought them to the outskirts of Nottingham and the throngs on the road were so thick as to slow progress. The town itself rose above the all-embracing forest as if the timbers of the houses were simply higher growths of the trees. Higher growths with doors and windows and roofs of thatch, but it was hard to tell if the town was starting an invasion of the forest or vice versa.

Hermitage's least-favourite, but very real invader of the moment, was already making his mark on the place. Clear signs of construction could be seen in the highest part of the town, near a bend in the River Trent, where King William was having a wooden castle constructed. It had to be William or one of the Normans; no one else was allowed to build anything anymore. Or if they did it would be burned to the ground in pretty short order.

Once this place was complete, it would command the entrance to the town and doubtless those who tried to enter. It looked as if the weavers had timed this just right. Another year and it would have to be a Grand Moot of Normans.

And that was not something that would attract friendly crowds at all.

Hemmed in by the trees that lined the path, the travellers now pressed forward to enter the town and begin their mooting. It looked like several of them had started some time ago, judging from the songs they were singing and the jostling that was going on.

Hermitage wondered why there was such a slow pace to their progress. Yes, there were lots of people, but this was a big place. Surely just walking into a town didn't cause such chaos.

It took quite a little while before they got within touching distance of the first building of Nottingham, and Hermitage immediately saw why there was delay. A table had been placed across the road and a group of fellows stood behind this talking to everyone who tried to pass by. He could understand that a Grand Moot needed organising, but surely they didn't need to know the name of everyone who came in.

When it was their turn to attend the table Hartle stepped to the front.

'Yes?' one of the men behind the table asked in a very impatient manner. He asked this without looking up from a pile of parchment he seemed to be simultaneously searching through and messing up.

'We've come for the moot,' Hartle said.

'Well, yes,' the table man sighed heavily at his parchment. 'Everyone has come for the moot. What group is this? Weaver or not?'

Hermitage saw that this fellow had a trying task to complete but surely he didn't need to be quite so rude.

'Weaver,' Hartle replied, in his own sharp tone.

The man cast a quick glance at the party, summing them

A Murder for Master Wat

up. 'Ninepence,' he said.

'What's ninepence?' Hartle asked, sounding confused.

'To come to the moot. It's ninepence.'

'Ninepence?' Hartle's confusion vanished and his anger and surprise stepped into the breach.

'That's right,' the man seemed unconcerned. 'One master, I assume, and the rest apprentices. Penny each plus an extra thruppence for the master.'

'To come to our own moot? I'm a master weaver, I should be entitled to come to this as an honoured guest.'

'You're entitled to pay more as a privilege. Moots don't just rise out of the ground you know. Things have to be paid for. It's not cheap putting on a moot this size. Ninepence.'

'What are my guild dues for then?'

The man sighed as if he had had this argument too many times for one day. 'The guild dues are for the work of the guild. The Grand Moot is an extraordinary event and extraordinary events have to be paid for.' He had clearly given the exact same answer many times as well. 'It's all in the guild rules and has been agreed by the committee of the guild at its duly convened gathering.'

'I bet you're charging the stall keepers as well,' Hartle growled.

'Take it up with the guild,' the man sounded rather bored now. 'It's either ninepence or you can go home again. Up to you.' At this point, a particularly large fellow, who had been standing a few feet behind the table stepped forward and folded strong arms across a massive chest. This was clearly the one who would help people leave if they were disinclined to pay.

Grumbling loudly and making tutting noises to the people behind him, Hartle reached for his purse.

'Workshop?' the man asked.

'Mine,' Hartle replied, fiercely.

'And who are you?' The man at the table did look Hartle in the face now and paid some attention to the rest of the group as he reached for a quill.

'Hartle,' Hartle said. 'Master Hartle the Weaver.' Hartle emphasised the word "master" and even nodded the man towards his parchment as if he should be making a note of this.

'And the rest are apprentices?'

'Apprentices,' Hartle confirmed nodding towards Gunnaug, who was the most visible of them all.

'And a monk?' the table man noticed Hermitage with some surprise. 'Have monks in your workshop, do you?'

'The king appointed him,' Hartle said, bluntly.

'What? The king appointed a monk to be a weaver's apprentice?'

'No,' Hartle corrected, calmly but with a piercing gaze at the table man. 'We do the weaving. The monk was appointed by the king to deal with all the murders.'

That did get the man's attention. 'Murders?' he squeaked and looked to the big man for some help. None was forthcoming. 'We can't have murdering monks coming into the moot,' he protested.

'Oh, don't worry. He doesn't do the murders, just sorts out who did what after the event.'

While Hermitage could see that this might be an accurate description of investigation, he thought that there was rather more to it than that. This didn't seem the moment to expand on the role.

Hartle was now leaning on the table and addressing the man quite directly. 'Our monk could be quite useful in a moot like this. You know, in case some man with a table got horribly murdered for being a pain in the arse.'

The man squeaked again.

'So, if we could come in?' Hartle slapped his ninepence on the table.

'Erm,' the man was clearly at a loss. 'Is that a woman?' He nodded towards Cwen. He sounded as if he didn't know which to be more shocked about, monks dealing with murders for the king or a woman at the weavers' moot.

Hermitage was about to suggest that Cwen might be his sister. In fact, those were going to be his very words, but he could already see that they weren't going to be terribly satisfactory. He thought that "might" was one of the most useful words there was. Others tended not to agree.

'She's with me,' Wat spoke up.

The man almost climbed onto his table as he looked at Wat. He clearly recognised the weaver and reached for his pile of parchment. He scrabbled to find the right piece, clearly thinking that something horrible was about to happen. 'I've got a note here somewhere. Where is it?' He sounded exasperated as he turned page after page looking for the right piece. 'It's direct from Master Hemling himself.'

'Old Hemlock,' Wat snorted. 'I thought he'd be in the middle of this somewhere. Trust Hemlock to block the thoroughfares of the country just to take people's names and their money.'

'Master Hemling,' the man at the table corrected, pointing a finger at Wat, 'is very much in command of the moot. He has been given the position directly by the Master of the Guild and he has left specific instructions about you.'

'I bet he has.'

The man turned back to his parchment. 'If only I could

find it.'

Hermitage felt such sympathy that he wanted to offer his help. He didn't like to see parchment being treated so roughly.

'Ah, yes, here we are.' The man had found the piece he was looking for and, perhaps like all men behind tables with bits of parchment, he suddenly looked more confident and official. 'Wat the Weaver?' he asked.

'Yes,' Wat replied, disconsolately.

Table man cleared his throat. 'You can't come in.'

There was a silence as if the group were expecting more. The man folded his arms and made it clear that that was all there was to it.

'He can't come in?' Hartle checked.

'That's right.'

'He can't come into Nottingham? To the whole town?'

'He's not allowed at the moot. We've had instructions.'

'But he's allowed in Nottingham?'

'Erm.' Table man was clearly adept at following instructions to the letter. When there weren't enough letters for the situation he got a bit lost. 'The moot's in Nottingham and he's not allowed to the moot, therefore he's not allowed in Nottingham.'

Hermitage sighed heavily at this nonsense and was keen to put the man's reasoning right. 'My dear fellow,' he explained, brightly. 'All of the moot may be in Nottingham but not all of Nottingham is the moot.'

The man turned his head to look at Hermitage sideways. It was a nervous glance as if the man could see murder sitting on Hermitage's shoulder. 'Is he all right?'

'Wat not being admitted to the moot is one thing,' Hermitage could see that he would have to make this very clear. 'But there are parts of Nottingham where it is not the moot. Surely?'

'Make him go away.' The man looked pleadingly towards Hartle.

'It's quite simple,' Hermitage went on, although he thought he'd already made it as simple as he could.

'It's alright, Hermitage.' Wat put his hands up. 'I said I didn't want to go to the moot anyway, so it's not a problem.'

'But,' Hermitage didn't want to give up like this. Never mind wanting to go to the moot or not, this was a point of principle. The principle being that this fellow's argument as to why Wat was banned was simply hopeless. People with hopeless arguments should not be allowed victory.

The queue behind them was starting to grumble now, and the name of Wat the Weaver was being bandied about as if it was the cause of all the trouble. Hermitage was briefly tempted to address them all on the fallacious arguments the Weavers' Guild put forth. He took a glance at the assembly and thought that "fallacious" was probably beyond them.

'It's alright, really,' Wat urged them. 'You go ahead and have a lovely time.' He sounded convinced that their time would be anything but lovely. 'I'll go home and put my feet up. Be nice to have the place to myself for a while. No one to bother me.'

Cwen gave him one short glance, shrugged and then pushed Hartle to pass the table and enter the moot.

'You coming back in?' the table man demanded as she passed.

'Coming back in where?' Cwen looked confused.

'Into the moot.'

'I'm only just going into the moot now. How can I come back in?'

Table man sighed. 'If you are intending to leave the moot at some point and then come back again, I have to give you the mark.'

'I'll give you a mark if you try,' Cwen growled.

'I have to put a mark on your hand. So we know that you've paid your penny. Or you could always pay another penny when you come back?' The man indicated a pot of ink on his table together with the stamp from a wax seal. He held out his own hand to show a blurry, inky stamp on the back of his hand. 'See. If you've got one of these you can come back in without paying again.'

Cwen looked at the man as if he would lose an argument between himself and his own table. Nevertheless, she held out her hand, onto which he stamped the ink. She looked at it once and then wiped it off with her other hand.

The table man sighed very heavily now. 'You'll have to pay again now.'

'Oh, you'll remember me,' Cwen informed him very directly as she passed into the moot, muttering about men and tables and ink.

Before Hermitage could get his stamp he turned to Wat. 'Will you be alright?' he asked, before realising the question was ridiculous. Of course, Wat would be alright alone on the road. It was Hermitage who would be in trouble if the moot didn't like monks.

Wat took Hermitage by the elbow and led him away a couple of steps. He bent to the monk's ear. 'I'll see you in there.'

'In where?' Hermitage asked, wondering where they were going now.

'In the moot,' Wat hissed.

'In the moot?'

A Murder for Master Wat

'Of course. I didn't want to go to their stupid moot in the first place, but I'll be blowed if some idiot with a table and a parchment is going to tell me what I can and can't do.'

'Er,'

'If he'd said, "Ah Wat the Weaver, most welcome, do come in sir," I'd probably have gone home.'

'I don't understand,' Hermitage said. And he didn't.

'You give it some thought, and I'll see you in a while.' He gave Hermitage a gentle shove back towards the table and then wandered nonchalantly off as if going to the moot was now the last thing on his mind.

Hermitage gave the man with the table and the parchment a nod as he received his inky hand. Like Cwen, he thought that the man should probably recall the only monk entering the place. He was also sure that his face was shouting out loud that Wat was going to sneak into the moot after all, but clearly, table men with parchments and ink don't pick up on that sort of thing.

Caput III: Moot

The first thing that struck Hermitage about this moot was the colour. Conclaves of monks and priests tended to be grey or brown or black. A splash of colour was seen as the first step into the quagmire of frivolity and light heartedness; expressions and symptoms of that most lamentable human indulgence, pleasure.

He thought it natural that there would be colour, after all, these people were weavers, but they seemed to be enjoying themselves as well. The chatter was loud and was frequently drowned out by street musicians or hawkers yelling at the tops of their voices. Most of the people milling the streets were dressed in leggings and jerkins and coats of the most outrageous shades. Red, yellow, blue and green all vied with one another for supremacy.

In a moment of his own frivolity he imagined old Father Dour being deposited in the middle of this street. It was that man's proud boast that he had never seen purple.

It was hard to tell if this was the actual moot or just the crowds gathered for it. If church conclaves were anything to go by, there would be a main chamber for the key debates and sessions; a place where the solemn functions of the assembly could be carried out. But then church conclaves were usually attended by a dozen people at most, not the throng that blocked the streets of Nottingham. In Hermitage's most recent experience of a conclave there had only been the main speaker and him. And even then the speaker had died.[5]

He wondered for a moment if the etymology of "conclave"

---

[5] Which conclave The Heretics of De'Ath goes into at enormous length

allowed for a gathering of one. It was a very new term and as the derivation was from the Latin, conclave, a room or chamber, he drew the only possible conclusion; a room was quite capable of being empty so there could be a conclave with nobody present at all. He further wondered how such an event, with no one there to say anything, would manage to resolve any questions put to it. He thought that he might quite like to attend a conclave of no one but realised that his presence would ruin the whole thing.

He soon felt himself disappearing into this rather knotty problem and only now realised he had lost sight of Hartle and the others. He scanned around, thinking that he should at least be able to see Gunnaug towering over every other weaver in the place. There was no sign and he was now carried along by the crowd. He just hoped they were going somewhere useful. At least the rest of the group would be dragged along in the same direction. He was sure they would meet up eventually.

He did get one or two odd looks, being the only monk in the place, but people seemed so taken up with the happy spirit that they either ignored him or simply pointed and laughed.

There were even one or two Normans about, but they seemed thoroughly confused by everything and just scowled at people. Hermitage imagined that they were here to build the castle, and perhaps didn't know that the whole town was going to be invaded by weavers. At least they didn't seem to think that there was any threat in such a gathering. That could make things really ugly. They would probably be best staying in their castle and letting the weavers get on with it.

As he walked on along the road he passed one alleyway off to his right and felt a sharp tug at his elbow as he was pulled from the main thoroughfare. The buildings here were close and tall and the sudden darkness made him anxious and reluctantly expectant about what was to happen next. Doubtless, in a gathering such as this there would be miscreants up to no good, and one lone monk would be an easy target. Not that he had anything worth taking. There were Normans though. They were just the sort of people to hide in alleys and grab passing monks. That made him quake.

'Here we are then,' Wat beamed at him from the gloom.

'Wat!' Hermitage almost shouted his relief. 'It's you. That was quick.'

'It's easy when you put an idiot in charge of stopping people getting in.'

'But surely, if they find that you're here they'll throw you out again.'

'Of course.' Wat winked. 'Just got to make sure they don't know I'm here.' He had a loose piece of cloth in his hand and held it up to show Hermitage. 'I got this.' He unfolded the cloth and revealed it to be a simple hood that dropped over the head. He put it on and held his arms out to demonstrate his perfect disguise as the thing flopped down over his eyes.

'Can you see where you're going?'

'Not really,' Wat admitted. 'I won't be recognised though.'

'You will when you bump into someone.'

Wat adjusted the hood until he could just see out from underneath it. 'How's that?'

'Very good,' Hermitage commented. 'I suppose your clothes are no more flamboyant than everyone else's so you may not be spotted.'

'Who cares anyway.' Wat's bright grin carried a rather worrying tint of mischief. 'Try and keep me out of their moot will they? We'll see about that.'

A Murder for Master Wat

'Well, you're in now, so there we are.' Hermitage had a horrible feeling this was not going to stop here.

'Oh, I'm not going to stop here,' Wat confirmed. 'Time to have some fun, I think.'

'Oh, dear,' Hermitage wilted. Fun was not a good idea at the best of times. This particular time, with Wat in the middle of a moot of weavers who had tried to keep him out, seemed a very bad time indeed.

'We'll follow the crowd,' Wat nodded back towards the main thoroughfare. 'With old Hemlock in charge the moot will probably open with a five-hour speech on the management of nettle cloth in warp-weighted looms.'

'Aha,' Hermitage said, actually thinking that sounded quite interesting because he had not the first idea what it was about. He liked things he had not the first idea about. However, even he suspected that five hours on the topic might be a bit much.

Wat led the way back into the crowd of happy folk, all heading in the same direction. He kept his hood low and hunched his shoulders, as if people were going to recognise it was Wat the Weaver by his neck.

They left the alley and pressed through the crowd again, making some progress as they were the only ones who actually wanted to get somewhere. Everyone else on the road seemed happy to simply amble along and then stop when they saw someone they wanted to talk to. Such was their attention that they only gave passing notice to a monk and a weaver with hunched shoulders and a hood.

Eventually, Hermitage spotted Gunnaug ahead and they pushed on.

'Want to buy a naughty tapestry?' Wat growled in a disturbing voice as they approached the back of the group.

'You decided to come after all, then,' Hartle said, without turning.

'Not going to let Hemlock the boring keep me out,' Wat replied. 'I might even go to his talk and ask questions.' The grin on the face was clear, even if it couldn't be seen.

'Behave,' Cwen instructed. 'You'll get us all thrown out.'

'Me behave?' Wat asked, as if he couldn't believe the accusation. 'You're the woman who claims to be a weaver. Let's see who they throw out first.'

The crowd on the road was still pushing them ahead and Hermitage could now see that this moot did have a centre. In an open space, in what he assumed was the middle of the town, a great tent had been erected. The thing was as big as Wat's entire workshop and was held up by ropes and poles as if some giant spider had started a web, but then abandoned it when someone dropped a tent in the middle.

Around this it seemed that a separate town had sprung up. There were stalls selling food and drink while others offered the products of the weaving trade. Simple canvas roofs had been erected over tables but every one of them was flamboyantly decorated and tried to outshine its neighbour. Ribbons hung everywhere and flags had been hoisted on makeshift poles. These badges of tradesmen fluttered as if there was to be some huge tourney; butchers fighting needle makers for the honour of the field.

Some stalls even had written signs upon them, although Hermitage wondered how useful these would be as none of their own apprentices could read. Even then, confusion reigned and he seriously doubted that any of the sign writers could read either. Some of them were in Saxon, some in French and one very erudite one was in Latin. In this instance Hermitage considered the structure of the sentence and

A Murder for Master Wat

doubted that the particular stall holder intended to announce that his fresh pork was doing the cooking instead of being cooked. Perhaps a monk might be useful here, after all.

The sign above the main entrance to the tent was very clear indeed. In all languages it clearly stated that this was the Grand Moot of the Weavers. It went on to specify that for the opening ceremony only masters were allowed beyond this point. To enforce the restriction another man with yet another table stood at the entrance scowling at anyone who even looked in his direction without permission.

Hermitage idly speculated whether being a man with a table was a profession in its own right or a particular role within the weavers' guild, and whether the man brought his own table or if it was provided. He concluded that tramping the country with a table would be a very tiresome trade indeed.

He also quickly determined what sort of motivation these obstructions were going to provide for Wat. Certainly the numbers actually entering the tent were relatively small, and they were all subject to interrogation by the man with the table. All of those passing beyond carried a mature and serious demeanour and that would clearly be a problem for Wat. Perhaps he could control himself for a few moments and adopt the appropriate behaviour if he really wanted to get in.

There was no way Cwen was going to be able to adopt the appropriate gender if she wanted to get in. Not only was she more female than the masters milling about, she was about half their size. Weaving was clearly a lucrative trade for a master and, judging from the size of them, most of the profit was spent on food.

'Right,' Hartle said, with a wave of his hand. 'I'll see you after the opening.' He turned towards the tent.

'Hold on a minute,' Wat called from under his hood. 'I want to see this.'

'Oh Lord,' Hartle muttered. 'Really? Why? You don't like the guild and you don't like the moot. Why do you want to cause trouble?'

'Trouble?' Wat sounded mightily offended. 'Here am I, a humble weaver, simply wanting to hear what the leaders of my trade have to say.'

'You? Humble? Anyway, they won't let you in.' Hartle gestured to the man at the table who was now sending an impertinent apprentice on his way with language that had nothing to do with weaving.

'There's probably a way round the back.' Wat winked at Hartle and beckoned him to go and distract the man at the table while he sneaked around the side of the tent.

Without a moment's hesitation Cwen followed on Wat's heels. After several moments' hesitation, Hermitage followed them both. He thought that Hartle was right, this could only lead to trouble and perhaps there was something he could do to prevent it.

Wat and Cwen had disappeared now, and when he caught up they were burrowing under the wall of the tent like rabbits. Or perhaps like weasels intent on causing chaos in the burrow.

'Oh, really,' he said, loudly enough to be heard by people with their head in a tent.

The area behind the tent was not guarded at all, but Hermitage thought that weavers probably considered it highly unlikely that there would be an attack on their moot. Hardly the sort of thing to interest anyone.

He considered the feet that were now disappearing under

the side of the tent and wondered whether he should follow or not. Going to a meeting he was not invited to went against everything he believed in. These weavers had been quite specific, masters only. And he was not a master weaver. But they didn't know that two other not-master weavers were, at that very moment getting into the meeting. Should he go round to the front and tell the man at the table? Should he just idly walk away and pretend he knew nothing of this? Should he, in fact, go home and give the whole moot up as a bad idea in the first place?

He found that he was even taking half a step away from the tent followed by half a step towards it as he prevaricated over his actions. The book of Proverbs was clear: He who conceals his transgressions will not prosper. Hermitage knew that he hadn't actually transgressed at all, but the concealment was a worry. But then did not Romans book 16 say keep your eye on those who cause dissensions and hindrances ... and turn away from them? If ever an example of one causing dissension and hindrances was wanted, Wat the Weaver was the man.

Turn away it was then. Hermitage forced himself to leave the back of the tent and return to find Gunnaug and the others. If there was trouble, then Wat and Cwen would have to deal with it themselves. This was only a moot of weavers, after all. It wasn't as if the king and his nobles were gathered in the tent, only too willing to lop the head off anyone who turned up uninvited.

When he returned to the main entrance there was no sign of any of the apprentices. They must have wandered off to pursue their own interests while Hartle was engaged. He thought that he might as well just tour the moot himself, looking at the stalls and entertainments and seeing what he might learn. It would be interesting to discover how the rest of the weaving world operated. He only had experience of Wat's workshop, which he now knew to be Hartle's anyway, and he suspected that it was different from everyone else in virtually every way imaginable.

Browsing around the stalls near the main tent he found some fascinating objects laid out on one particular table. They were strangely shaped pieces of metal and he had not a clue what they were. It was also clear that the stall holder had not a clue why a monk was examining his products so closely and was looking pleadingly around the field, hoping that someone would come and take this strange habit away.

Hermitage wouldn't dream of actually asking the man what his pieces of metal were, so he simply gave a friendly smile and walked on.

The stall holder wondered if there was someone he could report mad monks to.

The next stall was very obvious, it was that of a loom maker. He even had a tiny model of a loom on his table, a clear demonstration of his craft.

'Ah, there you are sir,' the stall holder called to Hermitage and beckoned him over.

Hermitage looked behind him to see if someone else was being summoned. This only caused the stall holder to double the pace of his beckoning, which made it somehow irresistible.

'This is what you need sir,' the stall holder enthused. 'Just what you've been looking for, I dare say.'

'Erm,' Hermitage said.

'The very latest thing in loom construction. Perfect for the large or small workshop. High warp, low warp, wool weft or linen, we can supply all needs.'

Hermitage tried his smile again. It only seemed to

encourage this ebullient fellow, who was now addressing the whole field over Hermitage's shoulder.

'You won't find a finer product in the whole of the moot,' the man shouted out to the passers-by. He was ignoring Hermitage completely and appeared to be simply using him to make the crowd believe that he had a real customer. Why they would think a monk was buying a loom of any height at all, Hermitage could not imagine.

'And for this moot only,' the man enthused. 'We are offering a full set of handcrafted shuttles at no extra cost.' He even waved his hands about at this, clearly considering it to be the most exciting thing anyone had ever heard. He picked up a small piece of wood from his table, probably a shuttle, Hermitage thought, and waved it above his head. 'And not just knocked-up shuttles, oh no. These are our very finest. You won't see a better shuttle at this moot, you can be sure of that. You sir,' the man now called to another one of the crowd, who quickly looked away and walked on.

Hermitage began to wonder how he was going to escape from this. It seemed very rude to simply walk away in the middle of the man's proclamations.

'This brother here can clearly see the quality of the product.' The man put Hermitage in a very difficult position. 'Come all the way from the finest monastery in Germany he has, just to see the looms of Robert the loom maker.'

'Oh, I say,' Hermitage had to speak up. It was clear he had been mistaken for another monk completely.

The man simply waved him quiet and hissed, 'Shut up and play along.' Hermitage didn't think that this was the moment for a game of some sort. 'So, come one, come all,' the stall holder shouted on, beaming at the whole field.

The need for Hermitage to engage in a detailed

explanation of exactly who he was and why he was here was dispensed with as a great cry went up from the main tent of the moot. He imagined that this was the mark of the ceremony that had now begun, probably with some grand statement that the moot was formally underway. The crowd inside had doubtless cheered loudly at the news and business would begin.

Indeed, several of the masters could be seen exiting the tent in a great hurry, probably anxious to be the first out. They didn't look very happy though. In fact, Hermitage thought they had the appearance of men in a state of shock. Surely the opening of a weavers' moot would not be such an alarming experience. It did cross his mind that there might have been some bizarre ritual accompanying the event. Perhaps that had upset those of a fragile disposition.

'Woe, woe,' one of them cried out as he staggered in the direction of Robert the loom maker.

'What's amiss?' Robert called out. 'Got a loom problem needs fixing?'

The man held him with a pale and stricken gaze. 'Master Hemling,' he announced, in a shocked tone.

'What about him then? In the market for a fine loom, is he? Couldn't do better than to come to Robert the loom maker.'

'No, he is not,' the man scowled his disapproval. 'Master Hemling is dead.'

Caput IV: Malicious In Tent?

𝕿he man who had announced this dread news suddenly seemed to notice that Brother Hermitage was standing there. 'Ah,' he cried. 'Just what we need,' and he grabbed Hermitage by the elbow.

'Pardon,' was all Hermitage could manage as he was hauled away to the main tent. This man, like many of the others, was a very large fellow and seemed to possess the strength to go with it. Hermitage concluded that this must be a master as he had come from the masters-only tent. He had little option but to follow but he had a horrible feeling about how being taken to see a dead body was going to go.

'Master Hemling is dead,' his assailant explained.

'Yes,' Hermitage replied, half-heartedly trying to pull back in the other direction. 'You mentioned that.' Surely death had not followed him to a weavers' moot of all places? Was there investigation all over the country, waiting around in tents just for him to turn up?

'And you're a monk.'

Observation was clearly not an issue.

'I am,' Hermitage confirmed as he was dragged across the threshold of the moot tent.

'So you'll know what to do.'

'What to do?'

'With a dead master.'

'What would I know?'

'You're a monk,' the master wearily explained. 'We're just weavers.'

'Well, what do you normally do with dead people? You must come across them now and again.' He considered the master who had appropriated him, and from his age concluded that he must have witnessed death at some point in his life. No one got through their first fifteen years without someone dying nearby.

'I'd send for a priest,' the master explained. 'If it was my death to deal with. But this really isn't my death to deal with, I just happen to be here. And I don't have a priest.' He was now sounding rather irritated. 'All I've got is a monk. So you'll have to do.'

'Ah, I see,' Hermitage felt a wash of relief. He was starting to seriously think that his role as King's Investigator was known and he was being summoned to yet another murder. That really would be too much. 'Perhaps there is a priest about somewhere?'

'Hardly likely, at a weavers' moot.' The master looked puzzled by the idea. 'I don't even know what a monk's doing here.'

'I, er, came with my sister.' Hermitage's lie crept from his mouth waving a huge flag that said, "I am a lie."

'A nun?' the master asked, not spotting the blatant untruth for some reason.

'No, no, my real sister. She's, erm, very keen on tapestry.'

The master now looked as if he was wishing he'd taken the trouble to look for another monk. 'Lovely,' he said. 'Perhaps we could deal with the dead master first?'

'Ah, erm, right oh. You'll still need a priest at some point though. Master, erm?'

'Thomas. Really?' he was disappointed.

'Oh, yes. I'm just a monk.'

Master Thomas was starting not to care anymore, by the look of him. 'At least you can tell us what we can do with him.'

'Do with him?' Hermitage thought that they could have

A Murder for Master Wat

discussed that outside.

'Of course. I can hardly leave him in there for the whole moot. It goes on for a week you know.'

Hermitage was about to confirm that the body could be moved and that he really had no need to observe it personally when he found himself at the back of the tent, with the dead Master Hemling.

'Aha,' said Hermitage, observing the prostrate figure.

Master Hemling was very old, very fat and very dead. None of these facts really required the expert testimony of a monk for confirmation. A small boy could have been brought in who would have been just as capable of verification. Granted, a small boy would probably have pointed and laughed and jumped up and down a bit, rather than feel slightly sick, which was what Hermitage was doing.

The deceased master was on his front, his huge stomach preventing him from lying flat on the ground. His face turned to one side as if looking for someone to come and help him stand up. There was no question of him standing up ever again. The pale face and the single staring eye that Hermitage could see told him all that he needed. A large bump was still emerging over the man's eye, doubtless where he landed when he fell. A man of this size landing on his head was certainly risking death.

'What happened?'

'What happened?' Thomas sounded very confused. 'He died, that's what happened. Was standing up at his loom. Then he fell over. Then he didn't get up again.'

Hermitage looked to the side and there was indeed a loom. It was only a small one, a very small one and Hermitage wondered what sort of weaving could be done on it. He would have to ask Wat. No, he told himself, he would not

45

ask Wat. This was just the simple death of an old man. There was no need to ask anyone anything about it.

Further over to the side, there was a small gap where the wall of the tent met the grass of the floor and he saw something else that gave him a start and caused him to cough and spin back towards the body of Hemling. The wall of the tent dropped back into place as the winking face of Wat retreated.

'He was at his loom you say?' Hermitage asked, feeling very flustered and thinking that it was something to say.

'That's right. It's part of the ceremony. Master Hemling casts the ritual shuttle that starts the moot and then gives his opening address.'

'I see.' Hermitage didn't, but it wasn't important. If Wat had been in the tent at the time he would be able to describe the event. 'Well, he seems to have been an aged fellow. Perhaps the exertion of the weaving was too much for him.'

'It's only a small shuttle.' Master Thomas picked the shuttle from the loom and demonstrated to Hermitage that it was simply piece of wood with a metal toe-piece, which fitted neatly into the palm of one hand.

'But he is old,' Hermitage nodded at the dead master.

'And has now stopped getting any older,' the living master pointed out. 'So we can move him, can we?'

'Oh, yes, of course.' Hermitage muttered a short prayer over the body of the deceased. Despite Wat's report that old Hemling was not the most entertaining company, he had clearly reached the heights of his craft and died doing what he probably enjoyed the most. And it was clear that he had a led a long and comfortable life. His clothing was of the very highest quality and of a pretty significant quantity as well. Just creating a decent jerkin for someone this size probably provided work for several tailors.

Death was always a sobering moment though, whenever, wherever and for whomsoever it came.

'There's one thing we can be grateful for, I suppose,' Thomas said, his head bowed in proper solemnity.

'What's that?'

'At least we didn't have to listen to his address. He had the decency to die before he could start talking.'

'Oh, really,' Hermitage chastised the comment. This fellow in Hemling's trade seemed to be taking the death with remarkable ease, if not a hint of irritation at the inconvenience.

'You never had to listen to him.' Thomas rolled his eyes. Then he had another thought. 'Still,' he rubbed his hands, apparently happy that this was all being sorted out. 'Guild problem now, they'll have to sort him out. I just want him to vacate the tent and as it doesn't look like he's going to do that of his own accord…,' he left the conclusion for Hermitage to draw.

'Are you, erm, not with the guild?' Hermitage thought it a bit odd that a passing master would stop to sort out a dead body.

'Me?' Thomas gave a sharp laugh. 'With that lot? Certainly not. Bunch of fat, lazy good for nothings, spending guild money on their own comfort. I'm supposed to be using this tent later for a meeting of masters from the south. Don't want a dead body joining us, even if he was a guild man. I suppose the guild will have to think about a replacement now.'

'Replacement?' Hermitage confused himself momentarily, thinking that they were going to remove this dead master and then bring another one to take his place. 'For the moot,' he nodded.

'Trouble is, old Hemling was a law unto himself, like most of the guild. The rest of them probably don't have a clue what he was up to.'

'He had no assistant or amanuensis?'

'Certainly not,' Thomas sounded rather offended at this.

'No one who took notes for him, or carried out his bidding?' Hermitage explained, patiently.

'Ah, no, not that I knew of. But then not being part of the guild I wouldn't, erm, you know…'

'Know?' Hermitage suggested.

'Care,' Thomas corrected.

Hermitage was confused now, which happened quite easily.

'You are a master?'

'Oh, yes, but not all masters are involved in guild work. Just because my workshop's near the guildhall I end up getting dragged in when no one else wants to help.' Master Thomas did not sound too happy about this. 'Still, guild problem now. They'll just have to try and pick someone. That's going to be a nightmare.'

'Because it is an honour and everyone will want to do it?' Hermitage smiled his understanding of the problem.

'You jest,' Thomas snorted. 'No one wants to organise a moot. Everyone was just thankful that Hemling was prepared to do it. There was a real danger the guild would choose one of the masters. Someone junior to blame when it all went wrong.'

'But surely it is an event of importance and great significance to the weavers' world.'

'Absolutely. So don't touch it with a long pole on the end of another long pole.'

A Murder for Master Wat

Hermitage just stood and looked as puzzled as he felt.

'You can't please everyone,' Thomas explained. 'So you end up pleasing no one. It's been a year in the planning, this moot, and all anyone has done since the guild came up with the idea is complain. They all complain about everything. Where it is, when it is, how it's been organised, why it's too big, or too small, or not long enough, or too long. They blame the organiser when things go wrong but don't offer any help or thanks when they go right. Every minute of the night and day there's one weaver or another moaning about something that isn't right.

'Then, when we get started, the tradesmen don't like where their table's been put or they don't want so-and-so next to them. And if they don't make sales they start asking for their money back.

'The townspeople complain about the noise and the behaviour, saying that all the weavers do is get drunk and cause trouble.'

'Ah,' Hermitage hoped they could get back to the dead body soon.

'And when the weavers do get drunk and cause trouble, you have to sort it all out. Who'd want a job like that?'

'Hemling did it willingly?'

'Seemed to. Even gave himself a chain of office.' Thomas nodded towards a fine chain that hung around Hemling's shoulders. Hermitage hadn't noticed it before, probably because it was round the neck of a dead man and he tended not to look too closely if he could avoid it.

'But he dealt with all these problems?'

'Lord, no. He just let people get on with it and went around looking important and saying how well everything was going. That was the bit he liked. If anyone wanted to discuss anything with him, he'd start off on one of his lectures and they'd soon give up. Either that or he agreed with everyone. If someone complained about someone else, he'd agree with them separately that they were both right. Then, when the trouble blew up, he'd be long gone.'

Hermitage had experience of people looking important but not actually doing anything helpful at all.

'Still,' Thomas clapped his hands. 'Can't hang about here all day. I suppose I'll have to get old Hemling out of the way or my meeting will be a very unusual affair. I'll get some apprentices to shift him.' He appraised the deceased. 'Mind you,' he added, 'I'll need a lot of 'em. Still, they'll probably enjoy dragging a dead guild master across a field, ha ha.'

'Some respect, surely,' Hermitage complained.

'Oh, don't worry. We'll give him all due ceremony. He had been around forever. I don't suppose we can just dig a hole and bury him?' Thomas looked pleadingly at Hermitage.

Hermitage was shocked by the very idea. 'Certainly not. You must get a priest and give him proper Christian burial in hallowed ground.'

'Hm.' Thomas reluctantly accepted that this was the proper thing. 'Bound to be some of that round here somewhere.'

'Where was he from?' Hermitage asked, thinking that Hemling's home town might welcome the return of a successful son at the end of his life.

'Up north somewhere, but we're not shifting him outside Nottingham.' Thomas strode off to the exit of the tent. 'We'll find a priest, and this can be Hemling's resting place. If his folk want to visit him, they'll know where to come.'

Hermitage was now alone with Hemling and felt that he really couldn't go. It was unfair to leave the deceased on his own, both for the sanctity of the situation and to prevent any disreputable types helping themselves to the old master's finery.

Rather than actually spend time too close to the deceased he wandered over to the small loom that had been the site of Master Hemling's final act. He considered the construction of the device. It was no taller than his head and would be dwarfed by any of the looms in Wat's workshop.

It was a simple frame of wood, like a doorway. Two uprights on either side supported a cross beam from which threads dangled to near his feet; Wat had told him many times to call them warps, not dangles. These threads were gathered together and tied to weights at the bottom to keep them straight and taut. And each of the threads seemed to glitter slightly, as if made of some remarkable material.

Across the middle of the whole frame, about the height of Hermitage's waist, a pole ran from left to right, resting in wooden hooks that stuck out from the front of each upright pillar. From this pole more threads ran back to the middle of the warp threads dangling from the top.

He could see that only every other dangling thread was attached to this pole and that the pole could be moved. If it was moved back and forth, the threads it was tied to would be pulled in and out of the main body of the dangling threads. The shuttle, with its own thread attached could then be passed behind these and so the weaving progressed.

He was glad that he could understand all this from a simple examination. It was actually a much less sophisticated version of the large looms Wat had. Some of his were like this but others were much more complex with foot pedals and all sorts of attachments.

'Aha, the old warp-weighted loom,' Wat strode into the

tent, rubbing his hands together. 'I remember this thing from my apprentice days.' He stood next to Hermitage and patted the loom as if greeting an old friend. 'Pile of rubbish,' he concluded.

Hermitage just looked on.

'It might have been useful once upon a time but not now. This thing belongs on a fire, warming people up. Probably the most useful thing it could do now.'

'The master who just left said it was used to declare the moot open.'

'That's right. It's certainly no good for making cloth, or anything else, come to that. Rumour is that it was Hemling's first ever loom and he kept it. God knows why.' Wat now gave the thing a good shake, as if expecting it to fall apart at the slightest provocation.

Hermitage only now realised that Wat had walked into the tent, and not crawled under the wall. 'What were you doing, skulking under the tent?'

'Skulking?' Wat sounded offended. 'I wasn't skulking.'

'What were you doing then?'

'Escaping.'

'Escaping?' That was much worse, surely.

'Absolutely. Cwen and I sneaked in to watch the opening. Squeezed under the wall. We were minding our own business at the back when old Hemling here did his dropping dead trick.'

'Minding your own business?' This really was too much. 'You weren't minding your own business at all. You were intruding on other peoples'. When you knew that you shouldn't.' Hermitage folded his arms.

'If you like,' Wat smiled. 'Point is, with Hemling going down, we thought that the last thing a crowd of shocked weaving masters would like to discover was Wat the Weaver and a woman, hiding at the back of their moot.'

'Just when their leader has dropped dead.'

'Quite. Funny bunch at the best of times.' Wat shrugged.

'It seems they all ran out.'

'Yes,' Wat said. 'I can imagine. Last one left might be asked to take over.'

'The master who was here has gone to get help to move Hemling.'

'Quite a lot of help, I should think.' Wat cast a glance at the body. 'Poor old Hemling,' he sounded quite sincere.

'You cared for him then?'

'Heavens no. He really was the most boring, tedious, dull and uninteresting weaver in Christendom. But he was sincerely boring, tedious, dull and uninteresting. Not a deceitful bone in his massive body. Full of his own importance, of course, but he'd talk to anyone, encourage apprentices or reprimand masters if he thought they were damaging the craft.'

'So, erm,' Hermitage just looked at Wat.

'Oh, he thought I was worse than a lop-sided loom. If he'd known I was in his tent he'd probably have died on the spot.'

'He did.'

'Oh. Yes. So he did. He didn't know I was here though, I made sure of that.'

'But you saw what happened?'

'I did. Only from the back, mind. He stood at the loom, cast his shuttle, pulled the heddle, staggered backwards and fell. And then didn't get up again. That was that.'

'You didn't rush over to lend aid?' Hermitage asked, the criticism quite clear in his head.

'Ha,' Wat gave a hollow laugh. 'Mind you, if poor old

Hemling had seen my face looming over him it might have brought him back to life, just so he could throw me out.'

Hermitage tutted.

'There were plenty of people running to help.' Wat excused his inaction. 'Well, one or two.' He looked at Hemling again and sighed. 'What a way to go. He would have approved.' As he nodded to himself at this thought, he ran his hands along the warp threads, as if strumming a lute. 'Ow, bloody hell,' he swore as he pulled his hand back.

'What is it?'

'They're metal,' Wat gazed at the loom, looking as puzzled as Hermitage usually felt.

'Metal?'

'Well, gilt, probably. On a silk thread. Used in the very expensive works, for kings and the like. What's Hemling doing carting around a loom strung with gilt thread?'

'He thought it appropriate?' Hermitage suggested. 'For ceremonial use.'

Wat nodded. 'You could be right. Just the sort of thing he would do. Have the very best thread on his private loom. Not because he wanted it for himself but because he was the leader of the moot.' He bent to examine the loom more closely. 'Hello,' he said, in a very thoughtful manner.

Hermitage looked around the tent.

'What's this then?'

Hermitage now looked at the loom, knowing perfectly well that he wouldn't know what it was.

Wat had squatted down and was looking at the weights hanging at the bottom of the warp threads.

'Something wrong?'

Wat now sat on the ground at the foot of the loom and started examining the weights, one by one.

A Murder for Master Wat

He turned a very serious face to Hermitage. 'I think you'd better go and find Hartle and bring him here.'

'Ah, right you are.' Hermitage nodded, happily. This was doubtless some fine detail of the weaver's trade that warranted close examination.

'And when you get back,' Wat added as Hermitage started to walk off, 'we'd better have a closer look at Hemling.'

'Really?'

'Yes. If I'm right we might need to start thinking about who killed him.'

Caput V: The Element in The Loom

Hermitage's mission to find Hartle was filled with dread. Dread that he would locate the old weaver, bring him to the tent and there they would conclude that Hemling had been murdered and that Hermitage was just the man to investigate the whole business and find the killer.

He knew that this was his curse, and there was nothing he could do about it. Wherever he went, or wherever he was summoned, there would be death and investigation. Was there to be no respite though? On the other occasions, there had been some mystery or catastrophe that prompted all the trouble. Here he was on a nice day out and someone went and got murdered.

He had no doubt that this was murder. He hadn't seen the body in detail, he hadn't examined the circumstances, he didn't know who was involved. All he knew was that he was here, in which case it would be murder. He could be walking along a clifftop when a lone figure, half a mile away was blown over the edge by the wind. That would be murder.

An old man passing peacefully from the world on his deathbed with his family gathered around would be murder. But only if Hermitage was there.

He wouldn't be surprised if the animals of the forest in his vicinity were being murdered daily. Even the small flying things and tiny creatures that crawled upon the earth were probably victims of crime. At least he didn't have to investigate them. He forced that thought from his head as he could easily imagine King William instructing him to investigate who was killing his bees.

He tried to calm himself by scanning the surrounding crowds for any sign of Gunnaug's head, poking over the top

A Murder for Master Wat

of everyone else. They must be nearby. Hartle was a master; he had gone to the tent to see Hemling's ceremony himself. He would already know what happened. What he obviously didn't realise was that Hermitage was at hand so the death was, in fact, a murder.

If only he had explained his situation to Wat and Hartle and Cwen they could have stopped everyone from leaving. At the moment Master Hemling fell they could have told the crowd that Brother Hermitage, the King's Investigator was within five miles of the place and therefore this was a murder. In fact, the whole crowd was at risk of being murdered, just because Hermitage had come to their moot. He foresaw a time when he wouldn't be welcome anywhere. Villagers would see the King's Investigator coming and simply flee for their lives.

He breathed deeply. One thing at a time, he told himself. Well, one murder at a time.

As he brought his attention back to the world around him, instead of the one his head had gone to, he saw that Hartle was right there, standing by a stall eating what looked like half a loaf with a pig inside.

'Hartle,' he called, raising a hand and walking over.

'Hmf,' Hartle mumbled through a mouthful of food. He wobbled his head around to indicate that he couldn't speak without spraying the contents of his mouth all over Hermitage. He was listening though.

'Hemling is dead.'

Hartle nodded, showing little concern. He chewed quickly, holding a hand up to indicate that Hermitage should wait. When he had swallowed he was free to speak. 'I know. I was there. He is dead then? Didn't just fall over?'

'Definitely dead.'

'Thought he might be. He landed like a tree. Of course, he was built like an ox.' Hartle mused on. 'Probably should have been built like a person, that might have helped.'

Hermitage didn't like to add anything about murder just at the moment. He was sure, but all he had to persuade others was the fact that wherever he went, people got murdered. He could see that this would not be a comforting hypothesis. 'And Wat wants you to come and look at his loom.'

Hartle frowned. 'That's a bit much, isn't it? Poor fellow only hit the ground a few moments ago and Wat's already after his loom?'

'No, no.'

'Wasn't any good anyway. Tiny thing. Useful for ceremonies and the like, no good for actually making anything.'

'Wat thinks there's something odd about it.'

'Odd about Hemling's loom?'

'Apparently.'

Hartle shrugged, took another bite from his pig-loaf and gestured Hermitage to lead the way.

At the entrance to the tent, the man with the table was doing a good job of stopping anyone from getting in. It almost seemed as if his life's work had finally come to fruition. He was not just telling select people that they were not allowed, he was at last able to tell absolutely everyone. The utopia of a man with a table's existence had come to pass. No one was getting past his table. A slightly maniacal grin sat on his face as he prepared to turn away master and apprentice alike.

'No,' he said, holding up a hand as Hermitage approached.

'I just came out,' Hermitage explained. 'I'm dealing with Hemling's death.'

A Murder for Master Wat

'You're not going in,' the man stated his fact.

'But you just saw me come out.'

'I'm not stopping people coming out,' the man explained as if to an idiot with not the first understanding of the function of the modern table. 'What I'm doing is stopping people going in. You're trying to go in, therefore I'm stopping you.'

'I can see that,' Hermitage acknowledged. 'But we need to get in.'

'They're all going to say that, aren't they?'

Hermitage looked around and saw that no one was actually trying to get into the tent at all, apart from him and Hartle. Hardly surprising, really, as there was a dead body in there.

'I think it's only me saying it.'

'There you are then,' the man nodded that this was conclusive. 'If you're saying you want to get in, you definitely can't come in.'

'I am Master Hartle,' Hartle announced.

'I know,' the man said. 'And you're not coming in either.'

'I was just in there with the other master,' Hermitage was finding this a bit frustrating.

'Master Thomas, aye. And it was himself who told me not to let anyone in.'

'So, when Master Thomas comes back,' Hartle reasoned. 'You're not going to let him in either.'

'Eh?'

'That would be quite proper,' Hermitage picked up on the idea. 'After all, Master Thomas said that no one was to enter the tent. He didn't say no one but him. Being a stout fellow you must follow your instruction and not let anyone in. Not us, not Master Thomas. No one.'

'Quite right,' Hartle agreed. 'Not even all the masters and apprentices who are going to turn up for the talk on the latest

59

thing in nettle retting.'

'What's going on?' Wat stuck his head out of the tent, doubtless wondering why entering a tent required so much discussion.

'What are you doing in there?' The man at the table sounded and looked horrified.

'I came in when you weren't looking.'

'So you let him pass,' Hermitage explained. 'I think you've already failed in your duties so you might as well let everyone in now.' He turned to Wat. 'This fellow has been left instruction not to let anyone in.'

'I see,' Wat said. 'And why, exactly, are you paying any attention to him?'

'Erm,' Hermitage didn't really have an answer to that. Following orders and instructions was just what you did.

'There's two of you, one of him and he doesn't even have a stick or anything. And there's a dead body in here, I think that takes priority.' Wat retreated to the tent with a grunt of disappointment.

Hartle just shrugged and walked straight past the man and his table. Hermitage tried to look very apologetic as he sidled sideways into the tent.

'I shall tell Master Thomas,' was the man's only riposte.

Hermitage gave his own shrug. He was used to being reported to higher authority for something or other.

Inside the tent, Hartle had joined Wat at the loom and they were both squatting down examining it when Hermitage joined them.

'I see what you mean,' Hartle was saying with a thoughtful nod.

'What is it?' Hermitage asked, his natural curiosity barging aside the worry of yet another investigation.

A Murder for Master Wat

'It's the warp,' Hartle explained.

'Ah,' Hermitage nodded. 'The dangling thread.'

'Yes,' Hartle sighed, 'the dangling thread.' He stood and drew Hermitage close so that he could demonstrate their findings. 'All the warps on the loom are gilt silk.'

'Wat said that's very expensive.'

'Yes, it is. But there aren't really very many on this loom as it's so small, and they're all pretty short. All the warps have weights on the bottom to keep them tight, which is quite normal, except several warps should be bundled together onto one weight. No point in having a weight for every single warp. You'd need a lot of weights and it's just not necessary.'

'And in this case?'

'There is an oddity. One of the warps has a weight all to itself.'

'Aha,' Hermitage said, thinking this must be significant but not having the first idea why.

'And that weight is heavier than all the rest by a long way.'

Hermitage pondered this and tried very hard to remember some of the things he'd been told about weaving. 'So that warp would be tighter than all the rest.'

'Very good,' Wat congratulated the conclusion. 'It would be a lot tighter. The weight is far too large for a loom of this size.'

Hermitage, encouraged by his successful application of weaving know-how, went on. 'Wouldn't the warp just snap?'

'It would,' Wat confirmed. 'Very good again. It would snap as soon as you put the weight on.'

Hermitage smiled.

'Or at least it would if there wasn't something different about this particular warp.'

'About the warp?'

'Exactly. The one warp tied to its own weight is not the same as all the others. This one,' Wat reached out to the loom and took hold of a thread that was hanging loose from the top, 'is not gilt silk. This one is a simple strand of wire. A strand polished up to look like silver.'

'Wire?' Hermitage frowned. 'Do people often weave with wire?'

Now Wat sighed and Hermitage could tell that he had started to get things wrong, again.

'No, they do not. It's possible, I suppose,' he gave this some thought and looked interested in the idea. 'It's used to make jewellery and chain shirts and the like but that's all by hand. If you built a loom strong enough…,'

'The dead master?' Hartle brought him back to the topic in hand. 'Or the one lying on the ground right in front of us, at least.'

'Yes, right. Where was I? Wire weaving. No, you do not weave with wire. Not on a loom at least and not with one single warp of wire when everything else is silk.'

Hermitage thought that this sounded suspicious. Or rather he thought that it would sound suspicious if he understood it.

'It looks as if the loom had been set with the wire warp in place, very tight, but not quite breaking.' Hartle now took over the explanation. 'However, as soon as Hemling pulled the heddle to swap the sheds, well!'

'Well indeed.' Hermitage nodded wisely, not having the first clue what any of that meant.

Wat sighed his sigh. 'When Hemling pulled this bar,' he rested his hand on the pole that sat across the front of the loom. 'Which is called a heddle, it would pull half the warps forward to create a little tunnel that the shuttle goes through.

A Murder for Master Wat

That's called a shed. One of the warps it would pull would be our metal one. The extra strain of the pull would snap the wire.'

'I see,' Hermitage said, and he really did, this time. 'But surely, warps snapping is a common occurrence.'

'Not if you've set your loom properly, it isn't,' Hartle huffed, taking on his teacher's voice.

'But it does happen, yes,' Wat confirmed. 'Except there's more.'

'More,' Hermitage said. 'Oh good.'

'Our wire had been weakened at the bottom, near the weight. It was a drawn wire.' Wat could probably tell that Hermitage was thinking this meant a drawing on some parchment. 'The wire was round. It was made by getting a length of flat, narrow metal and drawing it through a round hole in a stone. The metal comes out as round wire.'

Hermitage nodded. He was learning quite a lot today; most of it had to do with a possible murder, which was a shame.

'There are bound to be imperfections in the wire, drawing is a tricky process, but our wire has been made particularly thin where it joins the weight. It's as if it's been part-drawn for a second time, through a smaller hole in the stone.' Wat waited for a moment to see if Hermitage understood the implications. 'Which means it would snap at the stone end first and the tight wire would spring upwards.'

'Striking the person standing in front of the loom.' Hermitage got it.

'Exactly.' Hartle nodded but looked as if he was wondering why this was taking so long.

'I can imagine being struck by wire would be painful, but hardly deadly,' Hermitage speculated.

'Normally no,' Wat agreed. 'But what if the wire had also been sharpened along one side until it was like a shaving blade.'

Hermitage pondered this for a moment. 'That would be extremely dangerous,' he concluded with some shock at such a silly idea.

Hartle and Wat folded their arms and stood, looking at him.

He looked back. As the silence dragged on he realised that they were expecting something more from him. He looked at the loom again. Wat held out the wire for him to peer at. He peered at it. Closely.

'Good heavens,' he said, 'someone has sharpened this along one side.'

'Until it's like a shaving blade, yes,' Wat observed, rather dryly.

Hermitage then looked from the wire to the prostrate figure of Hemling.

'We'd better have a look, don't you think?' Wat offered.

Hermitage sighed. This possible murder was getting more and more likely. A loom loaded with killer wire could not be a coincidence.

Reluctantly, he moved over to the body of Hemling, with Wat and Hartle joining him.

'Big chap,' Wat observed as they squatted at the ex-master's side. 'On three,' he instructed, putting his hands under Hemling's waist while Hermitage took the shoulder and Hartle the legs. 'One, two, three.'

They all of them heaved at the same time and rolled Hemling over, not without much grunting and straining at the size of the task.

'Well,' said Wat, as he stood and noted the master's face

A Murder for Master Wat

and chest. And all the blood that had come out of the hole in Hemling's throat.

'Bit of a lucky hit,' Hartle commented.

'Lucky?' Hermitage couldn't see anything lucky about this at all. Not for any of them, especially Hemling.

'Putting a sharp wire on a loom is one thing. Getting it to snap at the right time and in the right place and actually hit the person standing there is luck. It could have gone anywhere. Got tangled in the rest of the warps, caught on the heddle, anything.'

'He was on the large side,' Wat said. 'Might be hard to miss. And he did tend to lean over his shuttle when he was weaving. Probably couldn't see it over his stomach otherwise.'

'But right in the throat?' Hartle clearly didn't believe this.

Hermitage had one last straw to clutch. 'You're sure it wasn't part of the ritual, having a loom with a single metal warp?'

'It is the guild of weavers,' Wat pointed out. 'Not the guild of idiots.'

'A moot of idiots would be real chaos,' Hartle noted. 'Probably dead people all over the place. Mind you, I've got a few names I could put forward to be master idiots.' He snorted and gave the others an apologetic glance for the distraction.

'I was just thinking that this is a ceremonial loom,' Hermitage pressed on, rather hopelessly. 'Could there be an element of risk in its operation? You know, like initiation ceremonies and the like.'

Hartle and Wat gave him sympathetic looks. 'No, Hermitage,' Wat said, quietly. 'There's not supposed to be a sharpened metal warp in the loom, deliberately set up to break as soon as the loom is used by the only person who was going to use it. It may have been luck, as Hartle says, but it wasn't very lucky for old Hemling. Someone has killed him. It could be that they didn't intend the wire to actually cut him, but the shock of the snap and getting him to fall over would probably be enough to do for him. And you know what happens when one person kills another one and you're nearby.'

Hermitage sighed. 'I'm beginning to think that it's me being nearby that makes people kill one another.'

'Oh, come now.'

'No, really. Think about it. Everywhere I go there's some murder to be investigated. It's as if the aura of the King's Investigator goes ahead of me and induces thoughts of murder in the heads of passers-by. Perfectly innocent people who hadn't had a sinful thought in their head suddenly turn to their nearest and dearest and stick a knife in them.'

'I think you're getting a bit carried away.'

'Hemling might have been perfectly fine if I hadn't turned up. A nice bit of weaving on his loom, a long speech and home to eat. But oh no. The King's Investigator is outside the tent so his own loom up and kills him.'

'Whoever did this went to a lot of trouble,' Hartle explained. 'This loom would have been set up days ago before you even knew you were coming.'

Hermitage frowned that this was a counter to his argument.

'And it's just nonsense,' Wat reassured him. 'Just think of all the people who are killing one another right now up and down the country. You're not near any of them, are you?'

'That's hardly comforting.'

'I expect that if any of us wanted to investigate a murder we could find one if we looked hard enough. We'd only have to peek around the right corner to find some foul deed being committed.'

'But I don't have to peek at all,' Hermitage wailed. 'They come to me.'

'You're probably just better suited to spotting them, being King's Investigator and all, you see things that other people miss.'

'What? Like a massive weaving master lying in front of his loom with his throat cut?'

'Ah.' Wat didn't really have an answer to that.

'I don't have to spot the dead bodies,' Hermitage moaned, gesturing at Hemling. 'I'm in danger of tripping over them.'

Wat and Hartle exchange hopeless looks. 'We don't even know this is murder,' Hartle said. 'I don't think anyone's skilled enough to lay a loom so it will kill. As I said, the broken wire could have gone anywhere. It was just Hemling's bad luck that it hit him where it did. I think someone set out to cause trouble, not to kill.'

Hermitage simply shook his head. 'I'm here,' he stated the fact. 'Believe me, it was murder.'

Caput VI: The Grey Guild

They left the tent and the body of Hemling in the care of Master Thomas and a selection of apprentices who had been carefully chosen for the task of moving the very large deceased. When Thomas asked where all the blood had come from, Wat wove a tale about it all being a freak loom accident. Thomas looked doubtful but was happy to accept it as he wanted the tent clear of corpses before the next session began.

Hermitage had taken some shameful satisfaction from observing the man at the table trying to prevent Thomas and the apprentices from entering the tent and being on the receiving end of a comprehensive and extremely personal criticism of his performance, intelligence and future employment prospects, with or without table.

They gathered back at the stand with the pork and bread to consider what the next step might be when Wat was approached. Or rather, he wasn't approached, he saw a slight figure darting by and put out a strong arm to stop it in its tracks. To this figure, he addressed a question, but it already sounded as if he wasn't going to like the answer.

'Oh, no.' He sounded full of despair and resignation as he uttered the words and addressed the figure in front of him. 'What are you doing?'

'Nothing,' a voice from under a hood retorted with a growl.

Hermitage frowned as he thought he recognised this boy. There was something about the hood, which was pulled far down over the face, and the leggings that tugged at his recollection.

'Nothing, eh? And where exactly are you going to do nothing?'

A Murder for Master Wat

The figure in the hood shrugged.

Now Hermitage had it. That shrug was one he recognised immediately. The rise and fall of the narrow shoulders had personality about them. It was the clothes that had put him off. He didn't know where they had come from. 'Cwen?' he asked.

'No,' the hood replied.

'Yes, it is,' Hermitage couldn't understand the reply. 'Where did you get those clothes?'

'She brought them with her,' Wat explained. 'Just so she could skulk about like this.'

Hermitage thought it a bit rich that Wat complained about Cwen skulking when she probably learned it from him.

'I am not skulking,' Cwen insisted, now using her own voice, but not removing the hood.

'You're going around the weavers' moot pretending to be a boy,' Wat pointed out. 'I call that skulking.'

'Call it what you like.'

'You might like to know,' Wat said, in a rather offhand manner, 'that we think Hemling was murdered. So, there's a killer in the moot somewhere. Perhaps you could take a bit more care than normal when you start annoying people?'

Cwen paused at that news. 'Murdered? How?'

'Killed by his loom,' Hermitage explained.

Cwen let loose a half-cough, half-laugh. 'I'll be sure to watch out for killer looms.'

'And if you get into one of the weavers' meetings dressed like that and they find you out, don't come crying to me,' Hartle wagged his finger. 'We'll say we've never seen you before.'

'This is only going to end in trouble,' Wat wiped a hand across his face. 'I knew I shouldn't have let you come.'

'Let me come?' Cwen was now outraged and on the verge of doing something rash. 'Let's be very clear indeed that you did not let me come. You don't let me do anything. If you're lucky I might let you go home with both your shins unbroken.'

'Alright, alright. But as Hartle says, you're on your own. Nothing to do with the workshop if anyone catches you.'

'Don't worry,' Cwen dismissed them. 'I'm not planning to mix with this bunch.' She waved her hand to encompass the moot as a whole. 'They wouldn't recognise a new idea or fresh thinking if it was woven on a loom that fell on them.'

Now Wat looked thoughtful and even more worried. 'What are you going to do?'

'Why should you worry? After all, I'm nothing to do with the workshop. You've never even seen me before.'

'But when we have to get you out of whatever trouble it is you're going to get in, it would be helpful to know where you are.'

'There isn't going to be any trouble. I am simply going to listen to some discussions about a new approach to weaving.'

'Oh, yes,' Wat didn't sound convinced. 'I've heard all about people at moots who have a new approach to show you. And all it needs is a few coins. Don't hand over any money, whatever you do.'

'I'm not an idiot.' Cwen was still sounding cross, but more in command, somehow. She leaned towards them and whispered from under her hood. 'I am going to the Grey Guild.'

The ensuing silence didn't seem particularly heavy with significance.

'What's the Grey Guild?' Hermitage asked.

'Yes,' Wat repeated, 'what is the Grey Guild?' He looked to

A Murder for Master Wat

Hartle who shrugged that he had never heard of it either.

'The Grey Guild is where new ideas are discussed and where the old order is not welcome.' By this Cwen made it clear that Wat and Hartle were the old order.

'Who told you that?' Wat scoffed.

'I overheard it. It sounds like just the thing for me. The Grey Guild don't want anything to do with tradition and ritual and the so-called rules of weaving. They're breaking new ground.'

'Well, be careful they don't break anything else,' Wat cautioned.

'And I suppose you think women weavers will be standing on this new ground,' Hartle said.

'Of course. It's obvious.'

'I wouldn't count on that.' Wat sucked air through his teeth. 'They may want to break with tradition, but my guess is they'll all be men.'

Cwen dismissed this problem with a wave.

'In fact,' Wat went on. 'My guess is that they will all be boys. Probably failed apprentices or ones who've been told that they're useless. Or been turned down for their journeyman status. In other words, weavers who aren't very good. The Weavers' Guild proper won't take them so they start their own. If that's the sort you want to mix with, good luck.'

'You're a fine one to talk, defending the Weavers' Guild.'

'I'm not defending that lot. I'm only saying that this Grey Guild of yours is probably a waste of time. You go along and have your little meeting and when you find it's a waste of time come and find us again. Ow.'

Cwen stomped off with the fumes of her departure leaking from her hood and the evidence of her presence even now turning Wat's left shin blue.

'Grey Guild,' Wat snorted once she had gone.

'Is it not real then?' Hermitage asked.

'No, of course not. Grumbling apprentices are always moaning about the masters and the guild. Every now and then they set up some little group of their own but they soon fall by the wayside. Usually, as soon as they get found out.'

'And I think we've got more to worry about than the Grey Guild,' Hartle reminded them. 'A dead master from the real guild.'

'Quite,' Wat said. 'Perhaps we'd better go and find somewhere a bit more private to discuss what to do next. If word gets out that we think Hemling was murdered there could be chaos.'

'Really?' Hermitage thought they were going to have to mention the fact at some point. It would be very difficult to investigate a murder if you weren't allowed to mention the fact that someone had been killed.

Wat shrugged. 'None of us will be safe if the apprentices think it's open season on Masters.'

...

Cwen's hunt for the Grey Guild was not as easy as she had hoped. As she wandered the field of the moot she thought that it was unlikely that they'd put out a sign saying "disenchanted weavers' meeting here." Mainly because it wouldn't be very secret but also because disenchanted weavers probably couldn't read.

Wat's comments, despite her throwing them back in his face, had struck home. It could be that this would be simply a gathering of moaning apprentices going on about how rotten their lot was. In her mind, she had seen a gathering of experienced masters who wanted to lead the craft in a new direction and had the inclusion of women at the top of their list of things to do. Her lonely search was creating some doubts.

She cast about the crowd, seeing if she could spot anyone who looked like they were sneaking off to a clandestine meeting. As she sidled along, face covered, she just wished one thing; that Wat wasn't right quite so often.

She had overheard two weavers, and come to think of it they did look like apprentices, talking about what a ridiculous thing this moot was and how it was only going to prolong the status quo. She didn't know what a status quo was, but the discussion had also included a lot of swearing about masters and how they wouldn't change their ways if they were walking into a bog. It was time for change, one had said, and the Grey Guild were the people to do it. Well, that was a better meeting to go to than one about yarn efficiency in the rigid heddle loom.

Most of the people around were chatting openly with one other or were striding along, clear that they had some destination of importance to reach. Others were wandering slowly through the stands and tents, trying their very best not to catch the eye of any of the stallholders, despite loud entreaties to take advantage of the marvellous offer that only this table had to offer.

The more desperate tradesmen even stepped from behind their tables to physically accost the passers-by, attempting to drag them by force to see the marvels they had on offer. Strangely, still others simply sat behind their tables and looked as if they wished they'd never come and couldn't wait to go home. The last thing they wanted was for anyone to actually approach them with business.

Amongst this variety, Cwen did spot two figures talking in quiet privacy, voices low and faces close. They even looked about themselves every now and again to make sure that no one was eavesdropping. And of course, to make them look as suspicious as possible. They were obviously weavers, the cut of their cloth was clear, but they were also young. Moaning apprentices again. Still, at least it was something, and as the two moved off into the moot Cwen followed at a safe distance.

The clandestine conversationalists seemed to wander without reason through the moot. They followed no direct path and were occasionally distracted by an interesting stall and paused in their wanderings to examine some product or other.

Cwen was starting to give up hope on these two and was on the verge of going over to demand to know where they were going and to berate them for wasting her time by meandering around like lost sheep. Before she could do so the two took one last, very obvious look around and then ducked, quite blatantly between two of the stands.

Her hopes dipped as she hoped that these two weren't exemplars of the discretion of the Grey Guild at its best. Nevertheless, she followed and found herself in a sort of back alley.

The fronts of the stalls all faced the walkway in the moot down which the customers wandered. Here, tables were gaily decorated and wonderfully bright. Whole tents or at least awnings provided cover from the weather, be it good or bad, and the stallholders smiled and beckoned their welcomes. At least the ones who could be bothered did.

Behind these bright enticements, the backs of those stalls

presented a very different picture.

Some stallholders sat, resting from a hard morning's something or other. Others were eating or drinking or relieving themselves against their neighbour's tent. It looked like all these stallholders had arrived some days ago to set up in advance of the moot, and had been using this back alley for everything back alleys got used for. The sights were revolting, the smell was awful, and the unconscious drunks littered the place.

Some were engaged in loud discussion of the merits of their trade and yet more had descended into fights, surrounded by their fellows urging them to greater violence.

Cwen noted one particular tradesman, obviously a baker, who was preparing his loaves for sale. He was doing this by digging out the mould that had grown up over the last few days and then spitting on the bread to make it shine. She tried to make a note of this man's face to make sure she avoided him at mealtimes.

Fortunately, her quarry, now out of the main moot, made no attempt to disguise their direction and were walking along briskly, talking normally.

It was easy not to be spotted herself in this area, a lot of people were walking around with hoods pulled down, either because they didn't want to be spotted or they couldn't stand the sight of the sun after so many meads.

Eventually, at the end of the alley, Cwen saw the two she was following enter what must be the tent of the Grey Guild. There was no marking of any sort, and the tent was grey through age and condition rather than as a result of any deliberate plan. Still, it was tucked away from the moot for some reason. She would just have to find out what that reason was.

With a confidence born of the knowledge that she could deal with most people who tried to get in her way, she strode up to the tent entrance. She fully expected to be stopped by someone, or at least asked what she wanted. There was indeed a man standing at the tent opening.

'Yes?' he said when Cwen approached. It wasn't an aggressive "yes" it was more of a confidential enquiry. She turned her hood left and right as if making sure no one was watching.

'The Grey Guild,' she said. She didn't ask, that would sound as if she wasn't already completely aware of the Guild and perhaps might not be entitled to enter.

The man at the tent simply nodded. 'Welcome,' he said and stepped to one side to let her pass. 'We don't believe in tables,' he added.

'Beg pardon?' Cwen had expected and anticipated many things to be said to her. This was not one of them.

'Tables,' the man now spat on the ground. 'Weavers' Guild tools of oppression.'

'Oh, yes?'

'Of course. Tables everywhere. Can't pass this table, have to pay at that table, leave your name at these tables. Men with tables? More like men with weapons.'

'The table as a weapon, yes, I see.' Cwen was having doubts about whether the Grey Guild was really going to be for her.

Leaving the man to a mumbling conversation with himself on what he would say to a table if he ever met one, as well as a few practice punches and kicks that would lay the table out in no time, she slipped into the tent. She immediately looked around to see if there was another way out.

The inside was dark and grubby. It was just an open space, nowhere to sit and certainly no tables. There were about

A Murder for Master Wat

fifteen people inside, not all of them hiding under their hoods but some were, which was a relief.

An older man approached her. At least he didn't look like an apprentice. Unless he was a very old one, which would not be a good sign. 'Welcome brother,' he said, quietly. He had dark eyes set back in a weather-worn face and a nose that looked like it had been hit by a flying shuttle too many times.

Cwen just nodded an acknowledgement.

'You come to challenge the old ways and forge a new path for weaving?' This sounded as if it was some sort of ritual.

'I do,' Cwen grumbled, keeping her voice as low as possible.

'You discard tradition and the rules of the weavers' guild?'

'I do.'

'You are open to ideas and practices hitherto unthought-of or practised?'

'Absolutely.' Cwen felt a swell of encouragement.

The man looked at her askance.

'I mean, I do.'

'Excellent,' the man was happy. 'Do come in. We're about to start. 'I am brother Shuttle.'

'Shuttle?' Cwen contained a snigger.

'Ah, this is your first meeting?'

'Er, that's right.'

'We all take secret names here. We know that the Weavers' Guild,' he spat, 'has its eyes everywhere and would pay dearly to know who we are. We must hide ourselves until the day comes when we can step into the light.'

Cwen nodded her agreement although she wondered about the level of threat from the main guild as neither Wat nor Hartle had ever heard of a grey version. She also wondered about these people accepting anyone in a hood into their meeting. She could be a Guild spy for all they knew.

'Do you have a name you would choose?'

Cwen thought about it, briefly. 'Cwen,' she said.

There was no reply for a moment. 'Oh, that's great,' the man enthused.

'Really?' Cwen asked, feeling elated.

'Yes,' the man nodded his enthusiasm for the idea.

'I'm pleased.'

'I wish I'd thought of that. We could have all used girls' names. That way no one would ever believe we had anything to do with weaving.'

Cwen's teeth did their best to grind themselves to dust.

'Come, come,' the man beckoned. 'We are about to have our opening ceremony.'

'Ceremony?' Cwen tried to contain her snarl.

'Oh, nothing like the Weavers' Guild.' He spat again. 'We don't believe in any of that nonsense.' He left Cwen, went to the front of the tent and raised his arms for silence.

All faces in the room turned his way and he spoke quietly, but loud enough to be heard.

'Brothers of the Grey Guild. Do you discard tradition and the rules of the weavers' guild?'

'We do,' the audience replied.

'And are you now ready to take action against those who stifle the craft and lead us down the path to destruction?'

'We are.'

'And do you silently cheer the one who sets our example, who leads where we will follow and who stands defiant against the tyranny of the Weavers' Guild?' Everyone in the room spat now.

'We do.' They all raised their right arms, clenched their fists and thumped them to their chests.

The man dropped his voice even lower. 'Let us speak his

name and take our inspiration.'

There was a profound and thoughtful silence before the whole tent whispered the name of the one they adored. 'Wat the Weaver,' they hissed.

'Nooo,' Cwen howled.

Caput VII: The Moot Money Motive

'Who would want to kill Master Hemling?' Hermitage asked the simple question when they had found a quiet spot where there was little risk of interruption or of being overheard. This spot was the stall where people could go to pay their dues to the guild. There was a wide space in front of the table as weavers of all descriptions walked in wide circles, simply to avoid coming close.

The two men behind the table seemed to have given up all hope as well and were simply lolling in their chairs at the back of the stall, gazing with disinterest at the world around them. They had obviously run out of idle conversation hours ago.

As the investigative party arrived, one man in the stall had stood with some excitement, perhaps thinking they had a customer.

'I'm all paid up,' Hartle reported.

'And I don't think you want me,' Wat added with a smile.

They had looked briefly to Hermitage but clearly realised that a monk was nothing to do with them. They went back to staring.

'I still say it was an accident,' Hartle said. 'A lucky or unlucky one, depending on how you look at it. There was no way anyone could expect the breaking wire to get Hemlock in the throat.'

'Let us assume it was a lucky one,' Hermitage suggested, considering his now well-established fact that anyone who died in his neighbourhood had been murdered. 'Someone put a sharpened metal warp in the loom. Why would they do that if not to cause injury?' He thought about this for a moment. 'Presumably, the first person to pull that hattle thing,'

'Heddle,' Hartle corrected.

'Yes, heddle. The first one to pull that would be in the way of the wire. Was Hemling the only one to use that loom?'

'Absolutely,' Hartle seemed to think any other possibility ridiculous. 'That was old Hemlock's ceremonial loom. Woe betides anyone who put a finger on it. You were allowed to look, but that was all.'

'So, our murderer would know that only Master Hemling,' he scowled at the other two for their lack of respect. 'Only Master Hemling would touch it. In which case we are back to the question. Who would want to kill him?'

'Maybe it was a joke,' Wat suggested.

Hermitage looked at him in horror. 'A joke?'

'Yes, you know.'

'No, I don't think I do. Knife-sharp wires strung to a loom so they'll break and slash the weaver to death isn't going to raise much of a laugh from anyone.' Hermitage knew that he didn't understand the things most people laughed at, but this one seemed clear.

'It's like sawing halfway through a heddle so the first time someone pulls it, it snaps in half, ha ha.' Wat smiled at them both and laughed.

'That doesn't sound very funny either,' Hermitage noted.

'Quite,' Hartle agreed. 'Sounds like the activity of some stupid apprentice.'

'But it is funny,' Wat insisted. 'The weaver goes to give a good haul on the heddle, it comes apart in his hands and he falls over backwards.' He looked at them, apparently puzzled that they couldn't see the humour. 'We've all done it, surely? Played a trick on a master.'

The look on Hermitage's face made it quite clear that he had been on the receiving end of too many tricks to be involved in giving them out.

Hartle simply folded his arms and gave Wat a withering look. 'Certainly not. And I can see why you and your master never got on.'

'You think someone put a sharpened metal warp on the loom as a joke?' Hermitage checked the proposal.

'Well,' Wat acknowledged. 'I suppose that might be going a bit far.'

'Going a bit far,' Hermitage repeated. 'Yes, I think it would be. Even if they didn't intend to kill, the thing would cause serious injury. Can we rule out a joke as the cause of death?'

'Please yourself, 'Wat muttered.

'Let's assume that we have a method for the murder, a sharpened metal warp. Presumably, Hemling did not keep the loom with him at all times?'

'It was in the tent before anyone arrived, I would think,' Wat said.

'So, we have an opportunity as well. Anyone could have entered the tent and strung the killer warp, which they had prepared beforehand.

'Now, motive. Why would anyone want Hemling dead? Hatred? It's always best to start with the simple.' As he said this, Hermitage thought that this investigation business really had gone too far and was starting to affect the way he thought. He sighed and plunged on. 'Who disliked him so much that they would want to do anything like this? I never knew the man, you've been weavers all your lives and from his age, I would judge that Hemling had been around all that time.'

'He certainly had,' Wat sighed, the memory not being a

A Murder for Master Wat

lively one.

Hermitage looked at them both for any possible answers. They in turn looked at the sky before considering the floor and all the people walking around them.

'He was very boring,' Wat suggested, eventually.

'Hardly grounds for an attack, I'd have thought,' Hermitage replied. 'What a world we would be in if people got murdered just for being boring?'

'Quite,' Wat said, with a rather peculiar look at Hermitage.

'Master Thomas told me that organising the moot was a thankless task and no one else would want the job,' Hermitage observed.

'Right,' Hartle confirmed. 'Being the most reviled weaver in the land, well,' he glanced at Wat, 'the second most reviled weaver in the land, isn't something most people would volunteer for.'

'Reviled?' Hermitage thought that sounded a bit extreme.

'Oh, absolutely. Everyone hates a moot organiser. The craftsmen, the traders, the town they've come to. Nothing's quite the way you want it and so that must be the organiser's fault. In this case, Hemling. And everyone thinks they could have done a better job with their hands tied behind their backs, but they wouldn't dream of trying.'

'It's unlikely that someone killed him so that they could take over the role then.'

'Hardly,' Hartle gave a laugh of disbelief. 'And this is the weavers' guild, not the Norman nobility. If you want to get on there are other ways of doing it than killing the person ahead of you.'

'And why do it now?' Wat asked. 'The moot is already underway. A few more days and it will be over.'

Hermitage was disappointed that this motive for murder

was dismissed so quickly. 'But he was not well-liked, apart from being boring.'

'Just at the moment, no.'

'Then there could be a lot of people who would wish him harm.'

Hartle considered this for a moment. 'Well, yes, but it's a bit much to go and kill someone for giving you a stall at the wrong end of the street, or putting your treadle design talk on straight after the noon meal when everyone's asleep.'

'But someone may have wanted to cause him some harm. Make things go wrong?'

'I suppose. But again, making a metal warp, sharpening it and going to all that trouble with the weight? Why not just saw halfway through his heddle.' Hartle rolled his eyes as Wat's grin spread across his face.

'And it's going to be over soon like I said.' Wat held his hands out to encompass the moot. 'All the people who called Hemling every name under the sun will be congratulating him for a job well done. Mainly because they'll want him to do it again if it ever comes up.'

Hermitage pondered this and recalled an experience he had had with an ambitious young monk, Brother Tredan, a few years ago. This man had been determined that he was going to rise through the ranks at a great pace, his natural authority and expertise would see him an abbot in no time and a bishopric was easily achievable.

Unfortunately, Brother Tredan's desire for authority outweighed his ability like a goose outweighs a sparrow's cough. He seemed to think that by simply telling people he was going to be in charge one day, it would happen. All he really managed to do was infuriate and annoy everyone around him to the extent that his chances of advancement

A Murder for Master Wat

diminished every time he opened his mouth.

In many respects, Hermitage was very happy to have him around. Brother Tredan became a fine distraction for those who might otherwise take out their exasperation on him.

Tredan did have one skill though, and one that he practised as often as the opportunity arose. The brother seemed to have an innate ability, some sort of instinct almost, to take credit for the work of others. And, despite all expectations to the contrary it seemed to work. Whenever anything of note was achieved, Tredan was there, being lauded for the results, even if he had nothing whatsoever to do with it.

It amazed Hermitage that people seemed to accept this. A group of brothers may have been working hard to create a herb garden in one corner of the monastery, and when the first crop was gathered there would be Tredan. Strangely, no one told him to clear off because he hadn't even known the work was going on, let alone been key to its success.

Before long, Tredan was being spoken of as a possible future sub-prior. It wasn't in Hermitage's nature to speak ill of anyone, but really!

Perhaps there were parallels in the world of weaving. 'Could someone have wanted to take the credit for the moot away from Hemling?'

Wat and Hartle looked at him with puzzled expressions, not having the benefit of the thought process that had gone on in silence.

'The credit?' Wat asked.

'Yes. You said that Hemling would be praised for organising the moot, once it was over. But if the very opening ceremony went wrong, he might be replaced. As it happened, he actually got killed. Is there any other benefit he gains?

Titles, payments? That sort thing?'

They considered it. 'I suppose he might get a scroll,' Hartle shrugged. 'No idea, really.'

'The moot will bring in a lot of money for the guild,' Wat said, looking thoughtful in that rather devious way he had.

'Really?'

'Of course. We all had to pay to get in; well, you did. And all the stallholders and tradesmen have paid. Good business opportunity, having so many weavers in the one place. Save a lot of trouble going around the country trying to meet them all one at a time. At least that's what the guild says when they charge traders an arm and a leg for the space to put a table up.'

Hartle nodded toward the guild fees stall. 'And even if we try to avoid them, the guild will find you if you haven't paid. Probably get a lot of money they've been owed by weavers who've forgotten to pay their dues for the last few years.'

Wat was now nodding with some enthusiasm. 'I wonder if Nottingham pays as well.'

'Why would they pay?'

'All this trade coming here. All these people spending their money. Any town would welcome an increase in income like this, as long as they can put up with the chaos and pay for the repairs afterwards. The ordinary folk won't want a moot anywhere near them but the head man and the merchants, they'd love it. It would line their coffers nicely. Knowing the guild, I wouldn't be at all surprised to find that they'd charged Nottingham a very healthy fee for being the host city.'

'Money.' Hermitage shook his head.

'I hate it when you say it like that,' Wat said. 'As if it's a bad thing.'

A Murder for Master Wat

'It's a very bad thing if someone got killed for it.'

'We don't know that Hemling was getting any money,' Hartle pointed out.

'That's the problem with investigating murder,' Hermitage said, with genuine despair at the whole business. 'You never know much at all when you begin. Then, the more you ask, the more you find out and what you find out is always positively shameful.'

'Being murder, I suppose it would be,' Hartle acknowledged. 'And this is the sort of thing you do all the time, is it?'

Hermitage sighed. 'Compared to most of the murders I've had to deal with, committing one simply to take money is quite wholesome.'

'Good Lord,' Hartle shook his head, seeming to have a newfound respect for Hermitage.

'Where would all that money go?' Hermitage asked. 'The pennies people are paying to get in, the stallholders, the town?'

Wat shrugged. 'Into the guild coffers, I suppose. So the guild men can lead comfortable lives.'

'I mean where does it go now?' Hermitage specified.

'Now?'

'Yes. People entering the moot are handing over their money. You gave ninepence, Hartle. Where is it now? Where's it kept. I can't imagine it's just left at the gate.'

'No idea,' Hartle rubbed his chin. 'I suppose it must all be gathered somewhere safe.'

'Under the watch of the moot organiser?'

Wat looked interested. 'So, even if Hemling wasn't in line for a share of the takings, he could have been looking after every penny of it in the meantime. Now he's dead, any fee he gets would go back to the guild. But where's the rest of it?'

'Quite. Master Thomas said Hemling had no assistant at all, no one who would be recognised as taking his place and so maybe all the money from the moot was with him when he died.'

'He didn't seem to have stacks of coin in his breeches,' Wat said. 'If he was looking after it, it's probably hidden away somewhere. And it's probably true that no one else was helping. Hemling was a difficult so and so. Who'd work with him?'

'But surely someone would have to take his place, as the moot isn't over yet? Who's going to deal with all those complaints?'

'Hm,' Hartle thought. 'Knowing the guild, they'll probably just tell someone they've got to do it and not pay them anything.' He nodded to himself. 'The guild might be quite pleased about that. Hemling could be awkward when the mood took him. Which was most days. Some of the guild might be glad to see the back of him.'

'Really?' Hermitage was intrigued to hear this.

Hartle tutted. 'Not so awkward as to kill him, for goodness sake. He was simply a stubborn old boy who thought he knew best about everything. If the master of the whole guild attends his funeral, he'll probably have a big smile on his face.'

Hermitage had more thoughts about the awful things people did. 'Maybe it's just plain robbery, then. If Hemling had all the money, that would be a very good motive for some people.'

'They're still paying their pennies to get in,' Wat pointed out. 'Not all the money will have been gathered yet. A bit early to steal it. If you waited a bit, you'd get even more.'

Hartle agreed. 'And if you were just going to kill Hemling

A Murder for Master Wat

for his money, why go to all this trouble? Why not just stick a knife in him?'

Hermitage considered the evil ways of man. He was getting quite good at it. He was quite enthusiastic about his latest horrible thought. 'This way it looks like an accident. No one would think of looking for the money if they thought Hemling had just died.' He thought on. 'They could probably even go on collecting it.' He shook his head that he was getting carried away. 'This is all just speculation though. Which is very good. I like speculation as much as the next man, but we have no facts. We need to find out what was happening to the money. The guild would doubtless want an account so it could already be in their counting-house. Who would know, now that Hemling's dead?'

Wat and Hartle exchanged looks of resignation at a very distasteful task that had just reared an unavoidable head. 'The guild,' they both said.

'No point me going.' Wat was cheerful at the prospect of not meeting the guild. 'They wouldn't even let me in, let alone talk about their money. Hartle's a genuine master.'

'Thank you very much,' Hartle grunted. 'I can't see the guild discussing their money with anyone, you know what a secretive gaggle they are.'

'But if a master demands to know what his guild is doing with his money,' Wat prompted.

'Said master might stop being a master altogether.'

'Can't do any harm to ask.'

Hartle looked wide-eyed. 'What on earth makes you think that? Asking is a very bad idea. You know the guild hates being asked anything. Remember old Nunty?'

'Nunty?' It seemed Wat did not remember.

'Old boy, used to do cloth work, mainly. Couldn't tell red

89

from green.'

'Oh, him, beautiful tapestry, "Green Sky at Night." Yes?'

'One guild meeting Nunty asked why the master got to have a fine gown and chain of office when the rest of them couldn't afford to eat.'

'Oh, dear.'

'Quite. No one ever heard from him again.'

'Good gracious,' Hermitage breathed.

'They sent him to Coventry.'

'What a horrible thing to do,' Wat said with some sincerity. 'I went there once. Ghastly place.'

'This is all very interesting,' Hermitage said, thinking that it wasn't, really. 'It doesn't get us any answers to our questions though. Where will we find the guild representatives?'

Hartle nodded his head towards the two bored men behind their table. 'They're sitting right there.'

'Them?' Hermitage didn't think that they looked like authoritative figures from the weavers' guild.

'Well, not them personally. They're just lowly functionaries. They'll know where the important people are though.'

'Probably in a private room above a tavern somewhere,' Wat suggested. 'Desperately avoiding having to have any contact with actual weavers.'

'This is their moot.' Hermitage thought that the leaders of the craft would surely want to engage with their craftsmen.

'And bishops pop round for a chat with the ordinary monk, do they?' Wat raised his eyebrows. 'It's going to be tricky enough to find out where they are, getting in to see them could be impossible.'

'One of their number has been killed,' Hermitage felt a

twinge of outrage.

'Yes,' Wat gave this some thought. 'That's true. They'll probably take it very seriously when they realise what's really at risk here.'

Hartle nodded his agreement. 'Their money.'

'Quite. Never mind dead Hemling. Although, with the old boy dying in the middle of their moot, they might think they've got a claim on all his property as well.'

Hermitage gave them both a baleful stare. 'I think that the masters of the guild will be more concerned to hear that one of their own has been murdered, right on their doorstep.'

Hartle and Wat looked at him and then started to walk off, laughing heartily.

'Oh, Hermitage,' Wat smiled broadly. 'You do say the funniest things sometimes.'

Caput VIII: Wat the Wonderful

'Brother Cwen?' Shuttle stepped across to her, being the only one who had cried out in despair at the mention of Wat's name.

'Ah, yes,' Cwen replied from under her hood. She noticed that the rest of the tent was looking at her, many of them still holding their hands to their chests as they had when they called out their chant.

'Something wrong?'

'Wrong? Well, no, not really, I suppose. It just took me by surprise a bit. Wat the Weaver and all.' She gave a light laugh. Being in a tent full of strange weavers, all of whom appeared to think that Wat was some sort of great leader, was a worrying situation. She was confident of her own view on Wat, but she was heavily outnumbered and didn't know how these men would react to the truth.

'He is our inspiration,' Shuttle said, solemnly and with his hand back on his chest.

'Does he know?' Cwen asked.

'Does he know?' Shuttle didn't seem to understand the question.

'Yes. I mean, does he know that you're all gathered in this tent being inspired by him? Chanting his name and, erm, so forth.'

Shuttle was shocked now. He spoke in slightly horrified tones. 'We would not presume to speak to the great man, or have contact with him.'

'Great man, eh?'

'Of course. He fights for all that we stand for. He opposes the guild and all its trappings. He makes his way without their permission or their connivance. Through the pure

A Murder for Master Wat

quality of his craft, he paves his success across the landscape.' Shuttle was getting a bit carried away now. He was looking to the roof of the tent in a declamatory pose, one hand now clamped to his chest, the other thrown forward as if the light of Wat was about to descend on them.

'You've never met him, then?' Cwen brought the adulation down to earth.

'Met him? Met Wat the Weaver? I would not...,'

'Presume, yes, I can imagine. But if you've never met him, how do you know that he's doing all these things. Defying the guild, paving his success and all that.'

'All that? His works speak for themselves.' Shuttle was now sounding a bit suspicious of Cwen's attitude towards the great Wat.

'They certainly do,' Cwen muttered to herself.

'Wat the Weaver leads where we can only follow. In his steps, we will tread and in his image we mould ourselves.'

'Right,' Cwen nodded, very cautiously.

One of the other brothers in the tent approached slowly, looking from Shuttle to Cwen and back again. His head was uncovered and he looked like a very young and very nervous apprentice, who wouldn't usually dare to speak even to his own master. He put his hand up.

'Yes, Brother Weft?' Shuttle invited the question.

If this new arrival spoke, Cwen couldn't make it out. The lips moved and some breath came out, but that was about it.

Shuttle leaned in close as if trying to catch the dying words of an old man. Weft spoke again, his eyes nervously and fleetingly landing on Cwen.

Shuttle leaned back, looking rather disgusted at whatever the words had been. He shook his head and turned to Cwen with a dismissive laugh. 'Brother Weft here wonders if you've ever met Wat the Weaver.' He looked around the tent at the other brothers, as if encouraging their amusement at such a ridiculous idea.

'Well, yes.' Cwen's words brought a silence into the tent and hung it from the roof where everyone could see it.

'Yes?' Shuttle didn't understand.

'Yes, I've met Wat the Weaver.'

Shuttle's mouth dropped open. Then it closed again and his eyes narrowed. 'You've met Wat the Weaver?' He clearly thought that Cwen was just making this up to get attention.

She was about to embark on a full explanation of her role and relationship to Wat when she paused. It wasn't like her to pause. If there was a hole to jump in, or trouble to be started, she was in the vanguard. There was something about this tent full of peculiar weavers, and something about Shuttle that made her think it better if she kept things to herself. Wat's warning about getting in trouble and them not coming to help came to her mind. She really hated it when he was right.

'His workshop is in Derby,' Cwen explained. 'Everyone knows that. And it's not far away.'

'We do not approach Wat,' Shuttle was appalled by the very idea. 'We are not worthy.'

'Not worthy,' Cwen nodded as if she was checking that she was getting this right.

'Did you speak to him?'

'Only to say hello.' Cwen thought it best not to report that she'd kicked him.

Shuttle now shook his head, sadly. 'Hello.' He offered this word to the rest of the tent, most of whom groaned at the very idea.

'What's the problem?' Cwen tried to sound as meek as she

could manage, which was not very meek at all. 'Wat's a weaver with a workshop. He must have apprentices and people he does business with. They talk to him. It's possible that he'd even be very pleased to hear that you're inspired by him. He might even come and give you a talk.'

The peculiar weavers took a step back from Cwen, probably driven backwards by the sharp intake of breath they all took.

Shuttle now pointed his finger at Cwen, from a distance and it was shaking a bit. 'Wat the Weaver is too good for the likes of us. Only when we have broken our own shackles can we dare to dream of being on his level.'

'Oh, God,' Cwen whispered to the inside of her hood.

'Wat inspires us to rise up against the Weavers' Guild.' They all spat. 'When we have done so, then we will be able to speak, but only then.'

'Rise up against the guild?' Cwen asked.

'Just so.'

'Well, I'm all for that. Rising up against the guild. Them and their stupid ideas.' She nodded her hood vigorously. 'I mean, they won't even allow women.'

Shuttle coughed. 'Well, of course, they won't allow women. We're against the guild in every conceivable way. Everything they think and everything they say is a stifling restriction on the true freedoms of weaving.'

'Good.'

'But no one's going to allow women.' Shuttle gave a sharp laugh, to which the rest of the tent added.

'Right,' Cwen said, very carefully. The members of Grey Guild had retreated in the face of her outrageous ideas and left the route to the door open. She was pretty confident that, while they may be opposed to most of the ideas of the guild, their attitude to Wat was something that she simply would not be able to cope with. It was bad enough when customers and the apprentices in the workshop said how wonderful he was, a whole guild full would be too much.

And their response to the idea of women weavers had been the last straw. Admittedly that only made two straws, but it didn't take many straws to break Cwen's back; and her temper, which she now struggled to control.

She took a step away. 'Well, I can see that you've got an excellent plan and a lot of good ideas but perhaps I'd better be on my way. You know, people to see, things to do.'

'Wat the weaver?' Shuttle sounded rather anxious now.

'Oh, probably not.' She took another step.

At a nod from Shuttle three of the hooded members of the guild moved around behind Cwen and blocked her exit.

'We have already struck our first blow,' Shuttle said, with a surprisingly effective tone of threat in his voice. 'We cannot allow anyone to report on us.'

'Report?' Cwen's voice came out as a squeak. 'Oh, I wouldn't report. Not to anyone. I'm with you, er, brothers.' She clamped her fist to her chest to show solidarity.

'You are now,' Shuttle said, as the three hoods took hold of her arms and pinned them to her sides.

'Phew,' she sniffed at one of her captors. 'Is that you Stinky?'

The captor stiffened.

'I mean, Master Stinley.' She looked at Shuttle, hoping he wouldn't know that there was already a master in their midst. 'You do know this is a master?' she nodded her head towards the source of the smell.

'Even masters want the guild to change its ways,' Shuttle retorted. 'But the person holding you is Brother Dye.'

A Murder for Master Wat

'Certainly smells like something died, ha ha.'

'We're going to tie you up,' Shuttle sneered. 'Don't make us gag you as well.'

. . .

'So, gentlemen,' Hartle leaned on the table in front of the guild men, who now seemed to be hiding in the back of the stall. They probably didn't expect anyone to actually come up to them, let alone anyone with a monk. 'I think you might be able to help us out.'

'Oh, yes?' one guild official asked in a rather nervous tone.

'Absolutely. You know that Master Hemling is dead, of course.'

The two men only nodded now, their eyes wide as they considered the possibility that they were going to be asked to look after the body.

'And Brother Hermitage here is the King's Investigator.'

This was getting worse and worse. The whimpers emerging from the stall indicated that the men would be willing to do anything to make these people go away.

'Without going into the details, it's important that we talk to someone in the guild.'

'Guild?' one man asked as if he'd never heard of anything called a guild.

'The Weavers' Guild. The guild you're sitting here taking money for, that guild.'

'Aha,' a very nervous laugh simpered out. 'That guild.'

'Just so.' Hartle smiled, but not in a nice way. 'Where are they?' His voice took on a darker shade and made it quite clear that Wat the Weaver and the King's Investigator could be let loose at any moment to wreak havoc on a couple of humble stall-minders.

'We're only tending the stall,' the second one explained through a pale face and trembling lips. 'We're not even members of the guild. We only live here. The guild was offering work for the moot. They never said nothing about monks and kings and dead people. Just take the money, they said. Ask everyone to pay their dues, they said.'

'So it will be easy for you to tell us where they are.'

It only took one brief exchange of looks for the two men to make up their minds. Their specific instruction not to tell anyone where the guild officials were did not cover situations like this. 'They're in the town.'

'Well, yes. Where, exactly?'

'They're staying in the great hall. Guests of the sheriff.'

'Ha,' Wat coughed. 'I wonder if the sheriff knows that.'

'It's Shire Reeve, actually,' Hermitage could not resist correcting the word. He knew that the young people, like Cwen, were shortening the word to sheriff, but where would that sort of thing end?

The man in the guild tent looked like he really didn't care what the pronunciation was, as long as it made these people go away.

'The great hall,' Hartle checked.

'Yes,' one man nodded vigorously. 'You can't miss it. It's right on the main street. It's a hall.'

'And it's great,' his companion added, helpfully.

'Greatest in the land,' the first nodded that the place was worth a visit even if you weren't on some sort of horrible mission.

'Right,' Hartle smiled and stepped back from the guild stall, which gave the men inside the opportunity to breathe again. He turned to Wat and Hermitage. 'Let's go and find the

A Murder for Master Wat

Sheriff of Nottingham.'

...

The great hall of Nottingham really was great and took their breath away. This was despite Hermitage spending the entirety of the short walk trying to persuade the others that they were, in fact, going to see the Shire Reeve of Snotingeham.

'Whatever you call this place or the people in it,' Hartle scowled at Hermitage, 'It is pretty impressive.'

The building was at least 100 feet long, a staggering distance. A tall roof dropped low eaves down to rest atop the windows and doors set into the side, and a chimney, perched in the middle of the length, puffed sweet-smelling wood smoke into the air. Outside, the place hummed with people coming and going on the business of the town, and the three of them standing there were of no interest at all.

'Right,' Hartle rubbed his hands. 'Let's see what we can see.'

'I'll wait here,' Wat looked around for somewhere to get comfortable. 'In fact, over there, probably.' He nodded towards a tavern opposite.

Hartle frowned hard at him.

'There's no point me coming in,' Wat explained. 'It'll only cause trouble. If there are any guild people in there they'll spend all their time going on about how awful I am and how they won't even speak to me.'

Hermitage smiled some encouragement to Hartle. 'He's probably right, you know.'

Hartle sighed.

'He is fairly awful,' Hermitage confirmed. 'Or rather, he

was. It's the business of Hemling we need to be looking into. We could end up in a horrible argument about Wat if we take him with us. He'll only cause a distraction.'

'Very well,' Hartle reluctantly accepted the situation. 'But you really do wait here,' he pointed a finger at Wat. 'And keep off the wine.'

Wat looked over to the tavern. 'More of an alehouse I'd say, by the look of it.' He gave them a friendly wave and strode happily over to find a seat. He called back over his shoulder. 'If I hear the sound of fighting, I'll pop over.'

'Fighting?' Hermitage asked, in some panic.

'There won't be any fighting,' Hartle dismissed the suggestion. 'He's only trying to worry you. Guild men don't fight. Not themselves, anyway. They pay other people to do it for them.'

Hermitage didn't find that much of a comfort as he followed Hartle toward the entrance of the hall.

Tall, oak double doors were as large and impressive as the rest of the building and they stood open to allow the constant flow of people in and out. This weavers' moot was clearly a very busy time for the town and while it may be bringing in lots of money, it obviously required a lot of work. Messengers were coming and going, well-dressed merchants loitered and chatted and officials, wearing badges of office, were instructing men hither and thither.

As Hermitage and Hartle passed through the door, one very burly fellow pushed past them, large leather buckets in each hand. He shouted back to the town official who had just despatched him. 'This is the last time,' he complained. 'If I have to clear up another one, I'm going home.'

The official waved him away and turned to the next problem. Hartle and Hermitage made sure that they did not

A Murder for Master Wat

ask this man where to find the guild.

If the outside of the hall was busy, the main entrance space was complete chaos. There seemed to be no one in charge, the noise of people shouting, demanding, reporting and complaining was immense and there was certainly no sign of the weavers' guild.

'They won't be getting involved in the actual running of the moot,' Hartle explained. 'They're probably in a back room somewhere, congratulating themselves on how well it's all going.'

'I don't care!' one man of the hall almost screamed into their ears.

They spun around and saw that he was berating a humble-looking fellow who was probably only reporting some problem or other.

'Tell him that's the only space there is and he will have to like it or lump it,' the man dismissed the issue.

'It's the lumps he's moaning about,' the humble fellow retorted. 'And what they're lumps of.'

They quickly moved on.

There was a second door to the back of the main entrance hall and they made their way to that, pushing and pressing past people who didn't seem in the least concerned who they were or where they were going.

Hartle opened the door and led the way into a much quieter place, the great hall itself. This really was an awe-inspiring space and demanded whispers and quiet conversation, not the raucous racket that pervaded outside.

This was clearly the space where the business of the town was conducted and would have room for virtually the whole population if needed. A huge fire blazed in the centre, the smoke finding its way up through the chimney they had seen from the outside. Even on a warm day, the inside of the hall was cold. The massive roof and small windows held back most of the light, as well as any warmth.

There were small groups of people in various corners of the room, talking quietly, most of them holding metal goblets, probably of wine. It was a markedly different scene from the one on the other side of the door.

'What do you want?'

Hermitage turned at the question and saw one of the reasons for the peace and quiet in here remaining undisturbed. The rest of the room stopped their quiet chatter and looked on as the very large man at the door held out just one of his very large arms to stop Hartle and Hermitage from progressing any further.

A couple of the chatting groups sniggered into their goblets, doubtless amused by the impudence of the common folk interrupting them.

'We're here to see the guild,' Hartle said. He nodded towards the far end of the room where a larger group sat in tall, padded, comfortable-looking chairs. The sort of chairs a person could sleep in. The sort of chairs people were sleeping in. A couple were chatting, but two others looked sound asleep. Tables of food and drink were set up next to them and the mess on the floor said that they had feasted well.

'There you are then,' the large man gestured towards the same people. 'You've seen them. Now get out.'

'If only it were so simple,' Hartle shook his head.

The large man was not impressed and moved to bundle them both back out of the door.

'I am a master of the Weavers' Guild,' Hartle complained as he was pushed. 'You can't push me.'

The man pushed some more to show that this was not the

case.

'Oy,' Hartle shouted towards the leaders of his guild, in a very unceremonial manner. None of them paid any attention.

'Hemling is dead, you know.'

One of the figures in the chairs raised a languorous hand to indicate that yes, they did know, and weren't particularly interested. The hand on the end of the arm then made a "go away" gesture, which the large man took as a direct instruction.

Hartle grunted as he fought back against his enforced departure; fought back completely ineffectively. 'He was killed, by the way,' he cried out, over the shoulder of the obstruction that was inexorably moving him towards the door.

No reaction to this from the guild gathering.

'And this is Brother Hermitage,' Hartle tried.

Hermitage thought that this was going to have no effect whatsoever. The hierarchy of his own church didn't know who he was, let alone an important group of weavers.

As they reached the threshold of the door and were about to be completely evicted, Hartle tried one more thing. 'Brother Hermitage,' he repeated. 'King William has sent his personal Investigator to find out which one of you murdered Hemling.'

That got their attention.

It got Hermitage's as well, as his knees stopped working.

Caput IX: Funny Shades of Grey

'This is ridiculous,' Cwen complained as two hands behind her bound her wrists with some rough twine and she was dragged to the back of the Grey Guild's tent.

'Silence,' Brother Shuttle led the way through an opening and out onto the field beyond. This was on the edge of the moot, and the edge of Nottingham as well. They were high on the main hill of the town and looked down on the River Trent, curling around beneath them.

'What are you going to do?' Cwen taunted. 'Throw me in the river?'

Shuttle stopped and turned to look at her. 'I hadn't thought of that,' he said, with a nice smile.

Cwen swallowed. This Shuttle had seemed such an idiot, even more so when he started praising Wat to the heavens. Now that he had her tied up on top of a hill leading to a deep river, she began to see his strengths.

'You can't kill me,' she half instructed, half pleaded.

Shuttle laughed. 'If we roll you down the hill the river will do the killing bit.'

'But, but.' Cwen strained at the ropes restraining her but nothing moved. She started to panic, thinking that these people might actually be mad enough to do this, and that simply shouting at them wouldn't work. Simply shouting at people worked in so many circumstances that she had come to rely on it as her main tactic.

Shuttle laughed again. 'We don't kill the likes of you.'

'Likes of me?' Cwen was mightily offended that she wasn't

A Murder for Master Wat

the sort of person they'd kill.

'Who do you think we are? The Weavers' Guild?'

The whole party spat on the ground.

Cwen felt a huge relief at this. She had been looking at the slope, trying to work out if she could roll sideways and avoid the water.

'What are you doing then?' she demanded, her old self returning in strength. Strength bolstered by a huge quantity of irritation that these people dared treat her like this.

'We are restraining you.' Shuttle explained.

'Well, yes, I picked that up from the rope. But why?'

'Because you would speak of us, obviously. You have had the temerity to speak to Wat the Weaver,' hands went to chests, 'and we have revealed to you that we have already struck our first blow. You might go and spread word before we are ready.'

'I don't even know what this blow is,' Cwen protested. 'How can I tell anyone what you've done if I don't know what it is myself?'

'You will find out.' Shuttle now took to pacing up and down in front of her. 'When you get back to the moot it will be the talk of the place. The action we have taken will be on everyone's lips. And you'll be there to say, "oh, I know, that was the Grey Guild."'

Cwen frowned under her hood. 'How will anyone know it's you who struck your great blow if you don't tell them you did it?'

'The time is not yet ripe.'

'Isn't it?'

'No.'

'I see. When will it be ripe?'

'In due course.'

'And how long is due course?'

'Who can tell?'

Cwen's anger at her treatment was melting to simple irritation as she concluded that these people really were idiots after all. 'This all seems a bit vague if you don't mind me saying. You've done something you won't talk about, you don't want anyone to know and you've tied someone up for not knowing what it is anyway.'

Shuttle pointed a finger at her. It seemed to be shaking with his own irritation. He stepped closer. 'The blow has been struck and now the moot will be in a panic. If we reveal ourselves too soon the guild will simply retaliate. They need time to reflect, a few hours to give it calm consideration, then we will come forward.'

'Ha,' Cwen scoffed.

'Look, Brother Cwen,' Shuttle was quite annoyed that his carefully thought out plan was being criticised like this. He reached out and took the edge of her hood, throwing it back to reveal her face.

The silence on that hill was so intense it could have been bundled up and rolled down to drown in the river.

Someone coughed. A shape at the back was the first to speak. 'It's a girl,' it said, in frank astonishment.

Shuttle was gaping.

Cwen appraised her captors, all of whom were simply standing and staring. 'Don't suppose you've seen a woman this close,' she said. 'The Grey Guild being a male institution. Or at least that's what your tent smelled like.'

'What?' Shuttle managed to get just the one word out.

'Are you doing here?' Cwen prompted.

Shuttle nodded his agreement.

'I'm a weaver.'

A Murder for Master Wat

The silence continued until someone let out a snort. 'No, you're not.' This was said as if Cwen had just cracked a very good joke.

'Yes,' she said, fiercely. 'I am.'

'I hardly think so,' Shuttle condescended.

If Cwen's hands hadn't been tied she'd have pulled his head off.

'Then what's all that weaving I do?' she spoke through gritted teeth.

'Oh, you may do some weaving. A lot of women do weaving. Making cloth for the family, a bit of tapestry for the rich, but it's not weaving, is it.'

'It's not weaving? What's weaving then?' She tried desperately to control the anger that wanted to roll the entire Grey Guild down the hill and into the river with rocks tied to their ankles.

'It's a craft,' Shuttle explained, wearily. 'Weavers are craftsmen of their trade and they belong to a guild.'

'The Weaver's Guild?'

They all spat.

'The Weavers' Guild you all despise? You're saying that you can't be a weaver unless you join the hated guild? So none of you is a weaver either?'

'No.' Shuttle didn't sound too sure of himself. 'We are members of the hated guild, but only because we have to be. We simply want that guild to change its ways.'

'So you are guild members. All of you belong to the Weavers' Guild.' Now she spat.

The voice at the back spoke up again, in a rather whining complaint. 'They won't let us be weavers if we don't join.'

'Oh, for goodness sake,' Cwen shook her head. 'You useless bunch. You're about as rebellious as a Saxon in a Viking longboat. What is it exactly that you expect the Weavers' Guild to change? And don't bother spitting again, I think we've had enough of that.'

'They must change their ways,' Shuttle announced, proudly.

'Yes,' Cwen pressed, 'which ways? What specific thing do you want them to do? If you've got one specific thing at all.'

'Masters,' Shuttle suggested.

'What about them?'

'They must change their ways.'

'I can see that you want a lot of ways changing but you haven't actually told me one yet.'

'Beating apprentices must stop,' Shuttle declared, to a round of applause from his fellows.

Cwen looked around the group. Shuttle was by far the oldest of those who had their hoods thrown back. The rest were all far too young to be masters. 'Apart from Stinley, who ought to be one, you're all apprentices.'

'We are,' the one at the back sounded quite proud of the fact.

'Including the ones who are hiding in your hoods, presumably in case your master spots you. And Shuttle here, who must be the oldest apprentice I've ever seen. What journeyman's tests did you fail? All of them?'

Shuttle's finger went back to pointing again. 'And that's another thing. These ridiculous tests that they make you do.'

'Like stringing a loom straight,' Cwen suggested. 'Or carding, dyeing and needle preparation.'

A little mutter of admiration ran around the group as they saw that Cwen seemed to know what she was talking about.

'You can't do any of them properly then,' she accused Shuttle.

'That is not the point,' the man retorted. 'The point is…,'

'The point is that you're not a very good weaver,' Cwen shrugged. 'Doesn't matter whether you're in the guild or out of it. If you can't put thread on a loom, you can't be a weaver. Not by anyone's measure, Grey Guild or not.'

This new silence was a bit embarrassing.

'But you're right,' Cwen went on. 'I am not a weaver.'

Various nods went around the group and Shuttle smiled that he had been right all along.

'By the definition of being an apprentice or a journeyman or a master or joining the guild, no, I am not a weaver. They wouldn't have me, would they? Not because I can't weave, but because I'm female.'

A couple of frowns appeared, which Cwen picked up on. 'Which is ridiculous. That's the sort of thing a Grey Guild ought to be trying to get changed. You're right again about the masters. In most workshops they have everything and the apprentices have nothing. Then, when those same moaning apprentices become masters they carry on exactly as their own masters did. Nothing changes.'

More nods of agreement.

'And the guild is the worst of the lot. They've become masters to the masters, rulers of their own little kingdom who don't want anything to change.'

'Yes,' a small group gave Cwen a little cheer.

'But I weave. I was taught by a master, a real master of the guild, even though I could never become one. And I make a very good living at the craft. I'm in a workshop with apprentices and I now teach them what I know. I work with a great master, who doesn't care that I'm the wrong size and shape for a weaver.'

Several of the Grey Guild sounded quite impressed that

such a place existed. Shuttle was looking a bit more anxious.

'What if the guild found out?' A nervous hand went up as the question was asked.

'If my hands weren't tied up I'd snap my fingers,' Cwen replied. 'We don't care an owl's second hoot for the guild. They never come near us anyway. Part of the reason I came to the moot was to see how the land lies for women weavers.' She cast a baleful stare upon them all. 'And I can see that it does not lie well. I might expect the guild to be horrified at the idea but when I heard about the Grey Guild my hopes were raised.'

Much nodding and agreement at this.

'Until I find you're no better.'

The nodding and agreement stopped.

'You don't want the guild to change, you just want to be masters. Preferably without your weaving skill being tested at all.' She directed this comment at Shuttle.

'And if you really were great weavers you wouldn't care whether you were in the guild or not.'

The puzzled faces said that no one could follow this line of thinking.

'I work with one weaver who never passed on to become a master.' She swallowed and hoped that there was no one she knew nearby to hear this. 'One whose work outshines anything made by any member of the guild. The very best weaver that I have ever seen, probably the best the world has ever seen. And one who doesn't give a flea bite for the guild. He shows that you don't need the guild to be a weaver.

'And does the guild care for him? No, it does not. It tries to thwart him and will have nothing to do with him because he's not one of them. A great weaver, even they know he's a great weaver, and they won't even let him into the moot. They left specific instructions that he was to be kept out.'

'No!' The Grey Guild was enthralled by this tale.

'Yes. But did he take any notice? No, he did not. He came anyway, ignored the guild's petty rules and even now he walks the stalls and streets of Nottingham.'

'Hurrah,' the Grey Guild was quite excited now, except Shuttle, who was frowning at his own men and their unwarranted enthusiasm.

'Who is it?' One member called out.

Cwen took a breath and looked at them all. 'Wat the Weaver.'

Various cries of "no", gasps of surprise, and hands put to mouths greeted this announcement.

'For God's sake,' Cwen muttered to herself. 'Who did you think I was talking about?'

The Grey Guild now seemed happy that they could draw close to this woman without something unpleasant happening.

'So that business about you talking to Wat was true?' one young voice under a hood asked.

'Of course,' Cwen huffed. 'He's only a man, you know. He's not some sort of angel. Far from it. His workshop's in Derby, for heaven's sake, you could walk up the road to meet him yourself.'

The crowd "ooh'd" as if they had just seen a conjurer's trick.

'In fact, if you like, I could go and get him. He could come and say hello.'

'Never,' Shuttle boomed out.

'Never?' Cwen asked. 'Why not?'

'Why not?' Shuttle was clearly not used to this level of rebellion.

'Yes, why not?'

'I've explained why not. Because,' Shuttle pointed the finger again, clearly making this up as he was going along. 'It is part of our mystery.'

'Wat not coming here is part of your mystery?' Cwen scoffed. 'Pulling your hood down doesn't make you mysterious, you know. It just makes you bump into things.'

'If Wat the Weaver came to meet us, word of the Grey Guild would be everywhere.'

Cwen nodded that she understood. 'And the time is not ripe.'

'Exactly. We move like ghosts among the guild,' Shuttle waxed lyrical. 'They see us not, they hear us not. The shades of the Grey Guild wreak their havoc and make fall the mighty.'

Cwen sniffed. 'And how long has the time not been ripe?'

'About three years,' another voice reported, with a weary sigh, heavy with boredom and three years of disappointed expectations.

'You'll see,' Shuttle addressed them all. 'You know that we have been waiting for this moot. The Grand Moot has not been held for many years and the Grey Guild would not affect change if we had to go round the country talking to everyone. The moot brings them all here, where we can strike.'

The crowd didn't seem impressed.

'We have been over this,' Shuttle reminded them, impatiently. 'Years of planning thrown away for the chance to meet Wat the Weaver? Our first blow is struck, we wait a few hours and go forward. When that is done we will be free to move openly.'

'Then we can meet Wat?' someone asked.

A Murder for Master Wat

'Wat will want to meet us,' Shuttle declared. 'Everyone will want to meet us.'

The Grey Guild seemed placated by this.

'In the meantime, this woman who claims to be a weaver must be kept here. She cannot be allowed to ruin our plans at this late stage.'

'Plans!' Cwen mocked.

'You will see, you will see.' Shuttle had regained his confidence now, and the Grey Guild stood at his back. 'Brother Cwen,' he sneered. 'Or whatever your real name is.'

'It's Cwen,' said Cwen, with a hopeless shake of the head.

'Oh. Right. Yes.' He turned to his men. 'Brother Treadle, Brother Heddle, guard her carefully while we return to the moot for the next step.'

'Heddle and Treadle?' Cwen sniggered.

'Shut up,' Shuttle instructed as he strode back to the tent. 'You will see the chaos that is about to descend on this so-called moot. The name of the Grey Guild will strike fear into the heart of the masters. It will all be in the name of the great Wat the Weaver and none shall be safe.' With a grand wave of his arms, he disappeared back into the tent. He seemed to be in a bit of a hurry, perhaps in case Cwen started criticising him again.

Caput X: The Sheriff of Nottingham

'King's what?' a guild member asked, without standing up.

All of the guild men remained in their seats. Hermitage thought that this was rather rude, but, judging by the amount of food and drink that littered this corner of the hall, he suspected that if they tried to stand they would probably fall over. Or be sick. Or both.

'Investigator,' Hartle repeated. 'Brother Hermitage is the King's Investigator.'

'Disgusting,' one of the guild slurred.

When they were allowed to approach the guild, Hermitage saw that there were only four of them here, it just looked as if there were more because of all the mess. It also seemed that they had been in their chairs for days and were used to being served whatever they wanted. And they were not used to being disturbed.

'It means he looks into things.'

'Vestigare,' Hermitage explained. 'The Latin, you know. To track. Vestigo homicidium, you might say,' he smiled. 'I investigate murder.'

It seemed the leaders of the guild weren't concerned about the Latin just at the moment.

'Murder?' one, who might be even more senior than the others raised his finger. He then looked puzzled about why he'd done this and put it down again. 'You were shouting something about murder.'

'Hemling,' Hartle spoke loud and clear. 'Hemling is dead and we think he has been killed. Murdered.'

'Oh, I doubt that,' another muttered. 'You can't go round shouting about murder, you know. Won't do at all. Upset the moot.'

'That could be the point,' Hartle was sounding impatient with this lot already. 'Is one of you in charge here? Who's the most senior.'

'That'd be me,' one who hadn't spoken at all raised his arm. 'Grand Master,' he announced, with a slur. His fellows huffed and jeered at his title.

'Grand Master Wulfstand?' Hartle asked, sounding surprised.

'That's me,' the man replied, sounding quite surprised himself.

'So you do exist?'

'Eh, what? Exist? Of course, I exist. Couldn't eat and drink if I didn't exist.'

'Well, no one's ever seen you,' Hartle reported. 'Never turn up to guild meetings, never appear at ceremonies. The Grand Moot is going on out there and you're in here.'

'Best place,' Wulfstand replied. 'Don't want to mix with all those weavers. Ghastly people.'

Grand Master Wulfstand hauled himself round in his chair and cast his gaze upon them. Hermitage could see why he hadn't got up, he suspected that if the Grand Master moved, the chair would come with him. From the size of the man he would judge that it must have taken considerable strength, and several assistants, to squeeze him into the chair in the first place. And it was a big chair.

Hemling had been a huge fellow but he was dwarfed by this Wulfstand. Perhaps the higher up the guild hierarchy you got, the bigger you became. Or vice versa. In a rare moment of levity, Hermitage imagined that the chair might be at its utmost limit and would, at any moment, expel Grand Master Wulfstand at great speed. That really would cause carnage and wipe out the leadership of the guild with one very heavy blow.

'And what's this about us murdering him, eh?' Wulfstand demanded. 'Haven't left this room since we arrived. And who are you, anyway, to go round making accusations like that?'

'Master Hartle.'

'Hartle, Hartle,' Wulfstand muttered as he tried to bring the name to mind. 'Never heard of you,' he concluded.

'I'm not surprised. I'm a weaver. One of the ghastly people.'

'We can check on the register, you know. Have you removed for your impudence.'

'If you can get out of your chair to find it,' Hartle hissed, quietly.

'Anyway,' Wulfstand collapsed back into his chair, which creaked its complaint. 'We've been here since before the moot began. Hardly likely to be out sticking knives in old Hemling.'

'He was killed by his loom,' Hartle informed them.

'Killed by his loom?' Wulfstand snorted. 'What? His loom got up and stuck a knife in him?' He laughed heartily at this and indicated that his fellows should join in. Which none of them did, two of them being asleep. 'Then take his loom, sir, and execute it. Can't have looms going around killing people, be the end of the trade.'

'His loom was so arranged that a metal warp snapped and cut his throat.' Hartle put a bit of wishful thinking into the "cut his throat" bit and seemed to be looking at Wulfstand's throat as he did so.

'I don't think any of us would be capable of that,' Wulfstand indicated his companions.

Hermitage looked at them and could well believe that none of these men was even capable of bending down, let alone

A Murder for Master Wat

getting into the workings of a loom to carefully replace a single warp.

'What is a warp, anyway?' Wulfstand asked.

Hartle just gazed at him. 'What's a warp?' He repeated, slowly and with naked incredulity.

'Some weaving thing, I suppose.'

'Yes,' Hartle informed the Grand Master. 'It's a weaving thing. Have you ever actually done any weaving?'

'Good God, no.' Wulfstand sounded mightily offended.

'But you're Grand Master of the guild for the whole of this part of the country.'

Wulfstand nodded. 'As was my father and his father before him. And my son will take over after me.'

'I don't suppose he's a weaver?' Hartle asked.

'How dare you? My son is a gentleman, not in some grubby trade.'

Hartle held his head in his hands and considered the other senior members of his guild. 'Any of these weavers?' he asked, rather hopelessly.

'Local guild officials, apparently,' Wulfstand shrugged his great shoulders. 'Don't know any of 'em. They were here when I arrived.'

'Great Gods of the loom,' Hartle exclaimed, loud enough for all to hear.

'Never mind us, young man,' Wulfstand grumbled. 'You say you're a master and this is the King's Investigator but we don't know that. You come in here shouting about the place, making outrageous accusations with no authority at all.'

'Apart from the king's.'

'So you say. However, I don't see the king.' Wulfstand's eyes narrowed. 'Perhaps we'll ask the sheriff.'

'The sheriff?'

'Yes.' The Grand Master seemed to have some scheme in mind that would put these two in their place. 'Fellow called William Peverel, he's new.'

'That's fine,' Hartle was confident.

'He's very, what would you say?' Wulfstand gave this some thought. 'Very Norman. Yes, that's it, very Norman. One of the most Norman people I've ever met. He's the new sheriff because he very effectively stopped the old sheriff from being alive anymore. Very close to the king, they say. He's the one building the castle you've probably spotted.'

'Good,' Hartle said.

Hermitage wasn't so sure. He'd never come across a William Peverel in his dealings with King William. Perhaps this Peverel didn't know about Hermitage at all.

'We'll be very happy to talk to the sheriff,' Hartle went on. 'But all we want to know is whether Hemling was looking after the money from the moot. And if anyone had come forward saying that they could take over from him, now that he was dead. It could provide a very good reason for murder.'

'Aha,' Wulfstand crowed. 'Now you change your tune, sir. Not accusing us of killing him anymore. Not now I threaten you with the sheriff.'

Hartle sighed, heavily. 'I only accused you because you wouldn't talk to us otherwise. I can see now that none of you is capable of even walking as far as Hemling's loom, and you probably wouldn't recognise it when you got there, as you don't have the first clue about weaving.'

Wulfstand raised his arm and beckoned someone standing by the door to come over.

A harassed looking and fidgety man came over, bits of parchment in his hand and a quill behind his ear. 'Yes?' he said, impatiently.

A Murder for Master Wat

'Ah, Grimly,' Wulfstand nodded.

'Gremwold,' Gremwold corrected for what sounded like the hundredth time.

'Summon the sheriff,' Wulfstand instructed.

'Do what?' Gremwold was staggered.

'Summon the sheriff.'

'Summon the sheriff?'

'That's what I said, man.'

'Summon William Peverel, the Sheriff of Nottingham?'

'What is the matter with you?'

'You want me to summon William Peverel, the Norman lord and Sheriff of Nottingham to come down from his castle and attend upon you?'

'At last.'

'You don't summon the sheriff, for God's sake.' Gremwold rolled his eyes at Hermitage and Hartle. He had clearly had several days experience of the Grand Master, every one of them a fresh trial.

'I am the Grand Master of the Weavers' Guild,' Wulfstand protested.

'You could be the Green Man on a night out with the King of the Faeries for all I care.'

'You have become increasingly troublesome over the last few days, Grimly. I shall have to take a note of your name.'

'Please do. Shall I spell it for you?'

'Just fetch the sheriff.'

'He's a bloody big Norman with a hundred soldiers at his beck and call. If you want to see the sheriff, you go to him.' Gremwold appraised the state of Wulfstand. 'And I don't think that's going to happen, is it? It's a steep climb to the castle and I don't think you're capable.' He turned to Hartle and Hermitage. 'Are you anything to do with this lot?'

'Not really, it seems.' Hartle replied.

'They say they're here with the moot but I've seen no sign of it. All they do is sit and eat and drink and don't pay for anything.'

'You're not with the guild then?' Hermitage enquired.

Gremwold replied with a very weary look of utter despair. 'No. I'm not. And if anyone mentions the Weavers' Guild after this I shall do something uncalled for. I'm supposed to be clerk of the town court. How I got the job of trying to manage this moot, I don't know. Must have upset someone.'

'You don't look like a cleric,' Hermitage noted. He knew that it was common for churchmen to take the notes for the court; they were the only ones who could write.

'I'm not.' Gremwold sighed again. 'My father taught me to read and write and one day the old sheriff found out. Made me clerk and that was that.'

'They'll be gone soon,' Hartle tried to sound encouraging.

'Not soon enough. And I dread to think of the mess they're going to leave behind.'

'Not to mention the dead body,' Hermitage said, then almost immediately thought that perhaps he shouldn't have mentioned it.

'Dead body?' Gremwold looked dumbstruck. 'What dead body?'

'An old weaver,' Hartle explained. 'Died at his loom.'

Gremwold shrugged with relief. 'It happens, I suppose. This many people in town all at once it's inevitable someone's going to choose this moment to die. Damned inconvenient. I hope the guild is going to pay to get him dealt with.'

'This weaver didn't choose to die.' Hartle raised his eyebrows to make the implication clear.

'Oh, hell. And that's why the giant wearing the chair wants

A Murder for Master Wat

the sheriff?'

'Sort of.'

At that moment there was a huge commotion at the main door to the chamber and much shouting and clattering of metal could be heard.

Hermitage recognised swords being brandished when he heard them; yet another terrible consequence of his being made King's Investigator. He'd only seen two or three swords before that, and they were very poor ones, mainly used as tools of the field instead of war. Now he knew what they looked like and felt like when they did what they were made for. The clattering of swords could only mean Normans. If anyone else clattered a sword these days their clattering days would be over in very short order.

The door was thrown open and sure enough, two Norman soldiers strode into the room. They appraised it quickly, pushed two innocent bystanders out of the way (who weren't in the way in the first place) and then stood guard.

Everyone in the room looked expectantly towards the entrance and simultaneously shrank discreetly into whatever shadow they could find.

Needless to say, the members of the Weavers' Guild couldn't go anywhere. Not unless they took their chairs with them, which would look a bit odd.

The cause of the disturbance now strode into the room and pierced everyone in it with his gaze. 'Silence,' he barked, which seemed unnecessary as no one was saying a word.

Hermitage had no doubt that this was William Peverel. From far too many encounters with the king and his court, he had come to recognise very important Norman nobles when they shouted at him. They did share common physical traits: quite big, strange haircuts, lots of weapons, but they also carried an indefinable quality that made you want to keep very quiet or ideally be somewhere else altogether.

This Peverel had the look of a mature and experienced soldier. Hermitage didn't recognise him at all, so he had not been present at any of his meetings with King William or his awful harbinger of doom, Le Pedvin; a harbinger who also delivered doom in person. It was easy to see that this man knew the field of Hastings very well indeed. He spotted Gremwold. 'Where are the weavers?' he demanded.

Strangely, the Grand Master did not put his hand up.

'Over there, my lord,' Gremwold bowed and smiled. And rubbed his hands with what looked like glee.

Peverel beckoned his guards to follow him and strode over to the chairs.

Hermitage and Hartle sidled away to make room. Peverel noticed this and simply gave them a sideways glance that carried the clear instruction that they were not to sidle any further.

'What's this about a murder?' Peverel demanded of the Grand Master.

That large representative of the weavers' fraternity was making valiant efforts to rise from his chair in the face of authority. Unfortunately, it seemed that the chair had grown so fond of him that it did not want to let him go. It shook and creaked beneath him and clung to his sides like some upholstered leech.

'Don't bother getting up,' Peverel said. 'I won't have to lift my sword so high when I cut your head off.'

'Eek,' said the Grand Master of the Weavers' Guild for the whole of this part of the country.

'What about this murder?' Peverel repeated, making it quite clear that one repetition was all you got.

A Murder for Master Wat

'Only a weaver,' the Grand Master managed to get out, making it sound just slightly worse than the death of a rat. 'An old weaver of the guild by the name of Hemling. He was the organiser of the moot. These fellows say he was killed by his loom.' He nodded towards Hartle and Hermitage.

Peverel turned his gaze on them. Hermitage nodded and gave a weak smile.

'A weaver?' Peverel returned to Wulfstand. 'A Saxon then?'

'Oh, yes. Most assuredly Saxon, my Lord. All the way through.'

'Pah,' Peverel turned away. 'I was told someone had murdered a Norman.' He sounded much relieved that this was turning out to be such a trivial matter. 'Brought me all the way down from the castle.' He glared at Wulfstand that this was obviously all his fault. 'Killed by his loom?' The Norman clearly thought this Saxon was as mad as all the others.

'So he says,' Wulfstand waved a hand towards Hermitage now, happily passing on responsibility for anything the Norman might not be happy about.

'And who the devil are you?' Peverel asked Hermitage. 'You're a monk.'

Hermitage acknowledged the observation. 'Brother Hermitage, my lord.'

'Hermitage?' Peverel frowned. 'Funny name for a monk.'

'Indeed, my lord.'

The Grand Master's face carried a slight smile now, relishing the fact that the big Norman with the sword and two guards had passed his attention on to these two annoyances.

Peverel looked thoughtful. 'King William has an investigator called Hermitage.'

'Just so, my lord,' Hermitage nodded again, although he now felt the weight of the world resting on the back of his head and wasn't sure he'd be able to lift it up again.

'What are you doing investigating the death of a Saxon?' Peverel sounded very confused. 'I don't think the king will want you wasting your time on this lot.' He waved his hand to take in everyone in the hall.

'I just happened to be here, my lord,' Hermitage tried the smile again. It hadn't had any effect the first time but he couldn't think of anything else.

'Just happened to be at a weavers' moot?' Peverel was clearly a man who liked order and everything in its place. Monks at weavers' moots was odd and he didn't like odd. 'Ah,' he raised a gloved finger. 'The other one.'

'Other one?' The horrible feeling that Hermitage usually had two or three times a day readied itself for action.

'Yes. The king was telling us all about Umair someone or other.' Peverel rubbed his fingers to help bring the tale to mind. 'Dead fellow,' he explained.[6] 'You and the other one sorted it all out.'

'I see.' There was no way Hermitage was going to offer the information.

'The other one's a weaver.' Peverel looked at Hartle. 'Distasteful fellow,' he granted Hartle a heavy Norman scowl. 'Wat the Weaver,' he snapped his fingers. 'Is that you?'

'No, my lord,' Hartle protested with some feeling.

'You?' Peverel demanded of the Grand Master.

'Certainly not,' the large man protested in high umbrage.

The room, which had been quiet anyway, now got quieter.

'And you want to investigate this dead Saxon, do you?' he

---

[6] The dead fellow, Umair, is the main feature in The Case of The Curious Corpse

A Murder for Master Wat

asked Hermitage.

"Want" was not a word Hermitage had ever used in relation to an investigation unless it was "want" it to go away. 'As I am here and there is some suspicion about the death, then perhaps I should?' He was half hoping that the Norman would forbid him.

Peverel didn't seem interested at all. 'Please yourself.'

Again, not something Hermitage had done, ever.

'But if we get a proper murder, a Norman of some sort, you forget the Saxon, yes?'

'Of course, my lord.'

'And you,' Peverel turned back to Wulfstand. 'Will give the King's Investigator every assistance or I will come back and deal with you and the chair together.'

Wulfstand swallowed and nodded.

'And by the time I've finished there will still be two of you, but the chair will be on the inside.' Another snap of the fingers and the Normans strode from the room and departed.

The Saxons started breathing again.

'Well,' Hartle said, looking at the space most recently occupied by a large and well-armed Norman. 'Wasn't that nice?' He turned and smiled at the leaders of the guild. 'The sheriff has made everything very clear, hasn't he.' His smile dropped. 'Now,' he leaned on the back of Wulfstand's chair. 'Those questions about Hemling and the money.'

Caput XI: Osbert the Expert

'Wat the Weaver?' Grand Master Wulfstand sounded well and truly disgusted, and not inclined to discuss Hemling and money.

'Not me,' Hartle assured him. 'But you do know a bit about weaving then?'

'We will have nothing to do with that man,' Wulfstand turned high and mighty once more.

'That's fine,' Hartle was light-hearted. 'I'll just go and tell the sheriff to start preparing the chair for your next meal, shall I?'

Wulfstand grumbled and looked to the other guild members, all of whom failed to return his gaze. 'Just don't bring him in here.'

'Agreed. Now. Hemling, money.'

'I have absolutely no idea.' Wulfstand waved the question away as if such triviality should not disturb the Grand Master.

'You have no idea? You, the Grand Master have no idea whether the organiser of the moot is looking after your money.'

'Of course not. I don't concern myself with details like that.'

'You seem to concern yourself with spending a lot of it on your food and drink.'

'There will be a count at the end of the moot. Until then I trust that someone is looking after it.' Wulfstand raised a goblet to his lips. 'Now, if there's nothing else?'

'Who would know?' Hermitage enquired, with a bit less of Hartle's irritation and naked contempt.

A Murder for Master Wat

'Know what?'

'Know whether Hemling was looking after the money, or had someone doing it for him? Where do the men at their tables take the money at the end of the day?'

Wulfstand shrugged, as much as the chair would allow. 'It's probably written somewhere.'

'Written? Where would it be written?'

'In the moot rules,' Wulfstand sighed that these idiots couldn't even understand that.

'There are rules?' Hartle sounded surprised that this moot had rules.

'Of course. The guild has rules for everything.'

'None of which you know,' Hartle concluded with a nod. 'Where are they then? Where are these rules?'

'In the books.' Wulfstand waved nonchalantly towards a large leather trunk that was against the back wall of the hall.

'Books,' Hermitage breathed. 'A whole trunk full.'

They left Wulfstand, tutting at his lack of cooperation, and headed for the trunk.

The thing looked as if it had travelled far and wide, going wherever the guild needed its rules up and down the country. It also looked as if it had been quite a while since it had been opened. The guild obviously didn't actually refer to their rules that often. There were two leather straps holding it closed and the buckles on these were rusted and stiff.

'We'll be lucky if the whole lot hasn't rotted to dust,' Hartle complained.

'Oh, don't say that.' To Hermitage, the thought of books rotting to dust was quite revolting.

Eventually, after much fingernail breaking and some muttered swearing on Hartle's behalf, they managed to shift the buckles and pulled the straps out of the way. Pulling the lid back did indeed reveal the rules of the weavers' guild. At least, they had to assume these were the rules as the mess of parchment jumbled about inside could have been anything from King Cnut's orders to the sea, to recipes for cooking eels.

'What a mess,' Hermitage moaned. It was a mess, but it was a mess of parchment, which was really quite exciting. 'If these are their rules they have put very little care into keeping them in any sort of order. We shall just have to go through them all one at a time.' He was now quite excited by the prospect.

'Hm,' Hartle didn't sound quite so keen.

'A problem?'

'Me not reading?' Hartle asked. 'I suppose it might be when it comes to going through parchment.' He idly picked one from the trunk, looked at it, upside down, and then put it back.

'Ah, you don't read.'

'The odd word here and there but not much call for it, really. I'm the weaver, you're the monk. It's only monks who have to read.'

Hermitage sighed. On the one hand, it was a disappointment that he would have no help with his interrogation of the parchment; on the other hand, it was marvellous that he would have no interruption in his interrogation of the parchment.

'Perhaps I'll go and find Wat. If we could find out where Hemling was living, there may be something there about the money.'

'Like the money itself?' Hermitage suggested.

'Possibly. Not much of a motive for murder if it's still there though.'

A Murder for Master Wat

'But if it's gone it might point us in the right direction.'

'True,' Hartle hummed and looked at the parchment again. 'Well, I'll, erm, leave you to it then.' He headed to the door. 'Come and find us when you've finished, or we'll come and find you.'

'Hm,' Hermitage acknowledged the instruction, which he hadn't really heard. Something about finding something when he'd finished. He smiled at the trunk. That could be days.

...

Outside the main hall, Hartle set off to the tavern opposite, looking for Wat, who he suspected would be just where he had been left. Except there would be tankards around him. There was no sign though, and he didn't like to ask if anyone had seen Wat the Weaver. That really could lead to trouble. Where had the wretched man gone? He thought the tent where Hemling's body had rested would be as good a place as any to start and so headed off. After all, it was the main venue of the moot.

It did occur to him to think that Wat might be keeping his head down. After all, this was the moot of the Weavers' Guild and he had been specifically told that he was not allowed to come in. In those circumstances, it would be sensible to avoid attention in case someone threw him out.

He told himself not to be so stupid. This was Wat the Weaver. If anyone was going to draw attention to himself and cause trouble it would be Wat. He'd probably quite enjoy being thrown out just so he could get back in again and taunt people.

Perhaps he should just look for signs of the biggest

commotion in the moot, in the middle of which he would find Wat. There didn't appear to be any fights going on nor were any instructions being screamed out by guild officials trying to remove anyone. Neither was there any enthusiastic gathering of apprentices seeking sight of Wat, and preferably one of his infamous works.

Back at the Hemling tent, as he now thought of it, all signs of the deceased had been removed. All signs that anyone had even done their deceasing here had gone. The place was full once more as another talk of the moot was underway. Well, it wasn't full, but there were a few figures inside listening to something or other.

He poked his head in and saw that the place now contained masters and apprentices as well as a warp-thin figure at the front who was pacing up and down and waving his arms as he addressed his audience with boundless enthusiasm. Hartle ducked out quickly before he was spotted. He had recognised the speaker and the last thing he wanted to do was find himself in the audience for a talk by Osbert of Loxwood.

Hartle was surprised that there was anyone in the tent at all, perhaps they hadn't realised who was speaking, or had just come in for a rest only to find they were trapped.

Osbert had a reputation in the craft, one that usually meant people went out of their way to avoid him. He had what he called ideas. Lots of them, on every single aspect of weaving. And he didn't restrict himself to just having the ideas, he told them to anyone who would stand still long enough.

His letters and notes to the guild on points of interest were things of legend. It was rumoured that there were hundreds of them and that they had all been carefully read by just one

A Murder for Master Wat

person; Osbert.

Hartle had a horrible feeling that Hermitage might come across some of these documents in the guild trunk. He might need to think about organising a rescue party.

To anyone unfortunate or ill-informed enough to give Osbert space in which to talk, his suggestions sounded quite reasonable, to begin with; what sort of wood was best for treadles and how to correctly select the right gauge for a warp, that sort of thing. The problem was the ideas came from what appeared to be a bottomless pit, and the further down the pit you went, the more ridiculous the ideas.

And one idea alone could lead down a labyrinthine path from which there was no escape. The wood for treadles would lead to forestry, seasoning periods, care of saplings, ground quality, felling and axe selection. Then it could move on to cover metalwork, sharpening stones, quarrying, masons, statues, church design and the problems with the Latin liturgy. Osbert had an opinion on absolutely everything but the most important thing was that he should share it with you. The only way of stopping the flow was to simply walk away.

It was incredibly rude, but the man seemed not to notice. If there was anyone else nearby he would latch on to them instead.

Doubtless, this particular talk was covering his suggestions for the development of the craft, which were endless. Hartle couldn't imagine which idiot in the guild had allowed him talking space. He was probably going on about his moving tapestry. All he said he needed was a loom ten times the size of anything anyone had ever built, a system of treadles that would need an army to operate, and he would be able to create images in tapestry that moved. The man was clearly as mad as a March hare in a loon's waistcoat.

There was no way Hartle was loitering in this area.

'That's rubbish,' a voice called out from within the tent.

Hartle dropped his head into his hands, 'Oh, Wat,' he moaned.

He darted back into the tent and sure enough, there was Wat. He was standing at the back of the tent and had interrupted Osbert with his vocal criticism.

'What, exactly, is rubbish?' Osbert asked, magnanimously.

'All of it,' Wat replied, his most mischievous grin shining from his face.

The other members of the audience were trying to shush him quiet. It didn't do to give Osbert any sort of encouragement.

'Wat,' Hartle hissed at him. 'What the devil are you doing?'

'I'm having a chat with Osbert,' Wat explained with a smile.

'You're setting him off, that's what you're doing. You should know better.'

'I think it's time the Weavers' Guild gave Osbert a proper hearing,' Wat actually sniggered as he said this.

'As long as it's not you doing the actual hearing.'

'Aha,' Osbert called from the front of the tent. His eyes gave away the fact that he had many years of experience behind him. How he managed to be ten times more lively and unbearable than any of his peers was a mystery.

'Oh, God,' Hartle murmured. 'He's got me now.'

'I see we have the renowned Wat the Weaver in the tent.'

The few heads of the audience turned in their direction and Wat gave them a wave.

The masters tutted, the apprentices sniggered.

A Murder for Master Wat

'Which particular aspect of my talk do you say is rubbish, master Wat?'

Any other human being would be ready to punch Wat on the nose for his impudence. Osbert sincerely wanted to know what the rubbish was, and then to have a jolly good discussion to get to the bottom of it. His whining, nasal voice only seemed to add to the irritation he was able to inflict from any distance.

'All of it,' Wat called out, the audience now getting audibly annoyed with him for prolonging their ordeal. 'Everything you say is rubbish.'

'Aha,' Osbert raised an admonishing finger. 'Now that can hardly be the case, can it? For instance, the thing that I am saying now cannot be rubbish because it is a response to your own statement. Unless, of course, you consider your own words to be rubbish as well, ha ha.'

'Now you've done it,' Hartle grumbled.

'I wonder if we should introduce Osbert to Hermitage?' Wat was clearly enjoying himself.

'Was it perhaps the proposal that a thread coated with goose fat might be used to create clothing proof against water?'

The audience groaned as they obviously didn't want to listen to all that again.

'Or my proposal for the use of metal as a warp for woven chain mail?'

'Yes,' Wat replied quickly. 'That's rubbish.'

'What did you say?' Hartle asked, much to Wat's surprise.

Osbert looked delighted to have had a genuine question, of sorts. "That a thread infused with goose fat before the weaving process might provide a level of protection against…,'

'No, not that, the other one. The metal.'

'Ah, yes, a very interesting area indeed. As I was only saying about half an hour ago…,'

Several members of the audience took advantage of the interaction between Osbert and someone else, anyone else, to get up and leave. Osbert gave them all a friendly wave goodbye, genuinely expecting to see them again at his next talk.

'I was saying that if metal wire were to be used as a warp material, then some level of armouring might be provided by the subsequent cloth. Obviously, a weft of wire would be difficult to handle but with the right weight on the loom, a wire warp could be kept taut. You see…,'

'Yes, yes,' Hartle interrupted. It was essential to interrupt Osbert. It was the only way to get him to stop talking. It was widely suggested that he had only been made a master weaver to get him to shut up. It was a rumour that had never been officially denied by the guild.

'Have you tried using wire as a warp?'

'Of course,' Osbert replied with a beaming smile. It must be years since anyone had shown such interest. Or any interest. 'All of my ideas have a very practical aspect.' He frowned now, 'Not that the guild would recognise anything new or interesting unless it was already old.'

Hartle hissed at Wat. 'Didn't you notice he was talking about wire on looms?'

Wat shrugged. 'I wasn't really listening.'

'Wouldn't it be dangerous?' Hartle asked.

'Dangerous?' Osbert was surprised by this question. He wasn't as surprised to notice that the tent was now completely empty and only the three of them were left. He walked over to join them, a move that made Hartle twitch

A Murder for Master Wat

through years of habit.

'Yes,' Hartle went on. 'A wire held taught on a loom might snap. Warps do snap, you know.'

'Not if you set up your loom properly, they don't,' Osbert pointed out in that very pointy way he had. 'And wire is much stronger than a normal warp thread.'

'You'd need a pretty heavy weight to hold it taut.'

'Of course. But that all depends on the gauge of the wire. You see, in wire manufacture, the drawing process successively reduces the size of the wire. I would always recommend drawn wire rather than swaged as a square section would cause the weft to snag. Now...,'

'But if the weight was too heavy, the wire would snap and could injure the weaver.'

'Oh, dear oh, dear,' Osbert shook his head sadly at such ignorance. 'Anyone who could not accurately install the correct warp weight should not be anywhere near a loom at all.' He seemed to think that this meant Hartle.

'Quite agree,' Wat said, although it looked like he was not listening, again.

'Could you examine a particular loom for us?' Hartle asked. 'I think it might be of interest.'

Osbert looked as if the sun had come down from the clouds just to shine on him. 'Be only too glad,' he beamed.

Wat seemed to wake up now. 'What are you doing?' he demanded of Hartle, while Osbert went to the front of the tent to collect his belongings. 'We know that Hemling was killed by the wire on his loom being too tight. What do we need Osbert for?'

'If Osbert knows how to set up a wire warp, maybe he did for Hemling.'

'Osbert?' Wat was incredulous. 'This Osbert? If he wanted

to finish off Hemling he could have just talked him to death. What a contest that would be. The two of them!'

'Bit of coincidence, isn't it? Hemling killed by a metal warp and here's Osbert talking about the very thing.'

'Hemling could have been killed by a bat with an axe and Osbert would have been talking about it. He talks about everything.'

'Still,' Hartle was beginning to regret his invitation. Even if it turned out that Osbert was the killer he wasn't sure it was worth the pain of the conversation.

'And why would he want Hemling dead? Why would he want anyone dead?' Wat thought about this for a moment. 'Might stop them walking out on one of his talks, I suppose. An audience of corpses would be the most attention he's had for years.'

Hartle hissed at Wat. 'It's quite possible all the money from the moot was looked after by Hemling. Hermitage is checking the parchment.'

'He'll like that.'

'He already does. But if it is the case, it gives us a very good motive for murder. Even Osbert could be tempted by money.'

Wat gave Osbert careful consideration. 'No,' he concluded, 'don't think so.'

'You're probably right. And he seems terribly enthusiastic about examining the loom, which would be a bit odd if it was his murder weapon.' Hartle pondered on. 'We could use Osbert and an examination of the loom as an excuse to go wherever the guild has taken Hemling. We might find a trail of the money, if not bags of the stuff itself. Unless it has been taken, of course.'

'And if it's all still there?'

Hartle looked a bit crestfallen. 'It means he wasn't

murdered for the money.'

Wat shrugged. 'Just got to hope there's no money then.'

Osbert was coming back now. 'Lead on, lead on,' he instructed with a happy smile and an encouraging wave. 'This loom of yours sounds absolutely fascinating, I must say. May I leap to the conclusion that it is, in fact, fitted with wire warps? It will be a most interesting examination. However, it would be a surprise if anyone else had considered the possibilities of wire in the weaving process other than myself. I believe I wrote a letter on the topic to the guild only some months ago, although I must say, the level of attention they give is very disappointing. You see, what I imagined…,'

Hartle and Wat led the way across the moot, keeping an eye out for Master Thomas or anyone from the guild who might know where Hemling's loom had been taken.

As they went, the words of Osbert droned on and on and on around them and they looked to the sky, sincerely wishing that it might choose this moment to fall on them.

Caput XII: Escape, Please

'Now then, Heddle and Treadle,' Cwen sniggered again. 'Let's talk about my escape.'

'Escape?' the one named Heddle sounded as if didn't know the word.

Both her captors were obviously apprentices as, although they kept their hoods low over their faces, their voices were as high as hers. Very young apprentices, by the sound of it. Doubtless, they were having a torrid time with their own master and had taken solace from Shuttle's assurances that everything would change for the better once the Grey Guild was in power.

'You're not going to escape,' Treadle assured her. He pointed his finger to make the situation perfectly clear.

Cwen observed that it really was the finger of a child. This wouldn't take long. 'I'm not staying here with you two. I've got things to do, places to go. I'm certainly not wasting a good moot stuck in a tent with my hands tied up.'

'Shuttle told us to keep you here so that's what we're going to do.' Heddle confirmed the arrangements and Treadle nodded agreement.

'Quite right too,' Cwen confused them mightily. 'But, you see, I'm a friend of Wat the Weaver.' She really hated to use Wat's name like this and was quietly confident that if her hands were free she would be able to deal with these two in no time. Her hands were not free though. They had been tied well, which was a bit of a worrying talent in a weaver.

'So?' Heddle challenged.

'The Wat the Weaver everyone wants to meet. The Wat the Weaver who won't be very happy to find that his friend has been tied up.' As she observed them carefully she saw that it was this latter thought that generated a slight twitch of shoulders.

'Doubtless, he's wondering where I am now, and he's no respecter of guilds as you know, grey or otherwise. If Wat the Weaver finds that you two have kept me like this? Well. I can't be held responsible for the consequences.'

'He won't find you,' Treadle said, with very little confidence at all.

'He will,' Cwen was supremely confident. She had no idea whether Wat had even noticed she was still gone, she was just supremely confident that Heddle and Treadle here were going to let her go. They just didn't know it yet. 'He's probably heard all about your first blow against the guild by now if it's the talk of the moot.'

'I'm sure he has.'

'And he's doubtless intrigued by the Grey Guild.'

'Ah,' Heddle sounded boastful. 'No one will know it's the Grey Guild yet.'

'Shut up, Heddle,' Treadle instructed.

'What's she going to do?' Heddle retorted. 'She's not going anywhere.' He turned back to Cwen. 'The first blow simply has the guild astonished.' He sounded like he was quoting Shuttle.

'Astonished?'

'Completely astonished. Something awful has happened but they don't know who did it, or why.'

'Very clever.'

'It is. And then, when they are in a state of, erm,' he tried to remember the word, 'confusion, that's it, we will strike again.'

'More astonishment,' Cwen suggested.

'No. Fear now.'

'Fear?'

'Of course. They won't know what's going to happen next.'

'And what does happen next?'

'Nothing. It is very clever, isn't it.' He didn't sound as if he was quite so sure anymore.

'Probably. And this nothing does what, exactly?'

'Keeps the guild on their toes.'

'I see. And I can see how this will bring things to a very effective conclusion.'

Her captors nodded their hoods vigorously.

'When the guild finds out that the Grey Guild has been keeping them on their toes, they will expel you all and you'll never be weavers again. Simple.'

The insides of the hoods were very quiet.

'How long have you been apprentices?' Cwen tried to make her voice sound friendly and trustworthy.

'How do you know we're apprentices?'

'Oh, come on. You sound like apprentices and act like them. I would guess that it's not long. I would further suggest that you have left home to become weaver's apprentices and have discovered that it's not actually very nice. Your master is awful when he speaks to you. You don't get to do any actual weaving at all. No one is teaching you anything and even the other apprentices look down on you and get you to do their chores.'

The hoods turned to look at one another.

'The Grey Guild must seem very attractive, promising you a way out of all that. But it's always been the same. That's how apprentices work. Give it a year or two and you'll start learning the craft. It's a test, you see. If you don't run away through fear and hatred in the first year you'll probably stick it and not waste the master's time.'

A Murder for Master Wat

'We can't run away,' Heddle said, quietly. 'We're not allowed.'

'Of course, absconding from an apprenticeship is a very serious offence. But mixing with the Grey Guild is going to be just as bad. Is this all there is? Just Shuttle and you lot?'

Treadle's hood nodded.

'Hardly going to challenge the whole of the Weavers' Guild, are you? I reckon Shuttle is a failed journeyman. He's probably been an apprentice for far too many years and has been thrown out of his workshop. He's had to make his own way doing odd jobs and hasn't got the skill to do any better. And he's never going to make it now.' She sensed that their devotion to their leader was wavering.

'Look. I'm no guild person, am I? I'm female, for goodness sake. I don't know who the guild will want to be dunked in the pond first, you for mucking about with the Grey Guild, or me for insulting the craft by being a woman. I'm not here to tell you to follow the guild. I agree with Shuttle on that, they are a useless bunch of old men without an idea in their heads. But I wouldn't want you throwing away your chance so soon. If you're found out, there will never be an apprenticeship, in this trade or any other.'

She left a pause. A nice long one so that these two could consider their options and which was worse than any other.

'What do we do?' Heddle released a quiet wail from the depths of his hood.

'Let me go. I don't know why Shuttle thinks I would tell the guild anything. I wouldn't tell them if their guildhall was on fire and they were all asleep inside.'

The hoods didn't leap into action.

'Who is your master?'

'We don't know his name.'

'You don't know his name?' Cwen shook her head. Were these two boys even weaver's apprentices at all? Perhaps they'd come to the wrong moot.

'He just calls himself The Weaver of Winchester.'

'Oh, God, him!' Cwen shivered. 'I'm not surprised you joined the Grey Guild. He's not a representative of most masters, you know. He's not representative of most people, come to that. Even the nasty ones. You let me go and I'll have a word with Wat. We've got more work than we can handle, he might have room for two more hands.'

Hoods were thrown back now, revealing, as Cwen suspected, two very young boys who looked like they shouldn't really have left their mothers. They couldn't be above ten years old, far too young to be mixed up in rebellion against the guild.

'Wat the Weaver has apprentices?' the one who was called Treadle asked. In fact, he was a thin, almost wasted blond-haired boy with grime on his face and a constant look of fear.

'Well,' Cwen began, 'actually he's not officially a, erm, yes. Yes, he does.'

'Coo,' Heddle looked thoroughly enthused. He was dark-haired but no better nourished. Cwen could well believe that these were apprentices of The Weaver of Winchester; a famous workshop where it was rumoured more apprentices went in than ever came out again.

'I'm not promising anything,' Cwen tempered their excitement. 'All I've said is that I'll have a word with him, and Master Hartle who runs the workshop.'

'That would be wonderful,' Heddle now skipped over and untied Cwen's hands.

She stood and admirably resisted the urge to clip these two

round the ear but rubbed her sore wrists instead. 'Now. This blow the Grey Guild has struck, what's that all about?'

'We don't know, exactly,' Treadle confirmed.

'What are your names? I mean the real ones. I can't call you Heddle and Treadle, it's ridiculous.

'I'm Edward,' Heddle reported.

'So am I,' Treadle agreed.

'What? You're both called Edward? You're not brothers, are you?'

'That would be a bit stupid,' Edward who was Heddle seemed to have found his confidence. 'Two brothers both called Edward?'

'I was named after the old king,' Treadle explained.

'So was I.'

Cwen shook her head. 'Perhaps I'll call you Heddle and Treadle after all. So, you don't know what's been done or what's planned?'

'No,' they shook their heads. 'Shuttle just said that he'd done something that would make the whole moot sit up and take notice. Something about the opening ceremony and showing someone for the fool they were.'

'Opening ceremony?' Cwen thought. 'Not old Hemling?'

'That was the name,' Heddle confirmed. 'I thought it was part of a loom.' He hung his head.

'Shuttle was going to do something to Hemling at the opening ceremony?' She now had urgency in her voice which frightened the two apprentices nicely.

'Could be,' Treadle suggested.

'Right. We really do need to find Wat now. And Hermitage.'

'A hermitage?' Treadle looked lost.

'This one's a monk.'

Heddle scowled. 'Funny name for a monk.'

'It certainly is. And he's a funny monk as well. Now, come on.' Cwen led the way back into the tent, Heddle and Treadle skipping along to keep up.

'If we do get to be apprentices to Master Wat,' Heddle began. 'Not that I'm saying we will, of course. Not taking anything as agreed, I'm just saying that if we did?'

'Yes?'

Heddle cast a glance at Treadle and a little gleam lit up his eye. 'Can we do work on some really rude tapestries?'

. . .

Hermitage's excavation of the guild's trunk was giving him so much pleasure that he didn't notice the time go by, or what the people in the hall were up to. His first encounters were with some of the old rules of the guild itself. They were in very poor condition as if they hadn't even been looked at for years.

He was intrigued to see that these referred to the collegium of weavers. That sounded much more learned than the people he had encountered so far. He suspected that most of them wouldn't even know they were in a collegium. Or if they did, how to cure it.

He knew that the Normans insisted on calling such organisations guilds but whatever the name, perhaps they might like him to bind all their documents into a handsome volume. He could index the main headings and topics and provide a fine title page. He almost hummed with pleasure as he considered the task.

Lower layers contained old appointments to office for people he'd never heard of, and to offices he didn't

A Murder for Master Wat

understand either. Quite what an under-silter of the master's standing closet did, he had not the first idea. It carried a salary of one penny a year so was probably not a very challenging role.

These parchments too were quite old, and he didn't recognise any of the names. They were all very Saxon and so probably long dead. Or quite recently dead, depending on how well they got on with the Normans.

Without realising he was doing it, he had started organising the various parchments. As he looked at each one, he took it out of the trunk and laid it at his side. When he looked down after a few minutes he saw that he had created several different piles. Glancing at each he saw that they were categorised according to subject; organisation, people, premises, guild standards, discipline. He was most gratified that he could organise parchment without looking.

As he dug deeper and deeper, the condition of the parchment improved. Doubtless, this was because they were seldom disturbed down here and were protected from prying hands. Not that it looked as if any hands had done much prying.

Picking one particularly splendid specimen, with a large red capital almost embossed on the parchment, he saw that this did indeed have reference to a moot. He was sure it couldn't be this moot, not this far down in the trunk, but he pulled it out and sat back on the floor to read.

He was grateful that whatever old official of the guild had called for this document to be created had engaged a fine scribe with a clear hand.

It was a moot document but seemed to be for some gathering of the guild, or collegium, as it was then, to discuss a change to the rules for masters' management of their apprentices. It all seemed to be fine details about accommodation and food, suggesting that both should be provided. He skipped to the bottom of the page where he saw that the proposal was rejected anyway.

He added this to the pile on organisation and dived back in. More routine material was cast aside, well, put carefully aside for detailed consideration later. At this point, he found himself at the bottom of the trunk and thought that there was nothing for it but to go back over everything again and read it more carefully this time. How lovely.

A last sheet seemed stuck to the floor of the box, which was not surprising considering how long it had probably been in there. He carefully pulled it away and glanced at the doubtful quality of this hand. He gave it a second glance when he saw the name Hemling. Well, Magister Hemlingus, which would be more appropriate.

It seemed odd that a reference to Hemling should be at the bottom of the trunk, under all the older material. Perhaps it was another Hemling. It could be that there were generations of them going back in history. Or maybe it wasn't his name at all, but his title. He was the Guild Hemling and in days gone by he hemelled away on their behalf. Could it be he carried a Hemel? Was there some particular weaving tool that Hermitage hadn't come across? He would have to ask Wat if the workshop kept a cupboard full of Hemels for when they were needed.

Of course, it could be purely ceremonial. Did an apprentice, on passing to become a journeyman get anointed with a Hemel by the guild Hemling? Or get given a Hemel of his very own? Had the word simply become corrupted over time and the dead Hemling simply used it as his name? Just as a master was called Master, so a hemeller was called Hemling.

A Murder for Master Wat

The excitement of this etymological romp was getting the better of him and he tried to calm down. He might find some older document that defined what it was.

He read the contents and was a little dismayed, and quite confused to find that it did refer to this Hemling, the dead person, and not some mystical rite of the collegium. It also referred to this moot. It was now doubly suspicious that this material was at the bottom of the trunk. He started to wonder if someone had buried it down here on purpose.

But it was what he was looking for. It confirmed that Hemling was the organiser of the moot and only had to refer to the Grand Master in exceptional circumstances. It also said that he would be paid for his role. Hermitage scanned the page to find a figure. There, towards the bottom, one shilling. One shilling? Hermitage knew that a shilling was a substantial sum of money, well, it was for a penniless monk, but it hardly seemed due recompense for organising a whole guild moot. What a paltry figure for such a task. Certainly not a sum to justify murder.

He read on and saw that the document listed Hemling's duties, which were many and detailed. One of them was specifically to gather all funds, fees and payments taken by whatsoever means and by whomsoever was duly authorised on behalf of the guild so to gather. He shook his head to get around the convoluted language. Why couldn't people write in plain simple terms? Like the Bible.

He tutted as he continued, but then stopped mid tut. There it was, the motive. Not only did Hemling gather all these funds, fees and payments but he kept them secure until such time as the keeper of the guild's treasury accounted for them. Wherever Hemling's accommodation was, it could be stacked quite high with money. If all those nine pences and the traders' payments and whatever had come from the town was gathered in one place it would be quite a temptation.

And more than that; Hermitage's mouth was open as he read on. A whole portion of the money would be kept by Hemling as his fee. The one shilling payment was just a symbolic amount. There was no mention of what the proportion was, but any share would come to a tidy sum.

There it was, then. A huge sum of money just sitting for the taking. And it explained the complicated nature of the attack. If someone had simply stuck a knife in Hemling the guild would probably have rushed to secure the money. If people thought it was an accident, the murderer would have time to find it and steal it away.

He jumped to his feet. He would have to tell Wat, straight away.

He dropped the paper in his hurry and stooped to pick it up. As he did so, a second sheet, stuck to the back of the first, came away. Doubtless just some addendum or annexe. He would normally be quite excited by an addendum or an annexe but this was not the time.

He glanced over this sheet and saw that it was in quite a different hand. It was not a second page of the document at all. It was separate and more like a letter than a formal record. It was addressed to the guild and he read it quickly.

'Oh, my,' Hermitage could not stop himself speaking out loud. He looked around to see if anyone had noticed his outburst. The men of the guild were still there, still in the chairs, but now fast asleep. The rest of the hall didn't appear to notice that he was actually there at all.

He glanced at the page again. Now he really did need to see Wat. And warn him.

Caput XIII: Where do Dead Weavers Go?

𝔋artle and Wat's meanderings with Osbert had got them very nearly ready to kill. Wat was sure that Osbert was breathing, he was still walking around, after all. How he managed to get all the words out while breathing at the same time was more of a mystery. There were words on everything. Every subject under the sun, including the sun itself, got the benefit of Osbert's detailed opinion.

Old Hemling was just boring, he went on and on about weaving but that was all he talked about. You couldn't even discuss the weather without the subject being immediately diverted onto a matter of weaving. But it was as if Hemling was an apprentice bore, very capable but only in a limited subject area. Osbert was a Master. He had whole lectures on subjects you didn't even know existed, just waiting to be let loose.

That would have been bad enough on its own, but it was accompanied by constant complaint that no one ever listened to his opinions. Wat was inclined to report that they were listening right now, as they didn't have any choice, but he didn't want to open his mouth; the one saving grace of Osbert's diatribe being that he didn't seem to expect any responses.

Their search increased in pace and urgency and they even started asking strangers if they'd seen Master Thomas, or anyone from the guild, come to that.

This got Osbert started on the guild itself, and there was another whole mine of comment and complaint just waiting to be dug out. And it was a very deep mine indeed.

The guild was the worst of the lot when it came to ignoring Osbert's perfectly reasonable suggestions and ideas. How anyone could be worse than anyone else when it came to ignoring a thing was the sort of question Hermitage would be best put to address. If keeping silent, saying nothing and looking the other way most of the time was not ignoring someone, Wat didn't know what was. He didn't know how he could do any more of it, but if someone told him he would give it a go.

The guild ignored letters, entreaties, talks, visits, missives, pleadings and every form of communication open to man, and a few more open only to Osbert. He said that he had told the guild he would be coming to the moot and would meet the Grand Master at a certain time on a certain day, surely there was no way the man could get out of that.

The next thing he knew was that he had been granted a space to deliver a talk on that very day and at that very time. And no, before they asked, the Grand Master had not turned up. Not that Osbert had noticed anyway. Nevertheless, he would be sending the guild a detailed report of his talk along with several of his more advanced thoughts, including diagrams where appropriate.

Wat silently congratulated the Grand Master on neatly avoiding a meeting with Osbert himself, while simultaneously inflicting it on the rest of the weaving community. Not that many of them turned up, and those that did had left as soon as they were able.

But Osbert was gratified that Hartle and Wat had taken an interest, even though he didn't approve of Wat, and he was sure that this would lead to a long and productive relationship.

'Please God, no,' were the only words Wat contributed to a good half hour of one-sided conversation.

Eventually, walking down one street of the moot, Wat gave

a great cry. He had never been so glad to see a master who didn't like him.

'Master Thomas, Master Thomas,' he called, waving his arms and stepping away from Osbert as quickly as possible. He turned aside to Hartle. 'No word of the money,' he hissed. 'Let's see if Thomas mentions it without prompting.'

Thomas had been in discussion with a stallholder when he found himself rudely interrupted by the rudest weaver in the country.

'What do you want?' Thomas looked positively shocked to be greeted in such a friendly manner by Wat the Weaver. He glanced quickly around to make sure no one else had spotted this. 'What are you even doing here?' he demanded, recovering his senses. 'I'd heard there were strict instructions that you were not to be allowed into the moot.'

'Ah, well,' Wat shrugged. 'You know me and strict instructions.'

Thomas now saw Hartle and Osbert approaching. 'Please God, no,' he whispered.

'That's just what I said,' Wat smiled.

'Wat the Weaver and Osbert of Loxwood, what a combination. Someone kill me now.'

'If we could find who killed Hemling we could ask them to do it,' Wat suggested, which brought a scowl to Thomas's face.

'Ah, Master Thomas,' Osbert greeted the man with a look of horrible intent on his face. 'I have written to the guild a number of times, and I understand you deal with some of their correspondence. I have not had a response. This is the perfect opportunity to outline several proposals I have for...,'

'Yes, yes,' Wat raised a hand and managed to stop Osbert in mid-flow. He examined his hand in some surprise at its power. He turned back to Thomas. 'We're looking for Hemling's loom. And wherever he was staying.'

'Why?' Thomas asked, looking deeply suspicious.

'Because the wire on the loom killed him and Osbert here knows all about wire on looms.'

'The what did what?' Thomas was now just confused.

'Hemling's throat was cut,' Wat reminded him.

'Yes,' Thomas replied, dryly. 'I noticed that when the apprentices picked him up. All the blood and the hole in the throat?'

'Quite. And the reason for the blood was that there was a wire warp on the loom. It was deliberately weakened and broke when Hemling pulled the heddle. It sprang up, cut his throat and killed him.'

Thomas considered Wat as one considers the man who wants to pass you secret messages from the owls.

'Seriously,' Wat assured him. 'Hartle and I examined the loom.'

'It's true,' Hartle confirmed.

'And we're here with Brother Hermitage,' Wat added.

'The monk? What's the monk got to do with anything?'

'He's the King's Investigator. He looks into murders and the like.'

Now Thomas looked horrified. Osbert, on the other hand, looked fascinated and clearly had many observations to make. Wat raised the hand again.

Thomas found his voice. 'You brought a King's Investigator into our moot? What were you thinking?'

'No,' Wat corrected him, firmly. 'We brought the King's Investigator into the moot. And we didn't bring him here to investigate, not expecting to find murdered weavers lying around the place. We just came to the moot. How were we to

A Murder for Master Wat

know it was the sort of place masters get done for?'

Thomas looked about as if someone was going to come up and make all this nonsense go away. 'He might not have been murdered,' he protested. 'Could have been an accident. Probably was an accident.'

'Putting wire on a loom? Only Osbert here has thought of that. And we all know what we think of Osbert's ideas.'

Osbert smiled at them all and then stopped smiling as he realised what had been said.

Thomas stood up straight and tried to look authoritative. 'If it is the case that Hemling was murdered, then it is a guild matter. The guild can deal with it. It happened to a guild master and it happened in the guild moot.'

'Oh,' Hartle put in, as if it was an afterthought and of only passing interest. 'The sheriff of Nottingham wants Hermitage to look into it as well.'

Thomas gaped. This was not turning out to be a good day. 'The sheriff?' he choked.

'That's right,' Hartle smiled. 'Big chap. Norman. William Peverel? Have you met him?'

Thomas nodded that he had indeed met Peverel. The memory was obviously not a comforting one. 'How the devil did he find out?'

'Who knows?' Wat didn't seem to think it mattered. 'Murder in his town? Not the sort of thing a good sheriff lets pass by, I imagine. Still,' he nudged Thomas in a friendly manner. 'At least Hemling wasn't a Norman, eh? That could have been real trouble.'

Thomas had nothing to say.

'He wasn't a Norman, was he?'

'No, of course, he wasn't,' Thomas snapped. He rubbed his chin as he tried to take all of this in and decide what to do.

'Why would anyone kill Hemling?' he asked, clearly not believing the tale.

'That's part of the investigation,' Wat assured him. He didn't want to mention thoughts of money. If Thomas, a master in good keeping with the guild thought that their money might be at risk, he'd probably do something stupid and get in the way. Like rush to Hemling's place, take all the money and the loom and lock it away where no one could get at it. 'Maybe they just didn't like him?'

'Nobody liked him,' Thomas pointed out. 'You don't go round killing people because you don't like them.'

'The Normans do,' Hartle pointed out.

'The Normans killed him?' Thomas was sounding utterly confused. 'I doubt they'd even met him.'

'No,' Wat dismissed the idea. 'The Normans didn't kill him, but someone did. That's why we need to look at the loom again.'

Thomas just shook his head, sadly. 'We took it back to his room, along with his body. We left him decently covered,' he added in response to some quizzical looks about whether that was proper treatment of the deceased. 'Your monk said we had to get a priest to bury him.'

'And there's none in Nottingham?' Hartle asked.

'We are a bit busy with the Grand Moot, in case you hadn't noticed,' Thomas huffed. 'I sent one of the apprentices to find a priest.'

'And Hemling's room is where, exactly?' Wat asked.

'Near the main hall. He took a room in the local weaver's workshop.'

'That weaver's kind donation to his guild's moot, I imagine,' Wat observed. 'No rent involved that way.'

Thomas said nothing.

A Murder for Master Wat

'Right, let's find the loom then. What are you going to do with it, by the way?'

'That thing?' Thomas dismissed it. 'Throw it out, probably. No good to anyone. Hemling insisted on using it for his ceremonies.'

'And who takes over from him?' Hartle asked, as innocently as he could manage.

'No one, probably. The moot's as good as done. I seem to be getting all the trouble at the moment.' He frowned at them as they were clearly included in this category. 'Once this moot is done there won't be another one for years. No need for Hemling. Not that anyone would want the job anyway.'

'Ah,' Osbert raised a hand.

'Right,' Thomas said, very quickly. 'Off to Hemling's room. I'll lead the way. And with that, he was gone.

. . .

In various parts of the moot, Hermitage and Cwen were searching for the others, Hermitage alone but Cwen still with the two Edwards in tow. They had put their hoods up again, fearful of being spotted by Shuttle now, who would doubtless have strong views on two of his guild who had not only let their prisoner go but who now appeared to be in her service.

'Look for a monk,' she instructed them. 'He should be easy to spot in the crowd.'

Edward and Edward scanned the people milling around without success. 'Shouldn't he be in a monastery?' Edward Heddle asked, quite reasonably.

'Not this one. He has been in monasteries, obviously, but now he lives with us.'

'He lives with you?'

'At Wat's workshop.'

'You and a monk live with Wat at his workshop?' Edward Treadle was starting to sound as if he would rather go back to the Grey Guild.

'That's right. And he's the King's Investigator.'

'Is he?' This question was very cautious.

'It means he, erm, tracks things. From the Latin, vestigare?' Cwen was quite shocked to hear herself say this. All that talk from Hermitage had obviously wormed its way inside and stuck. 'He tracks murders for the king.'

'Sounds interesting.'

Cwen turned and saw one Edward tugging the sleeve of the other, indicating that sneaking off into the crowd might be a good idea before they got murdered by the king's killer monk. She put her hands on her hips. 'For goodness sake. He's a lovely monk. Mild and friendly and helpful, not at all like most of them. King Harold made him investigator and then William followed. He doesn't want to do it at all. He just wants to read things and write them down.'

The boys clearly thought this was getting worse.

'You'll like him.'

They weren't convinced.

'There he is,' Cwen called. 'Hermitage, Hermitage.' She waved and beckoned across the crowd and caught his attention. Pushing through, making sure the Edwards were following, Cwen got to Hermitage's side. 'I have news,' she said, excitedly.

'Me too,' Hermitage replied. 'I was searching in the parchments of the Weavers' Guild and you'll never guess what I found.'

'No, you'll never guess what I found. This Grey Guild really exists and they have a leader, called Shuttle and all sorts of plans. And I think they killed Hemling at the opening ceremony.'

'A Grey Guild did?' Hermitage was confused. 'I thought it would be a him.'

'Well, it is. It's a character called Shuttle.' She turned to the boys, seeming to remember they were there. 'This is Edward,' she nodded towards Heddle. 'And this is Edward as well.' She held a hand out towards Treadle. 'And this is Brother Hermitage. See. He's not a dangerous killer, is he?'

Hermitage considered the two Edwards with some concern.

'They've never heard of an investigator before.' Cwen explained.

'I see,' Hermitage nodded. 'And, erm, who are they?'

'Oh, yes, they were holding me captive.'

'Captive, jolly good,' Hermitage nodded politely, wondering if he should grab Cwen and run.

'Shuttle had me tied up because I was going to tell the guild about their plans, except of course I wouldn't. The guild wouldn't talk to me, would they? So the Edwards here were told to guard me. But when I explained everything and told them I'd talk to Wat, they saw sense and let me go.'

'Well, that's good.' Hermitage could well believe that Cwen had been held captive by a mysterious guild. She was certainly behaving as if she had.

'So, we need to find Wat and then we can talk about their plan, and what they've already done.'

'What they've already done?'

'Hemling,' Cwen sounded impatient.

'Oh, yes. You said. You think they killed him?'

Cwen stood straight and spoke solemnly. 'I do. They had a plan and Shuttle's probably the one who carried it out.'

Hermitage frowned.

'You don't look very pleased to find out,' Cwen complained. 'This could be the end of the investigation.'

'I don't think it can be,' Hermitage was disappointed. 'You see, I looked at the parchments of the guild. I know who killed Hemling.'

Caput XIV: Room with a Loom

Hemling's room was indeed in the workshop of one of the local weavers, and the local weaver was not at all happy about the fact. He was rather sour-faced and seemed a miserable individual by nature. He was at least forty, thin and rather dishevelled as if the thought of a good meal and fine clothes might cheer him up, and he wouldn't want that.

His workshop was simply an extension of his demeanour. Quite what sort of customer would be attracted into a drab and dreary space without a splash of colour or a happy tone was a mystery.

The sign over the door said nothing at all. Once upon a time, it might have mentioned weaving and the name of the owner, but it had faded over the years and been battered by the weather. Now it looked as if someone had found a rotten old piece of driftwood in the river and nailed it to the wall.

Inside, apart from one rather horrible weaver, there was a loom, but it was an old and decrepit looking thing. Rather like its master. It would be good for a simple cloth but nothing sophisticated. And Nottingham was a large town; surely there would be good trade here for anyone who put in a bit of effort. The main task of this day seemed to be repairing the thing to get it working at all. The weaver was whittling away at a length of wood, doubtless some replacement part.

The man said very little to Master Thomas, just acknowledged his arrival and nodded that he expected him to go straight through into the back room.

When Thomas had disappeared, Wat, Hartle and Osbert made to follow.

'Bloody guild,' the weaver said to them, in a quiet voice.

'Oh, yes?' Wat asked.

'Come here taking my one room. I've had to sleep in the workshop, you know.'

Wat just tutted at this.

'And who did they give me? Hemling. Bloody Hemling of all people. I mean you know how boring he is when he's talking for half an hour. Imagine what it's like living with him!'

'Not joining the moot yourself then?' Hartle asked.

'That thing? Disturbing the town, throwing all the regular trade into turmoil. It's bad for business, I tell you.'

'Lots of visitors.'

'A lot of noise. And no one comes to the Nottingham craftsmen, do they?' He beckoned them close. 'You do know they've got foreigners out there.' He nodded his head towards the street.

'Really?'

'Oh, yes. Who's going to want to buy Nottingham cloth when you've got the low countries bringing their wares right to the doorstep? It's not right I tell you.'

'So you'll be glad when they've gone.'

'Then we'll have to clear up,' the weaver complained. It was pretty clear that nothing was going to make this man happy. Nothing at all. Ever.

'Apart from talking too much, Hemling was no trouble? And kicking you out of your room, of course,' Wat asked. 'Didn't have any visitors?'

'Who'd visit him out of choice?'

'Could have been anyone. He was organising the moot. I expect people had to come and find him. Drop things off and the like.'

'Oh, the money,' the weaver got it straight away. 'All hours of the day and night. Never mind my house, you just walk in as if you owned it.'

'So they did visit Hemling with the money from the moot?'

'Well, dropped it off and ran, really. No one wanted to spend too long in Hemling's company, did they?'

'Must be quite a lot of money,' Wat suggested.

'Piles of the stuff,' the weaver complained. 'Getting in the way, using all my good sacks to store it in. And do I get any pay for all this? No, I do not.'

'Poor recompense,' Hartle sympathised.

'No recompense at all. And now what do they do? Not satisfied that I had to put up with Hemling living in my house, they bring him back here when he's dead!'

'Shocking.' Even Osbert looked as if he would quite like to move on from this smothering blanket of complaint.

'Well, he's not staying. They say they've gone to get the priest but I don't know that, do I? The moment he starts to smell he's out in the street. Guild man or not.'

'How do you know we're not guild men?' Hartle asked.

The weaver shrugged. 'Not seen you before and virtually every member of the guild has been tramping in and out of my workshop for a week. Without a by-your-leave, of course.'

Thomas reappeared, a scowl on his face indicating that they should be following him.

'Well master, erm,' Hartle began.

'Grum, journeyman Grum,' the weaver was even unhappy with his name, quite wisely.

Hartle nodded. 'I am Master Hartle, this is Osbert and Wat the Weaver.'

'Wat the Weaver?' Grum sagged even lower as he turned back to his work. 'There goes the neighbourhood.'

'Cheery fellow,' Wat observed as they joined Thomas in the back room.

There was the loom, just as promised. And lying beside it was a very large shape covered in a plain cloth; a plain cloth with just a delicate splash of blood in one corner. Wat cleared his throat, making it clear that they were all going to studiously ignore the body in the room.

'No one's touched it?' Wat asked, appraising the loom.

'Just moved it from the tent,' Thomas confirmed. 'I'd have thrown the thing on the fire straight away, save all that effort.'

'Why didn't you?'

'Grand Master said it didn't show respect. As if he'd shown respect to Hemling anyway. So, we lumped the wretched thing all the way here. Help yourself.'

Wat nodded to Osbert who eagerly examined the loom and the loose wire hanging from the top of the frame. 'Aha,' he said, brightly, after only a few moments. 'This is it exactly. Just as I proposed.' He stood again and turned to Master Thomas. 'It seems that the guild has been paying attention to my ideas and has been using them without any credit given.' He folded his arms.

'Don't look at me,' Thomas retorted. 'The guild may get me to sort their letters for them but I don't read any of yours. No one does.'

'Hemling obviously did, otherwise how would he know to put wire in his loom?'

'You didn't put it there then?' Wat asked the question, bluntly.

'Me?' Osbert looked genuinely confused. 'Why would I do it?'

'Good question. You seem to be the only one who knows

A Murder for Master Wat

about putting wire in a loom. And you don't have a very good opinion of the guild, ignoring all your lovely ideas as they do. Perhaps you put it there to prove it could be done and to embarrass the guild? Except it all went wrong. The wire snapped as you'd planned but it actually killed Hemling, instead of just making a fool of him.'

'Ridiculous,' Osbert dismissed this out of hand. 'The guild is perfectly capable of embarrassing itself without any help from me. And if I'd fitted a wire it would have stayed fitted.' He held out his hand to direct their attention to the loom. 'What's the point of having a single wire warp anyway? My idea is to have a whole loom of wire. Then, when the cloth is made, it has wire running all the way through it. It would be a very popular product for the fighting man.'

'And virtually unwearable,' Hartle put in.

'I beg your pardon?'

'Well, think about it. One wire on its own is stiff enough, if you wore a whole cloth of it you wouldn't be able to move an inch. Be a good target, I suppose.'

'You don't understand,' Osbert condescended.

'You need a chain mail,' Hartle patronised back. 'Got to have movement. Fifty strands of wire running down your arm and you couldn't pick your nose, let alone lift a sword.'

'So, you say you didn't put it there?' Wat tried to stick to the question at hand.

'I certainly did not. I've never seen this loom before. As Master Thomas says, it is rather small and useless. Hemling obviously saw my idea and decided to steal it for himself. Unsurprisingly, he didn't do a very good job.'

'Perhaps he didn't put it there either,' Wat suggested.

Osbert looked confused for a moment. 'Someone did. Strands of wire don't make their way into a loom on their own.'

'Have you examined the bottom of the wire, near the warp weight?'

Osbert sniffed and took the wire in his hand. He looked at it and then bent to examine the weight that was lying on the floor. 'Oh, dear,' he said, in that way that only a craftsman can when he stands by and watches someone else fail spectacularly, exactly as he predicted. 'Oh dear, oh dear, oh dear. Who did this?' He even tutted and sucked air through his teeth. 'What a mess.'

'Precisely,' Wat agreed.

'Very shoddy work,' Osbert commented.

'Or deliberate?'

'Deliberate?'

'Someone weakened the wire at the bottom so that it would snap as soon as the heddle was pulled.'

'Or someone just did a very poor job of installation and it failed as soon as it was used.'

'Even put an extra heavy weight on that single warp?'

'Hm,' Osbert did seem to accept that there was something odd about this.

Master Thomas was observing all this with very little interest. 'Is that it, then? That's all you wanted to do.'

Wat sighed and cast a sidelong glance at Hartle. 'Yes, that's about it. Needed Osbert to confirm this wire warp business and he says that he didn't put it there.'

'I certainly did not. And I don't want it spread about that wire warps are liable to snap and kill the weaver. If a proper installation had been done the thing would have been perfectly safe.'

'Safe and useless,' Hartle muttered.

Thomas huffed. 'I didn't come here to have a discussion

A Murder for Master Wat

between you two pushed into my ears. I do have other matters to attend to so I think I'll be off.'

'By all means,' Wat bowed, sarcastically.

Thomas turned on his heels and left the room muttering. 'If you want the loom, you can have it,' he called back over his shoulder.

'I think I had best have words with Thomas,' Osbert said, quickly, and he scurried after the master before he could get away. 'I don't want this wire business being dismissed so lightly. Just because the first weaver who tried it died in the process doesn't make it a bad idea.'

'You do that,' Wat smiled at him as he left.

'Loon,' he said to Hartle when they were alone.

'Quite,' Hartle agreed. 'Wire cloth. Pah! Might as well take a whole sheet of solid metal and wear that.' He gave a dismissive laugh.

'Hm,' said Wat, carefully. 'There's a thought.'

Hartle frowned at him. He cast his eyes around the room. 'No money,' he said.

Wat came back to the real purpose of their visit. 'No. And Grum the grim weaver said there were sacks full of it.'

'Good reason to kill anyone, I'd have thought. And if we can find the money, we probably find the killer.'

'We'd better have another word with the weaving world's answer to plague.' Wat nodded back towards the workshop. 'I can't see our friendly local journeyman having the wherewithal to install wire warps on a loom, not without complaining about it all the time. But maybe he saw who did take the money.'

'Or helped himself to it when he found out Hemling was dead?' Hartle suggested.

Wat shook his head and kicked at the dust on the floor.

'This is not the workshop of a weaver who has just come into a large sum of money.'

'He'd probably complain that it was too heavy to lift.'

Wat led the way back to the front room. He folded his arms and gave the weaver a hard stare. 'Alright then, Grum, where's the money?'

Journeyman Grum glanced up from his whittling, which was obviously not going well. He held a much shorter length of wood in his hand now and was surrounded by a large collection of wood shavings. He threw the thing to the ground in disgust. 'What money?' he asked as if he'd never seen any in his life.

'The sacks of the stuff that were getting in your way,' Hartle reminded him.

'Hemling's money,' Wat pressed. 'Where is it?'

'How should I know?' Grum searched around for another piece of wood he could start on.

'You said there were piles of it here. Now there's none. Where's it gone?'

Grum shrugged. 'Back into the guild coffers, I should think. I get to see it come in, but do I get any of it for all the trouble I'm put to? No, I do not. Not even a penny rent.'

'If there was so much of it, you must have seen it go,' Wat insisted. 'You saw it all come in, how can it have gone out again without you noticing?'

'I'm not here all the time,' Grum complained. 'I do have to go out now and again. Get bread and the like. It's not my fault if the guild comes and gets their money when I'm not looking. I'm not being paid to look after it. I'm not being paid at all.'

'We know,' Hartle sighed. 'You mentioned that.'

Wat walked around the workshop, which didn't take long.

A Murder for Master Wat

He could see no sign of any money having been spent on anything for years. 'When did you notice it had gone? This great pile of money.'

'I didn't, did I? As I said, it came in and Hemling looked after it. I didn't go in his room.'

'You never went in your own back room to look at more money than you'd probably ever seen in your life? I don't believe it.'

'Hemling was in there, wasn't he? I'm not likely to go into a small room with Hemling in it on my own, am I?'

Wat had to agree that that would be a fairly rash thing to do. Still, a lot of money would tempt anyone.

'But Hemling had to go out as well, didn't he?' Hartle pointed out. 'He was managing the moot, doing the opening ceremony. You could have gone in when he wasn't there.'

'Could have,' Grum acknowledged with very little interest. 'But didn't.'

'Not even to help yourself to a few pennies that you were entitled to? As you say, you're not being given anything for this inconvenience and there's a pile of the guild's money right under your nose. They wouldn't miss a penny or two. Probably haven't even counted it yet. They'd never know.'

The look on Grum's face, which reached whole new levels of disappointed misery said that he hadn't thought of that. 'Oh, bugger.'

Wat shook his head at Hartle, a mixture of hopelessness, sympathy at such misfortune and despair at such stupidity. 'So you didn't see anyone take the money?'

'No,' Grum hung his head that his lot, which was the worst there could be, had just got worse.

'Well,' Wat said, with a resigned sigh and some enthusiasm for getting out of this place. 'We'd better move on. Get out of your hair.'

Grum stared at him and ran his hand across his completely bald head.

As they made for the door, Wat turned back to Grum's wretched workshop. He nodded his head towards the back room. 'Hemling's ceremonial loom is in there. Why don't you keep it,' he gave a wink of encouragement.

'A loom?' Grum sighed his disappointment and looked at the wood in his hand. 'Not another one.'

Caput XV: I Know Who Did It. No, I Do.

'It was the Grey Guild,' Cwen insisted. 'Shuttle was going to do something to Hemling at the opening ceremony. These two Edwards confirmed it. And what happened at the opening ceremony? Hemling was killed. There you are.'

'But the parchment says otherwise,' Hermitage insisted.

'Who does it say did it then?'

'Well,' Hermitage explained. 'It doesn't actually give a name.'

'Ha!'

'But it specifically says that there is one coming to the moot who wishes Hemling harm and that the guild must take measures to protect him. And root out the killer.'

'Hm,' Cwen sounded reluctantly convinced that this was on a level with her information about the Grey Guild. 'Where is it then?'

'Where's what?' Hermitage wished Cwen would stick to the subject.

'The parchment, of course.' Her tone reprimanded Hermitage for not keeping up.

'The one about the killer?'

'I think that's probably the one we're most interested in at the moment.' She rolled her eyes and folded her arms.

'In the guild trunk.' Hermitage thought he'd explained that.

'Yes, that's where you found it, but where is it now?'

Hermitage wished she'd stop rambling. 'It's in the guild trunk. Where else would it be?'

'In your hand perhaps.' Cwen was getting quite excited now. 'You found a parchment that directly mentions someone trying to kill Hemling and you left it where you found it?'

'Of course. It wasn't mine to take.' Hermitage really didn't understand Cwen sometimes.

'You're the King's Investigator.' Cwen now took to waving her arms about and raising her voice. That was usually significant, but Hermitage seldom discovered the cause. 'And there's been a murder. I think you can take whatever you want. It's a crucial piece of what-do-you-call-it.'

'Evidence.'

'Exactly. A crucial piece of evidence, and you left it where you found it.'

'Absolutely.'

'So what if the killer knows about it and goes to get it himself. Or herself.'

'What good would that do? I've seen it. I know what it says.'

'But if the killer challenges you and says that the thing never existed or that it never mentioned anything about murder?'

'He'd be lying.'

'Well, yes. But the guild won't know that.'

Hermitage stood a little more upright. 'I am a monk, Cwen. Who are they going to believe?'

Cwen collapsed a little and shook her head. 'I don't believe this,' she muttered. She took a deep breath and gave the problem some thought. 'This killer from the parchment could be one of the Grey Guild. It still could be Shuttle. Perhaps one of the other members decided that the plan to kill Hemling was going too far and tried to report him to the guild.'

Hermitage nodded as he thought this through. 'It is possible I suppose.'

A Murder for Master Wat

'There was no name on the thing? No signature.'

'No, it was, erm, what would you call it? Anonymous?'

'An oni what?'

'Anonymous,' Hermitage quite liked the word. 'From the Greek, you know.'

'No, not really.'

'An, without and onoma, name. Without name, see? Anonymous, nameless. A nameless parchment. An anonymous one.'

'Yes, yes, alright, whatever you like. But there wasn't even the name of a piece of weaving equipment at the end?'

Hermitage was lost again. 'It wasn't a list. It was a letter.'

'These idiots in the Grey Guild all take secret names. Shuttle's name isn't really Shuttle.' She glared at him as she'd expected him to understand this pretty basic fact from the off.

'Ah,' he said. 'I did think it was a bit of a coincidence, being christened Shuttle and then becoming a weaver.'

Cwen ran her hands all over her head and face as if she could somehow rub this conversation out of her head. 'And these two aren't called Heddle and Treadle.'

'I didn't think they were. You said they were called Edward,' Hermitage protested at Cwen's obvious irritation with him. He hadn't done anything. In fact, he'd found an important parchment.

'Can we get back to the matter in hand?'

'Yes please.'

Cwen breathed in through her nose and blew out slowly through her mouth, making "calm down" gestures to herself. 'Right. This Shuttle…,'

'Whose real name we don't know?' Hermitage checked.

'Whose real name we don't know,' Cwen confirmed. 'May

already have killed Hemling.' She held up a hand to ward off his protest. 'May have killed Hemling, I said. And he is now off to carry out the second step of the Grey Guild's plan.'

'Ah,' Hermitage saw the significance of that. 'And what is it, this second step?'

'Don't know.'

'I see.'

'And they don't know either.' She nodded to the Edwards, who smiled. 'But it could be another murder. If your anti-mouse letter writer was referring to Shuttle…,'

'Anonymous.'

'Yes, that. If he was referring to Shuttle then there might be another murder about to be committed. One we could stop.'

Despite his doubts about the letter referring to Shuttle and the Grey Guild at all, Hermitage liked the idea of stopping a murder before it happened. Quite apart from the moral questions involved, it would mean one less wretched investigation.

Cwen was now looking at Hermitage in a rather peculiar manner. Her face was pinched tight as if the thoughts inside her head were drawing on it for their strength.

'Are you alright?'

Now she nodded slowly. 'This parchment of yours.'

'Well, it belongs to the guild, obviously.'

'Obviously,' she still sounded impatient with this quite proper conclusion. 'It was written, yes?'

Now she was talking nonsense. Perhaps her captivity had got the better of her. 'Well, yes. That's how I was able to read what it said.'

'Quite. But there aren't many people who can write, are there? Apart from monks and the like of course.'

A Murder for Master Wat

'Well, no.'

'And you didn't write it.'

'How could I? When I found it at the bottom of a trunk of guild letters?' He was beginning to wonder if Wat hadn't been correct when he said that Cwen should not come to this moot. The excitement of it all seemed to be affecting her thinking.

'The bottom?'

'Yes. And that's a puzzle. It must have been put at the bottom so that no one would find it. It was being hidden.'

Cwen nodded that this seemed likely. 'But the writing. Was it a good hand?'

'Good hand?' Hermitage hadn't found a hand.

'The writing, Hermitage. Do try and keep up. Was the writing on the parchment in a good hand?'

'Oh, I see. No, not really. Certainly not a scribe. Lots of mess and bad spelling.'

'Not someone who does a lot of writing.'

'Absolutely not.'

'But enough to get by. Enough to write a letter to the guild warning them of murder.'

'I suppose so.'

'Which must cut out an awful lot of people at the moot. Most of the weavers I know could perhaps write their own name but that would be about it.'

Hermitage nodded.

'And the guild men themselves should all be able to write quite well, you'd think.'

'Either that or they have people to do it for them.'

'In which case, your parchment would be a nice neat job. You know. "To all and sundry whomsoever it may concern, be told that there is this day an killer amongst you. Your

173

obedient servant A nony mouse," that sort of thing.'

Hermitage was now looking at Cwen with a strange expression, but his face had gone completely loose.

'So,' Cwen carried on, full of the sort of enthusiasm Hermitage only usually saw from the inside. 'We know the parchment wasn't from the guild and it wasn't from a weaver. All we need to do is find out who could write enough to make something like it and there we are.'

'There we are, what?'

'Oh, really.' Cwen huffed. 'We find the parchment writer. We ask him who the killer is. We catch the killer.'

'Oh, I see. Good idea.' Hermitage smiled at the thought. He did wonder briefly if this was the sort of thing an investigator was supposed to think of. He supposed it didn't really matter who came up with it. 'And how do we do that?'

'Ask around.'

'Ask around?' Asking around sounded terribly impertinent somehow.

'Yes.' Cwen was nodding at her own thoughts. 'We ask around, pretending that we've got something that needs writing but we can't afford a scribe. Do they know anyone who could write a whole page for us?'

Hermitage considered this. 'It's a bit dishonest, isn't it?'

'So's murder,' Cwen pointed out.

'I suppose it is.' Hermitage hadn't really thought of murder as dishonest, somehow. Dishonesty was lying and cheating and stealing. Murder was way beyond dishonest. He couldn't imagine an honest murder, for example. 'Who do we ask?'

'Doesn't matter. Stallholders? They've been here a while, met most of the people.'

'The stallholders?' Hermitage said this very slowly. He didn't want to frighten off the sparkling pin-prick of

A Murder for Master Wat

recognition that had just lit a dim candle at the back of his head. This was the sort of thought that could vanish if you tried to examine it. Like recalling someone's name that is on the tip of your tongue only to have it fade the harder you think about it. Then, when you're not bothering it at all, it jumps up and down and shouts at you. He always had the same trouble with what-was-his-name, the father of Nahbi, of the tribe of Naphtali in the book of Numbers? There, that had gone again. It would come back when he wasn't looking.

'The stallholders,' he said again, trying to sneak around behind the thought and grab it.

'What about them?'

Hermitage snapped his fingers. 'I have it.'

'Good. What do you have?'

Hermitage was more satisfied that he had managed to capture his thought and bring it to the front of his mind, than that it might have something to do with the murder. 'I've seen that writing before.'

'Where?' Cwen looked quite impressed.

'On one of the stalls.' Hermitage almost jumped up and down with the excitement. Not only had he remembered something that he hadn't even been committing to memory, but it had to do with writing. No one else would have spotted it. Perhaps he could investigate after all. He put that thought firmly in its place and hoped that it would vanish never to be seen again.

'Which stall?' Cwen asked.

'Which stall?' Hermitage asked, coming down with a bit of a bump.

'Yes. Which stall? We can go straight to the stallholder and ask. It'll save a lot of time.'

'Which stall,' Hermitage repeated.

175

'Yes, which stall?' Cwen repeated as well but she sounded a lot less patient.

'Erm.'

'You don't remember which stall.' She folded her arms straight at him.

'I was more interested in the signs than the stalls. You know, the standard of penmanship.' He shrugged.

'Excellent.' Cwen shook her head and rolled her eyes, but in a friendly manner. 'So, we just walk the stalls until you find a sign that looks like the parchment.' She beckoned the two Edwards to follow as they walked off into the moot. They had been standing by gazing at this conversation with a mix of awe at the learning and terror that the learning was being used to find a killer.

As they walked, glancing at the few stalls that there were in this part of town, with no success, Cwen had another thought. 'What language was it?'

'The sign?'

'The sign, the parchment. Were the languages the same, or was it just the type of writing?'

Hermitage beamed. 'That's an excellent question. The stallholders used all sorts of different languages for their signs. If we find the one that was in the same language as the letter we'll be on the way.'

'Just so. And?'

'Unless the writer knows more than one language, of course.' Hermitage immediately saw the problem.

'If they can barely write one, they're not likely to know another, are they? What language was the parchment?' Cwen's impatience wanted to reach out to Hermitage, and slap him.

'I suppose not. Anyway, the letter was in a rough Saxon so

the sign must be as well.' He nodded at his first conclusion. 'That rules out the pork stall.'

Cwen clearly had a question in her head but couldn't find the right words, or didn't want to.

'The pork stall had a sign in Latin,' he explained. 'Bad Latin with the wrong case for the noun.'

'Fascinating. Absolutely fascinating. Who had a Saxon sign?'

Hermitage considered for a moment. 'I suppose a lot of them did.'

'So, a Saxon sign with this particular writing on it,' Cwen confirmed.

They continued to scan stalls for any indication of writing, but none of them in this area had anything apart from crude pictures indicating their wares. In some cases very crude pictures.

'It must have been near the entrance,' Hermitage said. 'It was when we first came in that I noticed the signs at all. It must have been one of them.'

'Right.' Cwen upped her pace and Hermitage and the two Edwards skipped along to keep up.

As they did so he had another thought. He turned to one of the hoods. 'Did your Shuttle person write?'

'Eh?' one Edward replied.

'This Shuttle. The leader of the Grey Guild, could he write?'

'No idea,' the Edward answered, plainly not seeing what this had to do with anything. 'Writing never came up, really.'

'Hm.'

Cwen turned to him and raised her eyebrows.

'I was just thinking that the letter might be a threat, not a warning. You know, if your Shuttle was going to kill

Hemling...,'

'He's not my Shuttle.'

'This Shuttle, then. If the fellow wanted to sow fear in the guild he might send a warning that a killer was coming?'

'I suppose,' Cwen agreed. 'But unless he's got a stall with a sign over it in Saxon saying "killer available", it doesn't tie up with your matching the writing.'

'Ah,' Hermitage saw the problem. 'Unless he got someone to write it for him?'

'That's going a bit far, isn't it? Getting someone else to write your threatening letters for you?'

'Perhaps they are in league? It could be that Shuttle simply asked Robert the loom maker to write the letter for him because they both want to damage the guild.'

Cwen stopped walking and stared at him.

'What?' he asked. He couldn't think of anything he'd said to offend Cwen. That was usually the cause of her stopping doing something and staring at him.

'What did you say?'

Hermitage couldn't see why he had to repeat himself. 'I just said that maybe Robert the loom maker wrote the letter for Shuttle.' He smiled that this was actually quite a good idea.

'Who wrote it for him?' she prompted.

'Robert the loom maker,' Hermitage repeated. 'Oh,' he cried out in surprise at what he'd just heard himself say. 'Robert the loom maker. It was his sign. He wrote the letter. So he knows who the killer is.'

'Yes,' Cwen sounded quite irritated with Hermitage for some reason. 'Either that or he is the killer?'

'Oh, yes,' Hermitage had a sudden queasy feeling that he had been loitering at Robert's stand when the man might have been a killer. Or was about to become one.'

Cwen started walking again, quite quickly this time. 'I think we need to find Robert the loom maker. If he hasn't run away already.'

'Or if he and Shuttle aren't already committing their next murder.' They all upped their pace, Hermitage hoping that they arrived just before or just after a murder. Before would be preferable, obviously, but arriving in the middle of one didn't bear thinking about. 'Vophsi,' he said with a smile.

'Pardon?' Cwen looked around. Perhaps Hermitage had just spotted something.

'The father of Nahbi, of the tribe of Naphtali. I knew it would come to me.'

Caput XVI: All Together Now

'Do you believe him?' Hartle asked as he and Wat made their way back into the moot.

'Grum?' Wat confirmed. 'The most miserable weaver in Christendom. Do I believe that his life and luck are so bad that he would miss a pile of money that was sitting in his backroom just waiting for the taking? Absolutely I believe him. That man could be commissioned to weave in gold thread by Saint Peter and the loom would probably fall on him.'

'So, our killer took the money then. Where do we go next? If I'd just killed Hemling and stolen all the guild's money, I don't think I'd wait around to enjoy the moot.

Wat thought as they walked. 'It could be the guild did take it. After all, once Hemling was dead the first thing of concern to our dear leaders in the guild would be their money. Dead weavers can be buried any time, sacks of money can get lost or stolen.'

'And dead weavers can always be replaced,' Hartle confirmed. 'There's plenty of weavers in the world, there's only a limited supply of money.'

'Priorities,' Wat nodded solemn agreement. Then they exchanged looks of hopelessness at their guild's callousness.

'Master Thomas was the one who got the body shifted.' Hartle said. 'If he'd seen a sack full of coin he'd have dropped Hemling down a well and dragged the money back to the guild.'

'Yes,' Wat agreed. 'He didn't seem bothered about taking us to see the place, apart from seeing me at all, of course. He obviously wasn't expecting there to be any money.'

Hartle gave this some consideration. 'Maybe he never knew

it was there in the first place? He keeps moaning about how the guild just get him to do their chores. Money isn't a chore so he wouldn't have been involved.'

They both walked on in silence for a few moments, turning the ideas over in their heads.

'The apprentices,' Hartle announced.

'What about them?'

'Thomas sent some apprentices to bring the body back. Think back to when you were an apprentice. What would you have done if you found sacks full of money?'

'You're right,' Wat nodded at the suggestion. 'I'd have taken it and run.'

'Me too,' Hartle said, which surprised Wat.

'You'd have taken the guild's money? And I thought you were such a decent fellow.'

'I've been with you for many years now,' Hartle replied. 'I think my claims to decency are long gone.'

Wat smiled. 'I'd probably have spent some of it on arranging a nice surprise for my master.'

'Oh, yes?'

'I could hire my own killer,' Wat gave a grim smile.

'Ha.'

'Oh, this isn't getting us anywhere,' Wat sighed his annoyance. 'There was some money, that's all we know. Was Hemling killed for it? Was it there when the apprentices went back with the body? Did the guild take it as soon as Hemling hit the floor? We've got more questions now than we had to begin with.'

'Do we look for Thomas again? Back to the guild? Ask them if they'd like to tell us what they've done with the money from Hemling's?'

'Ha!' Wat barked a laugh at that idea. 'The person who

tells them all their money has gone would be wise to do so from a great distance. Preferably by letter.'

'Not that I think the lumps in chairs at the great hall know what's going out here at all.' Hartle grunted. 'They know there's a moot and they're in Nottingham, but that's about it.'

'They'll soon wake up when their coin doesn't arrive.'

'Hermitage is still there, of course,' Hartle remembered. 'Although he's probably climbed inside that trunk of guild parchment by now. We might never get him out. Maybe he's heard some talk while he's been there.'

'Hermitage?' Wat ridiculed the suggestion. 'Brother Hermitage with a trunk full of parchment wouldn't notice if the Angel of Death brought Judgement Day in on a horse and cart while playing the trumpet and doing a dance.' He smiled at his own idea. 'Perhaps I should go and see the guild now,' he suggested. 'That'd horrify them into some sort of life.'

Hartle nodded at the idea. 'The shock might even kill 'em. Never know your luck.'

Having made up their minds they turned for the main hall of Nottingham, confident that the leaders of the guild would be just where Hartle had left them.

Before they had gone far, Wat heard a noise behind him and felt a tug at his elbow. He turned and saw a small boy grinning up at him. The child looked about seven or eight at most. A bit young for a moot.

'Hello?' Wat asked.

'Are you Wat the Weaver?' The boy sniggered slightly as he said it.

'Could be.' Wat looked around to see if this small boy was part of some sort of trap. The old saying of the weaving fraternity came to his mind. "If it's dangerous, send a child."

A Murder for Master Wat

'You are,' the boy was full of enthusiasm. 'My father said you were. He saw you earlier.'

'And who's your father.'

'Weaver Ailof.'

'Ailof of York?' Hartle asked.

'That's him.'

'I know him well, boy. Tell your father that Master Hartle sends greeting. Is he here?'

'I will, sir,' the boy agreed. 'Yes, he's here about somewhere.'

Wat smiled now. At least this seemed a genuine child. 'And why do you want to know if I'm Wat the Weaver?'

The boy sniffed. 'Because my father says I'm disgusting and if I don't mend my ways I'll end up like Wat the Weaver.'

'Oh, really?' Wat was not so happy now.

'You look all right to me,' the boy commented.

'Thank you very much.' Wat wasn't sure what to do with criticism from a seven-year-old.

The boy appraised Wat's clothes and appearance. 'I think I'd like to be a disgusting weaver when I grow up.' He stepped forward, gave Wat a hug around the tops of his legs and then turned and ran.

Wat turned to Hartle. 'And you can shut up,' he instructed.

'Never said a word,' Hartle replied, through barely controlled laughter.

'Come on then,' Wat grumbled. 'If I've got small children insulting me, the guild will be a piece of pudding.'

Picking their way through the crowd, which was at least fairly thin in this part of town, they were watching their feet to make sure they didn't tread in anything. Heads down, they rounded the corner of one building and bumped straight into a group of people coming in the other direction.

Before Wat could reprimand them for not looking where they were going he saw that one of them was wearing a habit.

'Aha,' he called. 'Not buried in parchment then, eh Hermitage.' He looked at Cwen and smiled. 'And not just buried in an unmarked grave in a quiet corner of the moot. Excellent.' Cwen scowled and Hermitage smiled.

Wat then looked askance at two boys behind Cwen who were just standing there, grinning at him.

'This is Edward,' Cwen introduced them. 'And so's this.'

Wat looked from one to the other. 'That's clear then.' He glanced at Cwen. 'Have you made new friends or are they just following you?'

The two Edwards were exchanging excited whispers at the sight of Wat; even though they'd never met him and didn't know what he looked like.

'They escaped with me from the Grey Guild,' Cwen explained. 'Apprentices of the Weaver of Winchester.'

Wat sucked air through his teeth. 'Oh, nasty.'

'Quite. Very keen on working with the great Wat the Weaver, apparently.' Cwen made it quite clear that she didn't think Wat was great and that anyone who wanted to work with him probably had something wrong with them.

Edward and Edward nodded vigorously.

'Who can blame them?' Wat's modesty was as false as a leg on a man with no legs.

'In fact, you wouldn't believe what the Grey Guild has in mind for you.' Cwen gave a mysterious smile. One that she clearly hoped would put the wind up Wat.

'Can't wait,' Wat said. 'But we've got more important matters. We've discovered that there was no money at Hemling's place. So, either it was taken back by the guild or

A Murder for Master Wat

our killer's already got it.'

'That's nothing,' Cwen dismissed Wat with a wave of her hand. 'We know who did it.'

'Eh?' Wat looked stunned.

'Well,' Hermitage had to step in. 'It's possible, that's all.'

'Who did it, then?' Hartle asked.

'Shuttle.'

Wat now just looked confused. 'No. It was the warp. I suppose it might have been the Heddle that caused the warp to break.'

'It wasn't me,' Edward protested.

'Pardon?' Whatever came after confusion was now moving in.

'Shuttle's not a what, it's a him,' Cwen explained.

'The Shuttle is a him?' Wat was looking at Cwen as if her time with the Grey Guild had done something to her.

'They all take secret names,' she went on, impatiently. 'The leader calls himself Shuttle. And these two are called Heddle and Treadle.'

'And not Edward and Edward,' Wat checked. 'Well, that's a lot easier.' He clearly thought it wasn't.

'Shuttle is the leader of the Grey Guild and he said that they were going to do something to Hemling to show up the guild.'

'Did they?' Wat did sound interested now.

'And then I found an anonymous note,' Hermitage reported.

'Never mind,' Wat sympathised. 'It'll probably wash off.'

'No,' Hermitage shook his head. 'An anonymous note. It means a note that isn't signed. No one put their name on it. No name, nameless, anonymous. You see?'

Wat nodded at Hermitage. 'Not in the slightest,' he said.

'The point is that this note said that a killer was coming to the moot.'

'The killer wrote saying he was coming?' Wat frowned deeply. 'Bit of a stupid killer by the sound of it, sending word that he's on his way.'

'Oh, Wat,' Hermitage pleaded. 'Do try and pay attention. There is no name on the note. Someone wrote saying that a killer was coming. The killer didn't write saying "Dear Guild, I'm coming to the moot, look forward to killing you." Someone else wrote a note warning the guild. But it was buried at the bottom of the trunk.'

'And,' Cwen announced, making sure they had everyone's attention. 'We know who wrote the note.'

'I thought you said it was Aunty Onymus.' Hartle looked very lost indeed. 'Don't we just look for her?'

'Anonymous,' Hermitage corrected with a weary sigh. 'No name?'

'So how do you know who wrote it?' Wat asked.

'I recognised the writing,' Hermitage said.

'After I prompted him,' Cwen put in.

'Quite,' Hermitage agreed. 'I knew I'd seen the hand somewhere else.'

'There was a hand?' Hartle asked with some distaste.

Hermitage sighed heavily. 'No, there was no hand. There was no Aunty. There was no name. I recognised the writing. I recognised it from one of the stall holders' signs. The same hand that wrote the sign, wrote the letter.'

Hartle nodded with understanding. 'Clever.'

'So, we're on our way to the stall now,' Cwen got them back on track. 'We'll ask Robert the loom maker why he wrote the note.'

Hartle nodded again but much more slowly this time.

A Murder for Master Wat

'Because it was his hand?' he tried.

'Exactly,' Hermitage agreed.

'Aha,' Hartle was happy now.

'Let's go then,' Wat beckoned Cwen to lead on. 'Of course, he may not know who the killer is either,' he went on as they walked. 'He may only have heard rumour or gossip or something. Didn't want to put his name on the letter in case the guild wanted to ask him all sorts of awkward questions.'

'Or he does know who the killer is,' Hermitage suggested. 'But just didn't want to put his name on the letter in case the killer wanted to kill him as well. Which would be even more awkward.'

'Ah, could be,' Wat nodded that this seemed sensible.

They soon made the main entrance to the moot and scanned about for the loom makers stall. The crowd was still thick here so it was awkward to make much headway. Every stall was pressed with people, except the one for the guild, obviously.

Hermitage raised his eyes and examined the various trade signs that were lofted above the stalls. A glimpse of a capital "R" pointed him to the loom maker and confirmed his conclusion that this was the writer of the parchment. The letter was instantly identifiable to anyone. This R was obviously the majuscule at the start of the name, but the hairline cross piece bore a strong resemblance to those on the letter. Clearly, this sign was made with brush rather than quill but the hand could not disguise itself.

Only as he looked did it occur to Hermitage that the loom maker himself may not actually have written either of the samples. Perhaps Robert the loom maker could no more write than the dung clearer, who had simply used a sample of his trade stuck on top of a pole to identify his stall.

Hermitage wondered why a dung clearer had come to a weavers' moot but he supposed it was a service required by all trades.

It was quite possible that Robert had commissioned a signwriter and it was the signwriter who had written the letter. He had obviously commissioned a very poor signwriter but perhaps he was the only one available. It didn't really matter. If Robert had no information himself, he could at least direct them to the right person.

He beckoned the others to follow and pushed through towards the stall.

As they arrived they saw that, although there was a crowd, no one was actually attending the loom maker. A loom must be an expensive thing to have made and so business would be light but lucrative.

There was a bit of added chaos in the area caused by the fact that one of the stalls had partly collapsed as a guy rope gave way. Hermitage considered that as well as shoddy sign work, these stallholders weren't even very good at building a stall that stayed up. He noted with some disappointment that it was, in fact, the guild stall itself that was falling down. A very poor example to set.

Eventually, they got to the loom maker's stall and Hermitage leaned over the table to call Robert's attention. He then saw that no one was actually doing business with Robert the loom maker because Robert the loom maker was dead.

He couldn't take it in at first. He thought that the man might just be having a lie down behind his stall as it had been a really busy day. Or he had taken his noonday meal and was resting it off. Or he had brought a skin of wine with him and had finished that off.

A Murder for Master Wat

That this lying down was not a normal part of the loom maker's day became clear when one considered the knife sticking out of his chest.

'Ah,' said Wat, as he stepped around the table to stoop at Robert's side. 'This looks suspicious.'

'Suspicious?' Hermitage asked, with incredulity. 'The man's been stabbed.'

'It appears so.'

The others pressed forward to get a look now, and in doing so started to draw the attention of the crowd.

'Oh, dear,' Cwen said.

'Quite,' Hermitage agreed. 'The man who might have known who the killer was, or whose signwriter was involved, has now been killed.'

'His signwriter?' Wat asked.

'Yes. It only just occurred to me that the loom maker may not have written his own sign. He could have got a signwriter to do it for him. In which case it was the signwriter who wrote the letter.'

Wat nodded towards the corpse. 'I think we can conclude that Robert used to do all his own writing.'

'And has been killed for it,' Hartle added as he considered the dead man.

'Can we look?' the two Edwards pushed forward.

'No, you cannot,' Cwen shooed them away. 'What now?' she asked Hermitage.

'Another murder,' he said, feeling the full weight of it. 'I come to a weavers' moot, a weavers' moot for goodness sake, and within hours two people are murdered.'

'I don't think you did it,' Wat assured him.

'I know I didn't do it, but it happens doesn't it? Wherever I go people start dropping like dead people.'

'I didn't think monks believed in curses,' Cwen pointed out.

'We don't,' Hermitage assured her. 'But it's a bit of a coincidence, isn't it?'

'I think Hemling would have died if you'd been here or not,' Wat said. 'The warp on his loom was interfered with long before you arrived.'

'And there's probably people being murdered right now all over the country and you're nowhere near them, are you?' Cwen tried a smile.

'That's not very comforting if you don't mind me saying so.' Hermitage let out a long and heavy sigh. 'Now we have to find Robert's murderer.'

'Probably the same person,' Wat tried to console him. 'Lots of murders but only one murderer. That probably only counts as one investigation?'

'Again, not much of a comfort.' As he contemplated this latest development, the crowd in the moot was disturbed as Master Thomas came striding up to them.

'What's going on here?' he demanded as he looked them over. 'You again,' he huffed. 'I might have known.'

'Robert the loom maker has been murdered,' Hermitage announced, reluctantly.

Thomas peered at the stabbed man. 'I see.'

'A knife.'

Thomas observed the body. 'It certainly is. Another death, eh?'

'Another murder,' Hermitage said, thinking that this sort of thing probably didn't show the moot in a very good light.

'Quite.' Thomas folded his arms and looked very stern. 'And one common factor, it seems.'

Hermitage nodded. 'I know,' he accepted the implication.

A Murder for Master Wat

Thomas beckoned that two large men Hermitage had not noticed before, should come over and assist him. 'Two murders when there's one person here who shouldn't be at a weavers' moot at all.'

Hermitage didn't know what his fate was going to be. Blame for the circumstances he could understand. Surely this guild man didn't believe that he had anything to do with the actual killings.

Thomas waved the large men to step forward. 'Wat the Weaver,' he said. 'I might have known. Take him away.'

Caput XVII: The Taking of Wat

'Where are you taking him?' Cwen demanded as they scuttled after Thomas and his large men as they almost carried a bemused looking Wat away. He was taken by the arms and dragged out of Robert's stand before he could say a word. He looked more surprised than anything and didn't struggle at all. He cast a look back at the others that said this was ridiculous and would be sorted out any moment now; and that if they'd like to do the sorting out he'd be very grateful.

'You can't do this,' Hartle added.

'I think we'd better just go along,' Hermitage said, quietly.

'This is exciting,' the Edwards enthused.

Cwen turned on them. 'You two can clear off. You'll only be in the way.'

They looked utterly crestfallen as if they had come within the grasp of their life's dream to be close to Wat the Weaver, only to have it snatched from their hands. Or to have him snatched from their hands, to be more accurate.

'Look for Gunnaug,' Cwen instructed. 'He's a great tall thing, probably the biggest apprentice in the moot. Tell him Cwen sent you and then stay with him and the other apprentices until we find you.'

The Edwards beamed once more and skipped off to find their new workmates.

'Are you really taking them on?' Hartle asked, nodding at the departing boys.

Cwen shrugged. 'Can't leave them with the Weaver of Winchester, they could be dead before they're fifteen. And the workshop could do with a couple more.' She smiled a winning smile at Hartle. 'Always assuming they're any good, of course.'

'Please yourself,' he said.

Her smile turned to rather smug satisfaction.

'Probably do you good, having a couple of apprentices to look after.'

The smile froze, 'Eh? What?' But Hartle strode on to catch up with Wat.

'And you can write to their parents and tell them that they're now working with Wat the Weaver,' he called back. 'Or get Hermitage to do it for you.'

He caught up with Thomas. 'What do you think you're doing?' he demanded. 'You're the Weavers' Guild for goodness sake, you can't go locking people up.'

Thomas snarled at him. 'I am not the Weavers' Guild. I am just a master innocently attending his moot who ended up having to deal with a dead body because no one else would do it. I am now getting every other whining complaint about the moot because I happen to be here and I happen to be a helpful person. Not one of those gargoyles from the guild has so much as got out of his chair to help.' Thomas was clearly happy to unburden himself. 'All they say is, "Jolly good, Master Thomas. We're sure you'll work it out, Master Thomas. Do let us know how you get on Master Thomas." Pah!'

'Nothing to do with any ambition you might have to join the guild's inner sanctum, then? Do a good job here and they might give you a chair to sit in next time.' Hartle suggested, with a lift of his eyebrows.

Thomas just waved the idea away. 'Now there's a dead loom maker. Hemling might have been killed by his loom, but if I see a loom that can wield a knife I'll burn it on the spot. A dead stall holder can't be left lying about and so I have to clear him up as well. Hemling on his own was one thing, but when the stallholders start dropping there's obviously something going on.'

'But,' Hermitage had to speak up as he skipped along to keep up. 'There's nothing to say that Wat had anything to do with it at all.'

Thomas did stop walking now and turned to Hermitage with a very jabby finger. 'Wat the Weaver should not have been in the moot at all. Hemling had left specific instruction that he was to be excluded. Why did he do that, do you think?'

'Erm, he didn't like him?'

'Didn't like him! Hemling didn't like lots of people. He only left instruction about one of them. He didn't like Norgot the wool merchant because he was rumoured to abuse his sheep. He didn't leave instruction about Norgot. No, He left instruction about Wat. He didn't want Wat here because Wat had probably been threatening him.'

'Oh, now really…,'

'And then who do we find standing over the dead body of the loom maker? Why it's Wat the Weaver.'

'But, we'd only just got there.'

'You had, yes, goodness knows when Wat did the deed. Have you been with him all the time?'

Hermitage's reluctant glance said that no, he had not. In fact, Wat had been on his own for quite a long period of time and could have been doing anything. Although he knew that Wat had not killed anyone, he thought it best not to appraise Thomas of this information. He would chastise himself for the dishonesty later.

'But Hartle's right,' Cwen chimed in. 'The Weavers' Guild can't go locking people up. And if you're not with the guild

A Murder for Master Wat

you definitely can't go locking people up.'

'I don't see anyone stopping me,' Thomas snarled. 'God! The sooner this wretched moot is over the better. I wish I'd never come.'

'You wish you'd never come,' Cwen gave a good snarl of her own. 'It's ridiculous. Wat did not kill anyone. He had no reason to kill Hemling and no reason to kill a loom maker he didn't even know.'

Thomas ignored her and returned to striding along, waving the two large men with Wat ahead of him.

'Ah, well,' Hartle mumbled to Cwen and Hermitage. 'It might not be too wise to say that Wat didn't know Robert.'

Cwen's look was half glare, half shock.

'They did some business a while back.'

'You never mentioned this,' Cwen accused him.

'Nobody told me the same loom maker would be dead with a knife in his chest,' Hartle pointed out.

'What business did they do?' Hermitage asked.

'Just some new treadles on one of the looms. We were too busy to do it ourselves so I managed to persuade Wat to pay a loom maker.'

'That must have taken some doing.' Cwen commented on Wat's well-known preference for keeping his money out of the hands of others. Any others. And preferably out of sight as well.

'It did. But the treadles would be replaced more quickly and we could get on with profitable work.'

Cwen nodded as her thoughts gathered themselves. 'Don't tell me, there was a dispute over payment.'

'Wat the Weaver arguing overpaying for something?' Hartle sounded incredulous and sarcastic at the same time. 'Surely not.'

'Was there a fight?' Cwen sounded as if there was usually a fight when Wat was asked to pay for something.

'Only a small one this time. I didn't realise how strong loom makers are. All that lifting wood and pulling on ropes and the like, I suppose.'

'A lot stronger than a weaver who barely even lifts a thread these days,' Cwen snorted. 'So they did not leave on amicable terms.'

'Not in the slightest,' Hartle nodded.

'Wat has disputes about paying for things all the time,' Hermitage said. 'He's never killed anyone about it before, why would he do it now?'

'He wouldn't, obviously,' Cwen was angry that Hermitage had even suggested it. 'But if Thomas finds out that there was animosity between Wat and Robert he'll draw his own conclusions. The wrong ones.'

'Ah, I see,' Hermitage nodded.

They now arrived at the great hall once more, and Thomas and the large men marched Wat inside.

'Is he being taken to the guild?' Hermitage asked. 'Surely they don't have the power to deal with deaths and such forth.'

'They can issue reprimands,' Hartle explained.

'A reprimand? For murder?' Hermitage was shocked. 'That's a bit lax, isn't it?'

'Death of an apprentice, usually. And unless there's solid evidence that the master actually did it, that's all they can do.'

And how many reprimands does it take until a master is removed?'

Hartle looked puzzled. 'As many as you like.'

'And if there is solid evidence?'

'Don't know,' Hartle shrugged. 'I've never heard of a case of a master actually killing an apprentice. Officially like.'

A Murder for Master Wat

'Officially killing him,' Hermitage shook his head in despair.

'But I imagine they would have to bring in the local sheriff or lord.'

'Which, in our case would be the Norman, William Peverel.' Hermitage nodded to himself at the thought. 'The same William Peverel who knows me as King's Investigator from William's own mouth. And he knows of Wat. He's hardly likely to do anything unnecessary if he knows us, is he?'

'A Norman?' Cwen sounded as if she thought Hermitage was making up silly stories. 'A Norman sheriff won't do anything unnecessary?'

Hermitage sighed. 'And this Robert was Saxon.'

'So?' Cwen asked.

'When we spoke to Peverel earlier he wasn't at all interested in the deaths of Saxons.'

'Unless he can cause them, I imagine.'

'So, even if the guild say that Wat did this and demand punishment, Peverel might not bother.'

Hartle gave a great sigh as they entered the inner hall. 'That's reassuring. Might not bother.

Instead of carrying on to the seated gathering of guild officials at the end of the hall, Thomas led them through a door to the left and out of the rear of the hall into a small yard. This was bordered by a roofed store of logs for the hall fire and a similar one for dry straw, to be taken in and spread on the floor when the old straw needed to go.

A pile of this old straw sat in one corner of the yard, gently steaming to itself as it waited to be taken away. Hermitage assumed that the dung clearer would only get to this once his stall at the moot was finished with.

Right next to the dung heap was the town lock-up. It really looked just like a store with a lock on the door, and a small store at that, but Thomas led the way straight to it.

'You can't put him in there,' Cwen protested.

Thomas turned on her with his pointing at full power. 'You people presume to tell me what I can and cannot do quite a lot. Who are you anyway? His mistress?'

Anyone who knew Cwen at all well would not have uttered those words. Hermitage and Hartle slowly slid backwards while Wat looked on with interest.

Cwen simply said, 'No I am not,' but the look in her eye gave the overwhelming impression that she now felt entitled to do whatever she wanted to Thomas. And it would be something quite unexpected.

The master blinked in the face of the onslaught and clearly thought better of further questions. He nodded that the large men should put Wat in the store, which they did, Wat ducking his head down to get in under the low door.

'It's not very nice in here,' he called back, brightly.

'Oh, dear,' Thomas said, as he shut and barred the door with a length of timber put there for the purpose.

'What now then?' Wat asked as he put his face and hands to two simple metal bars that were in a small window in the door.

'You wait there,' Thomas instructed, 'while I speak to the guild about what to do next. Though God knows why I'm bothering for all the thanks I get.'

'Why do you bother, then?' Wat asked. 'The moot is their problem. If people start getting murdered in it, let them sort it out.'

'They must have expected a death or two,' Hartle now suggested.

A Murder for Master Wat

This was much to Hermitage's surprise who thought a moot where deaths were expected was probably one to be avoided.

'You know what a bunch of drunk weavers away from home at a moot are like,' Hartle went on. 'They're going to come up with all sorts of stupid games. Daring one another to jump in the river. Getting in fights. Playing dodge-the-needle. Someone was bound to get injured at some point.'

'With a knife in the chest?' Thomas asked, dryly. 'Lying on the ground behind his stall stabbed to death? Flanbard of Hereford wove himself into his own loom and had to be rescued, but even he isn't stupid enough to stab himself to death.

'I only came to this moot to meet people and do a bit of trade.' He was now sounding very despondent 'I end up with Hemling dead, a master of the guild, and now a loom maker murdered. And it all happened at the guild's moot. It's guild business and the guild will have to sort it out.'

'If they can be bothered,' Hartle muttered.

'If they can't, I shall just leave it to the sheriff. I'm sure he won't mind executing a Saxon weaver for me if I ask nicely.'

'Execution?' Hermitage was horrified. 'Who said anything about execution?'

'I did,' Thomas confirmed.

'But Wat's a rich man,' Cwen protested. 'Not that he's killed anyone anyway, the whole idea is ridiculous, but he can afford weregild. If someone kills someone else they pay and that's that.'

'Ah,' Thomas said, wistfully. 'The good old days, eh? Under Edward and Harold that might have been the case, but the Normans seem a bit less keen on letting murderers walk around with fewer coppers in their purse and their heads still on.'

'I'm sure you'll sort it out,' Wat called to them, reassuringly, from his prison. 'What with a King's Investigator being involved and all.'

'King's Investigator, pah,' Thomas dismissed Hermitage's title. 'I'm sure the local Norman can sort this out, just the type of thing he does.'

'And if someone else gets killed as well?' Cwen pressed. 'That will show it wasn't Wat, won't it.'

'No,' Thomas said, lightly. 'It'll prove he didn't do the new murder, not that he didn't do the first two. And anyway, there isn't going to be another murder now we've got him locked up.' He nodded his head towards Wat, who gave a little wave in return.

Cwen's frustration was making her feet do a little dance as they tried to stamp the earth to dust. 'You simply can't do this,' was the best she could come up with.

Thomas looked at her, looked to Wat looked up and shrugged that it was done so that was that.

Hermitage had a thought and put his hand up. Only Hartle noticed. 'What is it, Hermitage?'

'Actually, I don't think he can do it.'

Thomas glared at him. 'If there's one thing I hate, it's people who start a sentence with "actually".'

Hermitage was very puzzled about that. There were a lot more important things in the world to hate than sentence structure. Although come to think of it, that would be top of his own personal list.

'I mean he's not allowed to do it. He's not allowed to do anything.'

Thomas folded his arms. 'King's moot organiser now, are

A Murder for Master Wat

you?'

'No,' Hermitage thought that should be obvious. 'But I read the terms of Hemling's appointment. In the trunk.'

Thomas looked very blank.

'The trunk of guild papers, in the hall. It says that Hemling is the organiser with all due power and authority delegated to him by the guild under the aegis of the Grand Master and that all such powers may be exercised at the discretion of the organiser under such circumstances as may from time to time arise within the bounds of the moot as it is so…'

'Yes,' Cwen barked. 'Why do you say it like that?'

'Like what?'

'As if it's all just one long stream of words.'

'Well,' Hermitage frowned. 'It is. That's what legal documents are like. I don't know if lawyers are frightened of capitals or word spacing but they never seem to use them. It's interesting that the Bible, for instance, would use a new line for…'

'Wat locked up?' Cwen prompted. 'Could we deal with that first and think about the layout of writing later?'

Hermitage looked forward to that. 'Oh, right, yes,' he tried to get back on track having been distracted mid-clause, which was always so frustrating. 'The point is that it is Hemling who is appointed to have all these powers and functions, not Thomas. Or anyone else, for that matter. I don't think any of his actions would stand up in a moot court.'

'And you're going to take me to moot court, are you?' Thomas challenged.

'I think the King's Investigator would have to,' Wat called from his prison. 'King William wouldn't want the locals taking things upon themselves, would he? He'd be sure to come and take them off again. Probably with one of his swords.'

Thomas glared at them all and seemed to be considering his position. 'Right,' he almost shouted. 'Please yourselves. Let's go and ask the idiots from the guild if it's alright if I lock Wat the Weaver up, shall we?'

When he said it like that, Hermitage could imagine that the guild might be quite pleased; Wat not being their favourite weaver.

They all followed Thomas back into the main hall, leaving Wat to his incarceration. They knew he was there because they could hear him whistling.

Upon arrival at the gathering of guild officials, Hermitage was surprised to see that they were all wide awake. This was mainly because it seemed to be mealtime, again, and the mess of food and drink that scattered the place made Hermitage wish he was back in the yard with the dirty straw.

'I've locked up Wat the Weaver,' Thomas announced, proudly.

The guild seemed quite interested in that. Not interested enough to stop eating but at least they raised heads as they chewed. 'Aha,' several of them grumbled in a non-committal sort of way.

'But these people say I have to let him go.'

The Grand Master heaved himself round in his chair to see what the fuss was. He found he couldn't manage it and simply waved that the group should present themselves.

'It's those two again,' he accused Hartle and Hermitage of coming back.

'The monk says I'm not allowed to lock Wat up because I don't have the authority of the guild.'

'Ha,' the Grand Master spat something onto the floor that landed with a thump. He looked at it, seemed to think momentarily about getting up to retrieve it but then decided that staying in his chair and simply getting another one was the better course of action.

Hermitage gagged slightly.

'Don't need authority, young man,' the Grand Master waved a chicken leg at Thomas. 'Best place for Wat the Weaver, locked up. You carry on.'

'There we are then,' Thomas crowed rather.

Hermitage didn't know what to do next.

'In fact, it's probably safest, just at the moment,' the Grand Master muttered on. 'Someone delivered this.' He waved his chicken in the air again, looked at it and saw that it was not what he meant. He dug around in his chair, dislodging the detritus of several meals, before retrieving a parchment. He handed it to Thomas who wiped some of the mess off it with his sleeve. He read. Very slowly. 'Well, well, well,' he sounded very smug indeed.

He handed the parchment to Cwen, who passed it to Hartle who handed it to Hermitage, who read it.

'Oh, my,' he said, for the second time in this room.

'What is it?' Cwen asked.

'It's from the Grey Guild,' Hermitage reported. 'It's a list of demands for change within the guild.'

'I'm surprised they can write,' Cwen commented.

'Not very well,' Hermitage confirmed, squinting at the page. 'But it says that their first action was against Hemling, their second against the trade of the moot, the third will be against the guild itself, and more will follow until their demands are met.'

'Never heard of the Grey Guild anyway,' the Grand Master complained. 'Who needs a whole guild just to make some grey?'

Cwen frowned as she considered this. Then she smiled. 'Aha,' she grinned triumphantly at Thomas. 'That's alright then. The letter proves that the Grey Guild killed Hemling and the loom maker.'

'It doesn't end there, unfortunately.' Hermitage took a breath before reading the signature. 'It says that these actions are the work of the Grey Guild in the name of their inspiration, Wat the Weaver.'

'Aha!' Thomas had a very good triumphant grin of his own.

Caput XVIII: Before the Killers Strike Again

Their departure from the hall was rude and rapid. Bundled out into the street by the large men, Hermitage had little time to consider what the Weavers' Guild was doing with large men anyway. Perhaps they'd hired them from the town for the duration of the moot.

Cwen stood gazing back at the great hall, fuming so intensely that people could have warmed themselves at her. 'They cannot hold Wat responsible for the actions of the idiot Grey Guild.'

'The idiot Grey Guild does,' Hartle pointed out. 'They even put it in writing.'

'But he didn't tell them to go and kill Hemling or the loom maker. They're just mad fools with their own stupid plan. We didn't even know they existed before we got here.'

'Before you went off and found them, you mean.'

Cwen's finger was shaking slightly as she pointed it at Hartle. Never a good sign. 'They were enthraled to Wat before I even turned up.'

Hermitage held his hand up before this descended into an unhelpful argument.

'The problem we have,' he explained, 'is that this Grey Guild seems to be out there murdering people in the name of Wat the Weaver. And I don't think the guild is too concerned about whether Wat knows about it or not.' He paused before stating the thought process he had gone through, the one that made him shake more than most things recently. 'As I read the situation, the guild is unlikely to give in to the Grey Guild's demands.'

'Ha,' Hartle gave a harsh laugh. 'The Grand Master will die of starvation first.'

'Quite. So,' Hermitage's conclusion was the only one possible in the situation. It was sensible, pragmatic and entirely reasonable. And also quite scary. 'We have to find them and stop them before they kill again.'

'What?' Cwen looked confused. 'The guild?'

'No, not the guild,' Hermitage sighed. 'The guild isn't going around killing people, are they?'

'Not that we know of.'

'Not in the name of Wat the Weaver, anyway,' Hartle put in.

'Ah, no.'

'How do we know they're going to kill again?' Cwen asked as if she was having trouble keeping up.

'Because the guild, the weavers' guild, not the grey one, will not give in to the demands.'

Cwen still looked a bit lost.

'The Grey Guild killed two people before they even sent their parchment. If the Weavers' Guild doesn't agree to their demands they will carry on killing.'

'Oh, yes.' Cwen looked pleased that she'd got it now.

'The ones we have to find and stop are the Grey Guild.' Hermitage spelt it out.

'Right.' Cwen now seemed quite keen on finding people and stopping them. Probably quite abruptly. 'And when we find Shuttle we'll want to bring him before the guild so we'd better not damage him,' she gave this as a clear instruction to the others.

Hermitage hoped that he looked horrified at the idea. 'We weren't going to damage him,' he insisted.

Cwen just looked at him. 'I was. He had me tied up.'

Hermitage just shook his head and gaped at the same time. He could imagine what sort of thing Cwen had in mind for

A Murder for Master Wat

people who tied her up. He couldn't imagine anyone had ever even dreamed of it before.

'We need to swap him for Wat. They can't do anything to Wat if they've got the man who did the actual murders.'

Hartle coughed lightly. 'I think they may still like to do something to Wat.'

'The question is,' Hermitage said, 'who will they kill next?' He posed the question and had a dread thought. 'They've killed a guild official and a trader, what if it was a Norman next?'

That made the others think as well.

'Trouble,' Hartle said, very seriously. 'Horrible, deadly trouble. If a Norman gets killed, that sheriff and his horde of Normans in their castle will be down on us like a horde of Normans from a castle.'

'Surely the Grey Guild wouldn't kill a Norman,' Cwen protested. 'I thought they were pretty useless when I met them. I can't imagine them taking on a Norman.' She shook her head. 'You've met Edward and Edward. They were an example of the Grey Guild. Probably quite a good one as they were given the task of guarding me while Shuttle went off.'

'Went off to kill Robert the loom maker, it turns out,' Hermitage said.

'And if he has the rest of his guild with him, they could be all over the place,' Hartle suggested. 'Maybe they're going to mount a mass attack.'

Hermitage swallowed. This was getting worse and worse.

'It's Shuttle who's the problem,' Cwen stated. 'The others all just follow him. They're sheep like the Edwards, Shuttle is the mad one, it's him we need to find and stop.'

'You're the only one who knows what he looks like,' Hartle said. 'We'll just have to go round the moot looking.'

'And when we find him?' Hermitage asked, not relishing the task of looking for a mad killer, never mind tackling one.

'We stop him,' Cwen said, in a very firm tone.

'Without damage,' Hermitage confirmed, although he was somewhat comforted that she seemed keen to go first.

'What about the Edwards?' Hartle asked. 'Presumably, they know this Shuttle character as well? They could help search.'

'They're just children,' Cwen sounded uncharacteristically sympathetic. 'And he might see them coming and be scared off.'

'He's going to see you coming,' Hartle said.

Cwen's smile was grim and full of foreboding. 'By the time he sees me coming it will already be too late.'

They set off through the moot, glancing continuously left and right to see if there was a glimpse of their killer. Hermitage and Hartle soon gave up as they realised they didn't have the first clue who they were looking for. Hermitage thought it unlikely that the fellow would be skulking, bent double with knife in hand as he searched out his next victim.

Hartle suggested that they just keep a weather eye out for anyone acting suspiciously. Hermitage agreed but knew that he was not going to find much success by that route. He tended not to spot suspicious people until they'd tied him up and locked him in a dungeon.

He knew this was a drawback to the duties of King's Investigator, but he had so many drawbacks where that role was concerned, one more wasn't going to make much difference. And no matter how many he collected he knew that he was not going to get out of the job.

They walked along behind Cwen, who was gazing at

everyone so intently that someone, sooner or later, was going to punch her on the nose for her trouble.

'One thing puzzles me,' Hermitage confided to Hartle.

'One thing? With a Grey Guild going round the weavers' moot slaughtering officials and tradesmen alike, just one thing puzzles you?' Hartle shook his head in disbelief.

'Yes,' Hermitage nodded to himself. 'Why would Robert the loom maker send a note about the Grey Guild? How would he know about them?'

Hartle gave a non-committal grunt. 'Could have overheard something? Chat in the moot, that sort of thing.'

'Possible, I suppose.'

'Maybe they confided in him? Maybe he's actually in the Grey Guild and they killed him because he betrayed them, having gone off the idea of murder?' Hartle sounded quite excited by this.

Hermitage shivered at the thought. 'And why didn't the guild do something about it?'

'That's two things.'

'Pardon?'

'That's two things you're puzzled about.'

'Erm, right.' Hermitage couldn't see that a count was particularly helpful. 'They had a note saying that a killer was coming but they did nothing.'

'I think they're probably very good at doing nothing. They have got some large men to protect them though. Probably not that concerned about other people getting killed.'

'I suppose so.' Hermitage shook his head at the lack of Christian brotherhood. 'And without knowing anything about the killer, how would they know where to watch out?'

Hartle mused on. 'And being leaders of the Weavers' Guild they probably get death threats all the time.'

'Really?' Hermitage was surprised at that.

'Oh, yes.' Hartle sounded as if it was the most natural thing in the world. 'You know, "you wouldn't accept my son into the guild so I hope you die of a horrible disease." Or, "My tapestry's fallen apart so I'm going to come round there and kill you," that sort of thing.'

'It's a bit extreme, isn't it?'

'People are,' Hartle shrugged. 'Particularly when they can put it in a letter and not have to actually face the person they're threatening.'

'Anonymous as well, no doubt,' Hermitage was finding his new word quite useful.

'Yes,' Hartle agreed absent-mindedly as he wandered on. 'Him too.'

Hermitage was about to explain the etymology once more when they saw that Cwen had darted into a tent. Following her through the entrance they came to a gathering of men standing about listening to a speaker at the front.

It was not a large tent, there could only be ten or twelve in the audience, but they were giving rapt attention to the man at the front.

Cwen clearly didn't recognise any of the faces as she hadn't leapt forward and grabbed one by the scruff of the neck to drag them away. She was looking over the heads and at faces so blatantly as to cause some ripples of disturbance.

Hermitage turned his attention to the nature of the event they had burst in upon. The man at the front was not an excitable or flamboyant fellow but was talking in the nature of a lecture of some sort. Hermitage recognised the tone from a three-day talk he had once heard on chapter two of the book of Ezra. He had been warned that the priest who gave it was renowned across the country as one of the dullest men

A Murder for Master Wat

alive. Hermitage dismissed these rumours as he had found the whole subject fascinating, and even now could recite all the names of the children who had been taken by Nebuchadnezzar.

As a result of this, he found the current talk on the selection of sheep to be enthralling. He had never known what significance the length of the wool had, nor that different coloured sheep attracted different interest. He was just about to ask a question on the advantages of combing over carding when Cwen grabbed him and pulled him away.

'No one here,' she complained at them both as they stood outside the tent.

'Do you think it likely that this Shuttle character will strike at one of the talks?' Hermitage asked.

'No idea,' Cwen shrugged, unhelpfully. 'It would obviously be spectacular if he could, but who knows. I'm just looking everywhere to see if I can spot him.'

'What does he look like?' Hartle asked.

Hermitage realised that this would have been a good question to ask before they even set off. He castigated himself silently, convinced, once more, that he shouldn't really be an investigator at all.

'Old boy,' Cwen described Shuttle. 'Dark eyes; mean, grubby little eyes, and a crooked nose.'

'Hair?' Hermitage asked.

'Yes,' Cwen confirmed that Shuttle had some.

'Grey?' Hermitage persisted, thinking that looking at all the people with hair could take quite some time.

'Oh, right, yes. And a bit thin.'

'Excellent,' Hermitage rubbed his hands as if ready for a satisfying task. Which he wasn't, but he thought it might help. 'Old man, eyes, hair, nose.' He nodded to Hartle who just looked blank. 'Next tent then.'

The next tent was virtually empty. There were only two people in there and they looked up with some surprise as the search party entered. They quickly stepped away from one another and one of them hurriedly put something behind his back.

Cwen simply tutted at them and retreated, clearly irritated that Shuttle had not been found in the first places they looked.

Walking along the roadway, she blatantly looked at everyone she passed, even reaching out to lift hoods and any loose hats that obscured faces. As people complained about this unwarranted treatment, a grumble began to grow. Those who had been examined complained as they walked away, and those approaching soon got the idea that something was going on.

'We're looking for someone,' Cwen retorted when one innocent individual had the temerity to ask why she'd taken his hat off.

'Well, there's no need to be quite so rude about it,' the man complained as he snatched his hat back and returned it to his head. 'Why can't you just ask, like normal people?' he demanded. 'I assume this monk is with you? He ought to know better.' The man walked on in a huff.

'Well,' Cwen called after him, 'have you seen Shuttle, leader of the Grey Guild?'

The man simply waved a hand behind his head to indicate that he wanted nothing more to do with any of them. Hermitage couldn't really blame him.

'On we go,' she waved Hermitage and Hartle on as if herding sheep. 'Next tent.'

Hermitage had to speak up, even though the consequences

could be well imagined. 'I'm not sure this approach is helping.' He tried to make it sound like a question.

He got a glare in return.

'If you, I mean if we make a fuss about looking for Shuttle we could frighten him off.' He added a smile, which seemed to make no difference. 'If you, I mean we, go shouting about that we're looking for him, he could hear us and hide away. Perhaps we need to be subtle?'

Cwen looked at him as if he was the most insulting monk she'd ever met. 'Subtle,' she repeated, trying out the word.

'Yes, you know, sneak about, that sort of thing. Cast an ear here and there, quietly observe, try not to be noticed.'

No, she still didn't get it.

'Just follow us,' Hartle sighed as he walked on. 'And don't touch anyone.'

Cwen gave a disgruntled shrug and followed.

They slid into the back of the next tent, which was more lean-to than actual enclosure. Two large poles had been stuck in the ground and a tatty sheet of canvas had been thrown from the poles into a tree that stood towards the back of the road. This did not have the look of a Weavers' Guild event, rather it appeared that some itinerant traders had stolen their way into the moot, and were ready to leave again at the first sign of trouble.

There was a man in charge of the goings-on here, but he was not making a great show of himself. He stood at the front of a small crowd, gathered around as if they were about to see the revelation of some great secret. Hartle and Hermitage gently moved their way into the group, careful not to upset anyone by pushing too hard.

Cwen snorted her impatience at this lacklustre approach.

'Dyes,' gentlemen. The very finest dyes.' The man spoke

only loud enough to be heard by those in front of him. He held up a small bottle. 'You won't see anything like this outside of the orient.' He said orient with a particular emphasis. 'The very far east.' The man nodded in a very significant way.

One member of his audience, impressed by this, turned to his young neighbour and explained. 'Norwich,' he said, knowingly.

'Let me just check though,' the man with the bottle addressed his audience. 'Do we have anyone from the guild with us today?'

That brought a round of derisive laughter from the assembly.

'I thought not,' the man went on. 'But you can never be too careful. These dyes are not the sort of thing the guild would approve of. Oh, dear me no. The guild would not approve at all.'

The crowd tittered conspiratorially at this.

Hermitage looked to Hartle for some explanation. Hartle was shaking his head as if he had seen all this before.

The man now held his bottle slightly higher and tapped the side of it with one finger. He beckoned his attentive audience to draw closer. They did. The man hissed for their ears only, 'Juice of lion,' he announced.

'Ooh,' went the crowd.

'For God's sake,' Hartle muttered.

'How do you get juice from a lion?' Hermitage asked, quietly. He'd never seen a lion but he'd heard about them, and of course, the Bible was full of them. They seemed quite fearsome creatures. He couldn't imagine they took kindly to being juiced.

'You don't,' Hartle grunted. 'It's probably his own piss in a bottle.'

Hermitage frowned and looked at the man and the bottle. Ah, he thought. Another suspicious character then. Perhaps he should take some notes.

A hand went up and the front of the crowd and the bottle was exchanged for some coins.

'Idiots,' Hartle complained.

'I've got camel's eye tint, squeezings of leopard and a very little elephant extract, but that's a very pricey item. Now then, what'll it be?' he tapped the side of his nose. 'Not a word to the guild, mind.'

His audience sniggered.

Hartle turned away and Hermitage went to follow.

'There he is,' Cwen shouted at the top of her voice.

Hermitage twisted around and saw that she was pointing to one figure at the front of the audience. This was indeed an old fellow with thin grey hair.

The target spun and saw Cwen pointing and jumping up and down. He ducked around the man with his dyes and skipped off behind the tree.

'Stop him,' Cwen instructed the crowd.

No one stopped him.

'Come on,' she waved Hartle and Hermitage to take up the chase.

'Subtle!' Hartle sighed and shook his head as they set off after Shuttle.

Caput XIX: The Chase is Moot

As Hermitage fully expected, by the time they got to the other side of the tree, there was no sign of their quarry.

'This way,' Cwen instructed, with no obvious justification.

The way she wanted to go was through a narrow alley between two houses, both of which overhung their route and looked ready to fall on it completely.

The other direction was back towards a crowded square where the moot-goers mingled and talked. Hermitage could see that it would be easy to spot someone barging through that crowd, but what if Shuttle was a clever fellow? What if he had run to that crowd and then simply joined in the mingling? The only option would be to accost everyone to try and find their man. He thought it a rather bad idea to give Cwen free rein on any accosting; the alley it was.

As he followed, there was a flash of light at the end of the alley, as if something had been blocking the exit and had just been removed. Shuttle, no doubt. They were on the track and he hurried forward, not thinking for one moment what they were going to do if they caught the man. Doubtless, Cwen would have some ideas.

Emerging from the darkness they were blinded for a moment as the bright sun, starting to drop towards evening, shone right in their faces.

'Which way did he go?' Cwen demanded.

As she had been first out of the alley, Hermitage thought this a somewhat unreasonable question. He lifted a hand to his head to shield his eyes from the sun and looked around. The passageway had opened into a small courtyard, trapped between humble dwellings that had cast most of their humility in a pile on the floor. He imagined that someone

A Murder for Master Wat

would come along and drag the heap of filthy straw away at some point, the quantity and pungency of the stuff said that the last clearance had happened quite some time ago.

The sun brushed the roof of the house directly opposite and cast its beams straight onto the opening of the alley. This was probably the only time of day the place got any illumination.

'He must be in one of the houses,' Hermitage concluded, quite reasonably.

'Well, yes,' Cwen replied in a very offhand manner. 'But which one?'

Hermitage cast about for any clue. 'That one,' he said, pointing.

'Why that one?' Hartle asked, turning his nose up at the straw.

'Because there is a trail of filthy straw leading to the doorway. Shuttle must have been just as blinded as us but in more of a hurry. He stumbled into the straw and then dragged some with his feet as he made his escape.' He was quite proud of this reasoning. Reasoning and observation in one go. Wat would be proud as well.

Cwen nodded agreement and headed in that direction.

To call the places houses was perhaps a generous step. They were single-storey buildings with walls and doorways and roofs and so the general definition was satisfied. The walls were plainly wattle and daub but made with too little of either. The doorways were just holes in the wattle and daub, presumably covered with skins in the winter but open now. And the roofs were thatch. Well, there was some thatch on the roofs but mostly it was gaps between the thatch.

Hermitage assumed the inhabitants simply moved about indoors as required. When it was raining they went to the bit of the room that had a roof over it. When it was sunny they could spread out a bit.

The doors opened into the grubby courtyard, and the alley was obviously the only way in and out of this small community. Hermitage considered the quality of the constructions and concluded that if Shuttle wanted to make good his escape, he could simply walk through the wall at the back of the house and be gone. Door or not.

Cwen was at the door of the hovel now and peering inside. It was as dark as the alley, this particular home having a greater share of the thatch. It was only one room though, so if Shuttle was in there she'd see him.

'Come on,' she called back, 'he went this way.'

Hermitage and Hartle followed and it was indeed the case that Shuttle had passed through the house, quite literally. Bits of the back wall lay scattered about and there was a real risk of the whole place coming down. Not that that presented much of a threat. If the house did fall on your head, you would simply brush the thatch off your shoulders and get on.

Out the back of the building, they were on open ground again. This collection of disgusting homes was on the edge of the town, doubtless the very latest stage of its expansion. Either that or the Normans had thrown people out of their own homes and they had had to make do.

At least the vista allowed them to spot Shuttle. It was rough ground here, sloping gently towards the hill that would drop to the river. The land was clumpy with tough grasses and hummocks and was obviously used for very little. It was not easy ground to travel over and Shuttle was picking his way across, only some hundred yards or so from where they were.

'Stop,' Hermitage called out.

A Murder for Master Wat

Shuttle didn't stop.

'Well, really,' Hermitage complained.

'How unreasonable of him,' Cwen snorted with a sidelong glance at Hermitage. 'Murderers not stopping, even when you ask them nicely.' She set off after Shuttle, nimbly hopping and jumping around the rough ground to make good progress.

Shuttle turned his head at the shout and Hermitage was gratified that he did at least look a bit worried. He even peered hard at them and seemed to recognise Cwen. Hermitage wasn't sure, but he thought he heard the man give vent to a pronounced "eek" before he set off again.

'We've got him now,' Cwen growled with horrible satisfaction.

'Really?' Hermitage couldn't see that this was a reasonable statement as they obviously didn't have him at all. He was yards ahead and still had time to get away.

Hartle stopped, bent with his hands on his knees and panted as he watched Cwen depart. 'I'm too old for this,' he breathed. 'I'm a weaver, for goodness sake. I only came to the wretched moot to find out what the weaving world was up to. No one told me I was going to have to chase murderers all over the fields.'

'How do you think I feel?' Hermitage asked, in a rare moment of vocal complaint. 'I'm a monk. I shouldn't be having to deal with murderers at all, never mind chase them. I might be asked to provide some biblical justification for a punishment or two, but that would be done from the comfort of the monastery. And it's not just this murderer. I'm inundated with the wretched people. At least you've got reason to be at a weavers' moot in the first place and the murder is an extra. Everywhere I go someone's killing someone else and I have to sort it out.'

He even enumerated his experiences, counting them off on his fingers. 'A monastery, a castle, a weaver at market, Normandy, for goodness sake, Wales, Shrewsbury, another monastery, King William's camp, my old abbot, Cwen's father and now this!'[7] As he went through his list he thought that it sounded very comprehensive, as well as quite scary. 'I've been to more places than most people. Certainly more than I ever wanted to go, and in every one of them someone gets killed. And you complain about one murderer running away across a field?'

'All right, all right.' Hartle gave Hermitage a sympathetic look from his position of being doubled up and panting for breath. 'Perhaps when this is over we can go home and you can hide under the bed.'

Hermitage sighed, the exasperation at his lot having subsided. 'I've tried that,' he said. 'It didn't work last time, and next time the corpse will probably be under there waiting for me.'

Hartle still looked in no condition to be bounding over the fields in pursuit of anyone. He waved Hermitage to leave him. 'You'd better go after her,' he said. 'There's no telling what she'll do if she catches him. You could have another murder on your hands.'

Hermitage saw the truth of this and thought he'd better get after Cwen quite promptly. Content that Hartle did not look in danger of complete collapse, he turned and set off after the now distant figure of Cwen.

As they pursued, Cwen in front and Hermitage following, Shuttle reached the far side of the open ground and dived back into the town where the hovels once more huddled

---

[7] And all of them Chronicles of Brother Hermitage, available now.

A Murder for Master Wat

against the boundary of Nottingham.

The houses here were still rude and simple and were crawling up against the old walls of the town. These were wooden palisades, high and impenetrable - unless you were a Norman army of course, and no one was putting up a fight. Doubtless, there was some gate nearby around which the outer hovels nested, and Shuttle could soon be back in the chaos of the moot and lost to them once more.

'He's getting away,' Cwen called back to him.

Hermitage didn't like to say I told you so and that her presumption of proclaiming that they'd got him had been premature. The look on her face expressed her disappointment that Hermitage had not kept up and that Hartle had given up completely.

Hermitage increased his pace, as much as the restrictions of his habit would allow, and was just a few yards behind. They were both too late to see where Shuttle went as he vanished in between the buildings.

They passed the first house to see that it was in no better state than the ones they had left behind. Perhaps this was just the style of places around here, or more likely there simply wasn't enough building material to go around.

In front of the town walls, there was a rough street, if the gaps between the hovels could be called a street, and this led up to a gate in the wooden defences, which was busy with people loitering and chatting. There was no actual coming and going and there really wasn't anything around here worth coming or going for.

There was a man at the gate though. With a table.

'A penny,' he said, holding a hand up to stop them as they ran up.

'We've already paid,' Cwen snapped at the man as she

dodged around his table.

This was obviously a quiet end of the town, and this particular table man probably didn't expect any business at all. It was unlikely the occupiers of the hovels would have a penny at all, never mind be willing to spend it on a moot. This table was probably just a precaution, in case people of a devious nature tried to avoid the main entrance.

'Here,' the man called after Cwen, far too late to do anything. 'You can't just barge past the table like that. This is an official table.' He sagged as he seemed to give up hope of ever seeing Cwen again, never mind getting a penny out of her.

'A monk,' he turned his surprised attention to Hermitage. He looked as if no one had told him what to do about monks. He was doubly surprised when Cwen came up behind him.

'Where did he go?' she demanded loudly, making the man almost jump up onto his own table.

'Argh, what?'

'The man who went through before us, where did he go?'

'Where did who go?' The man looked in no mood to be helpful. He hadn't got his penny, his table had been barged around, and now he was being shouted at.

Cwen held him with one of her best glares, the sort that could probably get the table to talk. 'The man who came through here in front of us,' she enunciated very clearly indeed. The one we saw come through. The one you must have taken a penny off.'

'He was with the moot,' the man was defiant.

'How do you know?' Cwen demanded.

'He was wearing his moot badge.' The man held up the back of his hand to show his ink stamp.

'How lovely for him,' Cwen sneered. 'And where did he

A Murder for Master Wat

and his badge go?'

'Into the moot.'

'Obviously. Which direction?'

'Why should I tell you?' the man stood his ground; well, some of it as he backed off a little bit.

Cwen smiled. 'Because I am the woman who will take your moot badge and rub it out with the business end of some good, strong nettles.'

'To the left, he went left,' the man crumbled.

'Right. Come on, Hermitage,' Cwen commanded.

Hermitage shrugged an apology to the man and his table and followed on her heels.

'Where's Hartle?' she asked.

'He had to stop for a rest. He's not a young man you know.'

Cwen's snort was the impatient sort. 'Can you see him?' She was casting her eyes about this area of town for any sign of Shuttle, or anyone at all who looked like they were trying to run away from her.

'There,' Hermitage pointed to their right.

'Where?'

'By that stall. The man there is picking up his wares as if someone has just knocked them to the floor and he doesn't look at all happy. He's facing down the street which is probably the direction the person who did the damage has gone.'

Cwen nodded. 'Very good. Anyone would think you'd done some tracking before.'

Hermitage shook his head as she headed off quickly. 'Investigation?' he muttered to himself. 'From the Latin, vestigare to track? Yes, I've done a bit.'

Questing down this particular street of vendors like a dog

that's broken into a butchers' moot, Cwen looked and pried and peered and examined for any sign of Shuttle.

Hermitage followed like the dog that's been caught in a butchers' moot, shuffling along, glancing apologetically at the vendors for the rudeness of his companion who has stolen all the sausages.

Most of those he passed tutted at him for having anything to do with Cwen, while others gave him looks of some sympathy. One just grumbled noisily and another simply ignored him completely as he went on after Cwen.

She had reached the end of this road now and was at the space where it joined another route crossing from left to right. She looked frantically all over, obviously frustrated at having lost Shuttle in the crowd.

Hermitage joined her, and she glared at him as if this was his fault. 'Where's he gone?'

'Erm,' Hermitage said, hoping that this was a rhetorical question.

'He can't have just vanished. He must have passed all the stallholders.' She turned back to indicate the path with her arm.

'Absolutely,' Hermitage agreed.

'We'd better go and question some of them.'

'Question them,' Hermitage said, slowly and thoughtfully as something occurred to him. 'Yes.'

'What is it?' Cwen asked, obviously wondering why Hermitage's mind wasn't on the problem in hand.

'Let's go and question one in particular,' he said.

Cwen shrugged as if it didn't matter to her which one they went for. 'They're all the same.'

'They are,' said Hermitage. 'Except they're not.' He led the way back up the road, Cwen looking at him as if some

A Murder for Master Wat

madness had crept in.

'Why are we going backwards?'

'Because when I came by, all the stallholders complained about you,' Hermitage nodded that this was very interesting.

'That's their problem.'

'It is indeed. You caused disturbance, were rude and intrusive and gave no indication of what it was you were about.'

'I am looking for a murderer,' Cwen explained, impatiently.

'So why did one of the stallholders not pay me any attention at all?'

Cwen shrugged. 'Doesn't like monks?'

'Could be,' Hermitage acknowledged. 'Or it could be that he didn't want to draw any attention to himself. It could be that he wasn't a stallholder you had abused at all, but rather someone trying to hide by pretending to be a stallholder.'

'Shuttle,' Cwen hissed.

'Possibly.' Hermitage tried to issue some caution but he knew that Cwen never took caution, even when it was offered.

'Which one is he?' Cwen whispered in Hermitage's ear as they walked slowly back up the street.

'If it is him, and it may not be, it's the stallholder on the left. The one selling what look like rakes.'

'Nettle rakes,' Cwen explained.

Hermitage nodded that if someone wanted a nettle rake then this stall was obviously the place. Why anyone would want to rake their nettles was another question.

'For making nettle cloth,' Cwen went on. 'For when you ret the nettles.'

'Ret the nettles,' Hermitage was none the wiser.

'Soak the nettles to make the fibres come loose,' Cwen

tutted that everyone should know this. 'Very often it's done in a stream or pond. Getting the nettles in is easy. Getting them out, you need a rake.'

They walked nonchalantly up the road, idly examining stalls as they went. This was a bit difficult as only moments before Cwen had stormed down the place poking her nose in where it was not wanted.

The grumbling of the stallholders began again and before they could even approach the stall of the nettle rakes, its owner pulled his hood down over his face, skipped out from behind his stall and ran back up the road.

Cwen and Hermitage arrived at the stall with their quarry only a handful of paces away. Cwen pressed ahead while Hermitage stooped and picked something up from the ground.

'It's him,' Cwen shouted. 'Get him,' she now instructed the rest of the stallholders.

It seemed that these men had had enough of Cwen, and if she was after one of their own she was going to have to go through them.

Normally that would not be a problem but there were a lot of stallholders and they all now emerged into the road, effectively blocking the path for everyone. There was no way they were going to let the rude young woman and her monk pass by.

'He's getting away,' Cwen complained.

'Good for him,' said one of the stallholders.

'He's a murderer,' she announced.

This did generate some consternation, but people soon decided that they didn't believe her.

'Who's he murdered, then?' one voice demanded.

'Master Hemling,' Cwen retorted.

A Murder for Master Wat

There was some muttering at this.

'And Robert the loom maker.'

Now there was rumbling anger that one of their own had been killed. Perhaps they'd been wrong after all.

'And the next one to die is written here,' Hermitage announced, holding a small piece of parchment in his hand. He leant over to Cwen's ear. 'He dropped this by the stall. It must have fallen from his robe.' He held out the document with the most damning information on it. Why else would this Shuttle be carrying a list of the dead if the next name on the list was not to be the next victim?

'Who is it?' one of the crowd called out. 'Who is to be next?'

Hermitage read the name and gasped. 'It's the Grand Master.'

Silence fell. Then it went on a bit. Then there were a couple of coughs and fidgets.

'Grand Master, eh?' that voice in the crowd said as if considering the idea. 'This murderer's not all bad then?'

Caput XX: A Very Grand Murder?

'If we save the Grand Master from the killer, he's bound to release Wat.' Cwen was quite breathless as they made their way back to the main hall as quickly as they could.

Hermitage, who took breathlessness quite seriously and was doing it very well indeed, panted a few incoherent observations but waved his hands that his thoughts would keep until he could stop moving.

'I just hope we're not too late,' Cwen called over her shoulder as she skittered into the entrance of the hall.

Hermitage did think that arriving to find the Grand Master already dead would not do anything for Wat's prospects.

He was quite a way behind now and wasn't too sure what they were going to do if the man was still alive. Stand guard? Fight off the killer? He was fully prepared to reason most vigorously with the murderer, but his experience told him that murderers were seldom reasonable. Dealing with them in a sensible and pragmatic manner was really Wat's area of expertise. Naturally, he was worried about the killer, but he was also concerned about what Cwen might do in this situation.

He followed a few steps behind and passed through the vestibule to enter the main hall, gasping and resting with his hands on his knees.

As far as he could see, nothing had changed at all. Cwen was now in the room, obviously, but the guild men were still in their chairs. Of course, it was quite possible that the Grand Master was already dead and just hadn't moved. There would be no way of telling until Hermitage went up to him and checked his breathing. Or looked for knives sticking out.

As he drew near he saw that the seated men were all still alive, although Cwen was glaring at them as if looks could kill. She had her hands on her hips, but her piercing gaze was just reflecting straight back from men who were probably used to ignoring people.

'We have found the killer, you know,' she said, quite loudly.

The Grand Master stirred at this, but just to look around as if he was searching for some servant to come and remove this disturbance.

'It's Shuttle of the Grey Guild.'

The Grand Master's search for help now got quite agitated and Hermitage stepped forward.

'It's that monk,' one of the guild members accurately observed. 'He was here a while ago, looking at our papers.'

'I was,' Hermitage confirmed, over the sound of Cwen growling and grinding her teeth at people who would speak to a monk but not to her.

'Aren't these people with that awful Wat the Weaver?' the guild man rummaged through his memory.

The other guild members harrumphed their agreement and distaste in the same noise.

Hermitage addressed the Grand Master directly. 'Mistress Cwen is right, we have located the killer, well, she has.' He nodded towards her, but the men of the guild still seemed determined to ignore her.

'The Grey Guild you were warned about,' Cwen snapped. 'You know, the parchment Hermitage found telling you that a killer was coming to the moot. And the letter they actually sent telling you that they'd done for Hemling and the tradesman?'

'Done for them in the name of Wat the Weaver, if I recall,' one unhelpfully astute guild member pointed out.

The eyes of the guild men returned to Hermitage, obviously hoping he would speak to them. Cwen wasn't having any of that and moved about so that she caught their eyes whether they liked it or not. 'And we found the killer's list. He's done the first two, Hemling and a trader and now he's on to number three.'

The guild men looked almost ready to stand on their own two feet to avoid this unwarranted intrusion. But only almost.

'The next person to be murdered is…,' Cwen paused as if she was about to announce a prize. 'The Grand Master.' She held her hand out.

This did get a fidget from the Grand Master in his chair.

'I wonder how he'll do it?' Cwen mused. 'Obviously, Hemling had his throat cut, Robert the loom maker was stabbed to death. Perhaps a beheading?' She illustrated this option with the noise of someone being beheaded. Whether it was really the noise of someone being beheaded or just the noise children make when they're playing a beheading game was irrelevant. The Grand Master's hand went to his throat.

'Shuttle?' he croaked. And this was addressed to Cwen.

'Of the Grey Guild,' she pronounced it carefully.

'A shuttle is part of the weaving process,' one guild member did actually speak directly to her. 'It's not a person.'

'The Grey Guild take secret names,' Cwen sighed her impatience. 'And this one's called Shuttle, and he's the one who does all their killing for them.'

The looks of the Grand Master now took on a more urgent and personal importance as he peered around the hall for aid.

'We're here now,' Cwen reassured him.

A Murder for Master Wat

Hermitage didn't feel reassured at all.

'And it's obvious that this is nothing to do with Wat,' Cwen pressed her advantage. 'The killer is called Shuttle, and he's got it into his head to revere Wat for some reason.' It was very clear that she couldn't think of such a reason. 'He knows nothing about it. So, if we can get him out of the lock-up, he can come and help sort out the real murderer.'

'Why would this Shuttle character want to kill anyone?' The Grand Master was in a much more talkative mood now, the prospect of a violent death doing wonders for his social skills.

'He wants the guild, your guild, to change your ways. He wants you to challenge masters who treat their apprentices poorly, and he wants the process of becoming a master made easier.'

That brought more grumbles than the suggestion that the Grand Master was about to be killed in his own chair.

'Oh,' Cwen added as an afterthought, 'and he's mad. Just the sort of mad to go round killing people to make the Weavers' Guild change a few rules.'

The Grand Master's eyes narrowed slightly as he thought about this. The early signs of panic at the thought of a stranger wandering in and removing his head were replaced by a more natural and comfortable demeanour; low cunning.

'And this fellow thinks the best of Wat the Weaver, does he?'

'He does,' Cwen confirmed. 'Just part of the madness, I suppose,' she shrugged.

'Quite,' the Grand Master agreed. 'Wat the Weaver, eh?' He mused some more and no longer looked like the chicken cornered by the fox. Now he looked like the chicken who is going to turn out to be a wolf in disguise. 'Summon Wat the

Weaver,' he commanded no one in particular.

'Right,' Cwen huffed her impatience that it had taken them this long to sort things out. She headed for the back of the hall and the courtyard beyond.

'Where's that Thomas fellow?' the Grand Master asked, casting his eyes about as if expecting Thomas to be waiting upon his beck and call. The question seemed directed at Hermitage.

'Erm,' Hermitage said.

'He's dealing with this business. Go and find him.' The Grand Master waved a hand, indicating that Hermitage was to do his bidding. Hermitage knew that this was just the sort of situation he needed Wat or Cwen for. Saying no to someone in authority, anyone in authority, just wasn't in his nature. The fact that the Grand Master of the Weavers' Guild had no authority over monks anyway, made no difference. Hermitage had been told what to do, and he usually did it.

'Aha, erm, yes, Master Thomas.' He thought frantically about how he could mean no while actually saying yes. 'I could, of course, go and find Master Thomas but, erm, if this Shuttle character should arrive before Wat and Cwen get back, there will be no one to deal with him. Perhaps I should remain here?' he asked very meekly, not for a moment thinking that he was capable of dealing with anything.

The Grand Master gave this some serious thought. He considered Hermitage in great detail and clearly agreed with the conclusion that this polite, inconsequential monk was unlikely to be much help when it came to diverting the attention of killers. Even if he was this King's Investigator thing.

On the other hand, he was an extra body, and killers

A Murder for Master Wat

probably liked extra bodies. 'Very well. You may stay.'

Hermitage resisted the strong temptation to say "thank you."

'Just go to the men on the door and tell them not to admit anyone.'

Hermitage looked over at the men by the door and thought that they looked as if they had very little interest in the welfare of the weavers' guild. He strolled over anyway. At least the main entrance to the hall would be the way Shuttle came in. There was no danger of him sneaking past Hermitage and doing the awful deed.

'Aha, hello,' Hermitage said to the first person he came across.

This person obviously had a dislike of monks as he turned his nose up and looked very puzzled. 'Clear off,' he said. 'I'm not giving you anything.'

'I'm not asking for anything,' Hermitage replied, imagining this fellow thought that alms were being requested but wondering why he needed to be quite so rude.

The man just scowled. He was tall, well dressed and important looking, and that he wasn't sitting with the guild made Hermitage think he was probably something to do with the town. He had been talking to another man who had left as Hermitage approached. Which was just as well, as Hermitage never liked to interrupt.

'What do you want then?' the man demanded. 'You been talking to the guild people,' he accused Hermitage. 'I saw you doing it.'

'Well, yes.' Hermitage had to agree as it was true. He couldn't quite see why it was such a problem. 'It's just that the Grand Master of the guild has asked that no one be let into the hall.

'I bet he has,' the man snorted. 'And perhaps he'd like it turned around so that it faces in a nicer direction?'

It didn't take Hermitage long to realise that this was said with some annoyance and so probably wasn't a genuine suggestion. If this man represented the views of the town, Nottingham was fed up with the Weavers' Guild in general and with its master in particular.

'No, no,' Hermitage said, quite genuinely. He leant in and dropped his voice as if imparting a confidence. Which he was. 'There is an individual abroad in the moot who does not wish the Grand Master well.'

'Just the one?' the man sounded surprised. 'There aren't enough Normans in Normandy to deal with all the people who don't wish the Grand Master well.' He looked at Hermitage with a gaze of incredulity. 'Do you know why the hall is so empty?' He cast his arms about to indicate that there were very few people in the great room.

'Erm,'

'Because he's in here,' the man nodded towards the Grand Master. 'This place is usually busy with trade, but no one wants to go near him so they're all staying away. Getting people who don't wish the Grand Master well to come in in the first place is your problem.'

Well, thought Hermitage, he had followed his instructions and got his reply. The Grand Master had not been any more specific and so felt that he had done his duty. He turned to leave the strangely annoyed man to his own devices, whatever they were, and just hoped that Cwen and Wat would come back soon.

'Ha,' the man called out loudly enough to make Hermitage jump. He turned back to face the town official who was holding an arm out towards the other end of the hall. 'Maybe

A Murder for Master Wat

now we can get back to normal.'

Hermitage followed his gaze and saw the Grand Master quite plainly at the other end of the long hall. He was quite plainly being removed from the building by four fellows with hoods pulled down over their faces, who had lifted Grand Master, chair and all, into the air and were carrying him towards a small door that Hermitage hadn't noticed before. 'What are they doing?' he asked, thinking this must be some sort of guild ritual or ceremony.

'Taking the wretched man away at last.' The townsman said. 'And with any luck, they don't wish him well.'

As the bizarre sight of the Grand Master, hoisted aloft on his chair, vanished through the door, Hermitage thought that perhaps he should make after him. This was the man they had come to protect from the attentions of the Grey Guild. Then he thought that it could well be the Grey Guild that had just carried him off, which would be a very bad thing. His second thought was that this was going to take some explaining to Cwen and Wat. Just then, Cwen and Wat arrived.

'Ah, Hermitage,' Wat called brightly. 'I knew you'd sort it out.'

Cwen punched him on the arm

'I mean that Cwen would sort it out and that you would be there as well.' He rubbed his arm and gave Cwen a friendly scowl. 'So. Shuttle and the Grey Guild, Cwen tells me.'

'Erm, yes,' Hermitage said, slowly, wondering what the opportunity to mention that the Grand Master had just been taken by the Grey Guild would look like, and when it would arrive.

'And they're after the Grand Master?'

Here it was. 'And they've got him,' Hermitage nodded that

the plan was complete.

'Beg pardon?' Wat frowned and shook his head. 'They've got him. What do you mean, they've got him?'

'Hermitage?' Cwen did her growly voice.

'Well,' Hermitage began. 'I was talking to this gentlemen here,' he turned and saw that the gentleman had gone. 'Erm, the one who was here.'

'Yes?'

'The Grand Master told me to come over and stop anyone entering into the hall. I think he was worried that Shuttle would come and take him, or worse.'

'And?'

'While I was over here, Shuttle came and took him. Or worse.' He gave a modest grimace. 'It might not have been Shuttle,' he added quickly. 'I couldn't see faces. But four men lifted the chair up with the Grand Master still in it and left. There was another door, you see. At the back. Which no one knew about. Apart from the Grey Guild, obviously.' As he gave this explanation, it got slower and slower under the gaze of Cwen and Wat.

'So,' Cwen said as if getting things straight in her head. 'The man we came to protect from the Grey Guild has, in fact, been taken from the hall by the Grey Guild, while you were watching.'

'Not exactly,' Hermitage protested. 'I just noticed, I wasn't watching, not as such.'

'Not as such,' Cwen sighed. 'How long ago did this happen?'

'Oh, just this moment,' Hermitage said as if that would make it better.

'Chasing after them might have been an option then?' she called as she stepped quickly across the hall towards the

A Murder for Master Wat

gathering of chairs in which the other guild members still sat. Wat and Hermitage followed.

'They took him,' one of the guild members protested from his chair. Protested in the strongest possible terms.

'We know,' Cwen snapped at the man. 'And what did you do about it? Sat there and watched.'

'Certainly not,' the man objected. 'We weren't watching, we were, what might you call it? Witnessing.'

'You mean you watched and didn't do anything about it.'

'What could we do against four strong men?'

'Standing up might have been a start.' Cwen left them and went over to the door set in the back room of the hall.

This was not a big entrance, more like a service door through which supplies might be taken, but it was obviously big enough for a Grand Master in a chair. Cwen would have to admit that these men must have been pretty strong to lift that great weight and carry it away. A bunch of weak at the knees apprentices couldn't manage it. Shuttle must have had help. She pushed the door open and saw that it simply led into the street at the side of the hall.

She was joined by Wat and Hermitage who had not stopped for a critique of the situation with the remaining guild masters.

'Ah,' Hermitage said, pointing to the chair leg that now sat, incongruously in the middle of the street. People were looking at it and he was sure it wouldn't be too many moments before the thing was taken away for a fire. He stepped quickly over and picked it up, examining it carefully, as if it might contain a clue as to the direction the Grand Master had taken.

'Powerful men, these Grey Guilders,' Wat observed. 'Not only could they lift master and chair together, but then they managed to break one of the legs off the chair. Perhaps it's a sign.

'A sign?'

'Yes. Unless the guild does what they're told they get the Grand Master and his chair back one piece at a time.'

Hermitage frowned at this dramatic idea. 'It probably simply fell off and they took the rest away.'

'Right,' Cwen said, in that disappointed voice she used when it was time to fix something that had gone wrong and which was someone else's fault. 'Now we've got to go and find him.'

'Really?' Wat obviously didn't like the sound of that.

'They're going to kill him,' Hermitage pointed out, with some surprise at Wat's reaction.

'I know,' Wat nodded. 'But Grand Masters die all the time. They have to, otherwise, there wouldn't be new Grand Masters. And he was pretty old.'

Hermitage could not believe this and just folded his arms and stared at Wat.

'Alright, alright,' the weaver relented. 'Got to stop a murder, I know.'

'Quite.'

'The other guild masters won't mind if he's dead,' Wat muttered.

'That is not the point. We cannot leave a man to be murdered at the hands of the Grey Guild.'

Wat shrugged that he still wasn't convinced.

'Of course,' Cwen added, nonchalantly, 'the sheriff and the guild and so forth will want to take action against the killers if they do manage to finish the job.'

'So?' Wat asked.

'Nothing really. It's just that as the Grey Guild are doing

A Murder for Master Wat

all this in the name of Wat the Weaver, they could probably hang you instead.'

Wat looked at them both. 'Time to rescue the Grand Master,' he said, full of enthusiasm.

Caput XXI: Follow That Guild

'Have you seen four men carrying another one away?' Hermitage asked a perfectly innocent couple, walking along, enjoying a stroll among the stands and entertainments of the moot.

The man looked at Hermitage in a very strange way, took the arm of his lady companion and moved them both away.

Hermitage held his arms out to indicate that this was a perfectly reasonable question and that he couldn't understand why they were being so unhelpful.

Wat was being Wat and was leaning close to people to whisper the question in their ears as if it was just their little secret.

Cwen was being Cwen and was frightening more people than Hermitage as she demanded that everyone tell her where the Grand Master had gone.

They had come to the end of the street now, where it joined the larger thoroughfare that passed along the face of the great hall.

'Someone must have seen something,' Hermitage complained. 'How can four men carry another one down the street and no one sees a thing?'

'Not very popular, the Grand Master,' Wat explained. 'They probably thought some great harm was about to fall upon the man and didn't want to get in the way.'

Coming down the main thoroughfare, at a leisurely and gentle pace was Hartle, recovered from his exertions across the fields of Nottingham. He greeted them all with a smile and nods. 'So,' he said. 'How's it going? Just seen the Grand Master being carried along shoulder high. Some sort of ceremony? Need strong fellows to get that great lump all the

A Murder for Master Wat

way up there.'

'You saw him?' Hermitage almost shrieked. 'He's been taken by the Grey Guild.'

'Oh,' Hartle nodded with interest. 'That was them, was it? Must say, he looked very surprised. Probably not been that far away from the ground in his life.'

'Which way did they go?' Hermitage asked, thinking that this was far more pertinent than whether the Grand Master was enjoying the experience or not.

'Headed back towards the main entrance.'

'They haven't killed him yet then,' Hermitage said, with some relief.

'Surprised him,' Hartle confirmed. 'But definitely still alive.'

'They're probably taking him away from the moot,' Hermitage speculated. 'Too much risk of them being found out in here.'

'And no risk of them being stopped as they carry the Grand Master of the weavers' Guild for half of England on their shoulders?' Cwen asked.

Hermitage didn't want to stop to consider that question, a man's life was in the balance. Quite good balance if the Grey Guild was still carrying him after all this time. 'Come on,' he called to the others as he headed off.

As he scurried along, his habit restricting him to a sort of hobbled hopping motion, the others seemed to be taking it far less urgently. 'Come on, hurry up,' he urged.

'Yes, yes,' Wat waved him to calm. 'We're just discussing the dear old Grand Master in the hands of the Grey Guild.'

'And?'

'Probably doing him the world of good,' Hartle said. 'Bring him down a notch or two.'

'Not if he's dead,' Hermitage pointed out. 'By that time he will have run out of notches.'

'Well, yes,' Wat was thoughtful. 'But if they just wanted to kill him they'd have done it there and then. In the Great Hall in front of the other guild men. Why take him away first?'

Hermitage had no idea. 'Do it in private?' he suggested.

'Not going to get much change in the guild if you quietly kill the Grand Master and don't show off about it.'

'Maybe they want to show off about it by telling everyone they have the Grand Master and then kill him so that it's obvious?'

'Or they keep him as a hostage and if the guild doesn't change its ways, they'll kill him.'

'How awful.' Hermitage thought that sounded more heartless than actually killing someone, somehow.

'Not going to work, either,' Hartle dismissed the idea. 'Asking the rest of the guild men, the ones who aren't Grand Masters, to stop their leader being killed? Ridiculous. A dead Grand Master means there's a vacancy for a Grand Master. And with this one out of the way quickly they could even avoid his son just stepping into the job.'

'We still need to find them,' Hermitage pointed out. 'Hostage or murder victim, never mind the moral imperative of not treating people like this, the Grey Guild are doing it all in the name of Wat the Weaver.' He looked directly at Wat. 'So we know who's going to get the blame, and the blame for murder doesn't usually end well.'

Wat shrugged that this did seem a good reason. 'What is it about me anyway?'

'Very good question,' Cwen scoffed. 'I don't know what they see in you but apparently, you're an example of how to rebel against the guild.'

'I've never had anything to do with the guild.'

'Exactly. If you can make a good living by weaving outside the guild, so can they.'

'Good luck to 'em.' Wat seemed to think that they could do what they liked.

'Problem is,' Cwen explained, 'I don't think any of them are actually any good at weaving.'

'Ah. If you're trying to make your fortune from weaving that can be a problem,' Wat accepted.

'And they obviously don't know the guild very well if they think taking the Grand Master is going to make any difference at all,' Hartle concluded.

'The Grand Master may not be the end,' Hermitage said, urging them to keep going. 'If killing him makes no difference, who will they choose next? Clearly, they are desperate men.'

They had reached the main entrance of the moot again now, the crowds still busy but starting to thin as the day wore out. The vacant stand of Robert the loom maker stood testament to the work of the Grey Guild and even the tent where Hemling had met his end gave Hermitage a cold shiver.

'What are you doing walking about?' a loud voice demanded from across the space.

They turned and saw Master Thomas beckoning them and they stopped, waiting for him to join them.

'I locked you up,' he protested to Wat. 'Who let you out?' he glared at the others.

'The Grand Master,' Wat said, which had the desired effect on Thomas.

'Why?'

'Probably because he knew that the Grey Guild killed Hemling. Nothing to do with Wat at all,' Cwen sneered slightly.

'And that the Grey Guild was coming for him next,' Wat said, with a little too much glee in his voice.

'Eh?' Thomas was nicely confused.

'And they got him,' Hartle added.

Thomas looked from one to the other as if some explanation was going to emerge from all this nonsense.

'The Grey Guild came to the great hall and took the Grand Master,' Hermitage said. 'At least, we assume it was the Grey Guild.'

'No one else would want him,' Hartle put in.

'We think they've taken him away from the moot and are either going to kill him or hold him hostage.' Hermitage nodded at what was really quite a simple situation. A horrible one, but simple. 'And we're going after them.'

'You are?' Thomas appraised them all and seemed doubtful that an old man, a woman, a monk and Wat the Weaver were capable of dealing with a gang of merciless killers.

As Hermitage saw the doubt on the master's face he began to see his point. 'Perhaps you could help?' he asked.

Thomas just laughed. 'Rescue the Grand Master from a gang of merciless killers? I don't think so. As I said, I'm nothing to do with the guild. I was in the wrong place at the wrong time and ended up having to deal with Hemling. I'll be blowed if I'm sorting out their Grand Master for them as well. Leave him to his fate, that's what I say.'

'Ah, yes, Hemling,' Wat said as if only now remembering that this had all started with Hemling's demise. He looked hard at Thomas and held his gaze. 'Where's the money?'

Thomas looked as if had not understood where this question had come from. 'What money?'

'The money from the moot. All the pennies we have to pay

A Murder for Master Wat

to get in. The traders' fees, the money Nottingham probably paid to have all these weavers here.' He gave a short laugh. 'And would probably pay again to make them go away now.'

Thomas nodded that he now knew what Wat was talking about. He wasn't concerned though. 'Safely in the hands of the guild.'

Hermitage felt a flush of disappointment at that. Money was such a wonderful motive for murder, it seemed a pity to let it go to waste like this. Not that it was much of a waste as they were currently chasing a band of crazed killers through a weavers' moot as they made off with a Grand Master. As he thought that through, the money as motive was preferable, somehow.

'You cleared Hemling away and had his loom taken to his room. Which was probably where the money was.'

'Of course, it was. Old Grum the weaver is a complete idiot but even he'd have worked out that the money was there for the taking after a few days. I had it moved back to the hall and into the guild's keeping.' He gave Wat a disappointed look. 'You should have asked when we were at Grum's place. Have you been thinking this was something to do with me because I had the money?' The accusation was clear.

Everyone found somewhere else to look.

'Honestly,' Thomas complained. 'I bend over backwards to help this guild and then I get accused of stealing their money. I found it, I gave it back to the guild and put it somewhere safe.' He folded his arms as a teacher, more saddened than disappointed by the stupidity of his pupils.

'Somewhere safe?' Hermitage asked.

'Under one of the chairs.' Thomas shrugged that this was as safe a place as any, the chairs not being likely to move.

'Not under the Grand Master's chair?' Hermitage asked,

with a note of panic. 'The Grey Guild took him and his chair.'

'God, no. It would have been in his purse before we could count it. No. Under Master Tremlet's chair. He hasn't been able to reach his own knees for twenty years, not much danger of him getting down there.' Thomas sounded confused now. 'So this Grey Guild want the money as well?'

Hermitage liked the sound of that. 'They could indeed.' He smiled at the others. 'Yes, they want the guild to change but there's also a large sum of the guild's money lying about. If I understand this guild of yours correctly, they'd be much more concerned about getting their money back than they would about their Grand Master coming to a nasty end.'

'And desire for money is probably another trait they pick up from the great Wat the Weaver,' Cwen noted with an accusatory glare at Wat.

Ignoring the comment, Wat and Hartle nodded sombre agreement at this suggestion.

'But they chose the wrong chair,' Hermitage pointed out. 'They got the master but not the money.'

Wat agreed and looked sombre 'We really need to find the Grey Guild,' he urged. 'Killing people in my name is one thing. Having designs on the guild's money in my name could get me in real trouble.'

'Perhaps I will come along,' Thomas offered. 'I've had more trouble in the last day than I deserve. Seeing the Grand Master discomforted will be some recompense.'

Hermitage thought that this was a rather heartless reason for trying to rescue someone from death, but if they did have to deal with the Grey Guild, an extra pair of hands would be useful; even though he doubted that Thomas would get those hands dirty if trouble arose.

A Murder for Master Wat

'Where will they have gone though?' he thought out loud.

'We'll ask the man with the table,' Wat said. 'He's been busy enough stopping people coming in, you'd think he'd notice the Grand Master on the way out.'

Back at the main entrance the man and his table were still at work, although the demand was lighter at this time of day. People who had left the moot during the day were now wandering back for the evening and a few were just arriving, perhaps to see what excitements the falling darkness would bring.

Those returning were waving their hands, showing the stamps that allowed them admission. Others were being charged again, including those who protested that they had been stamped but that the ink had come off. Table man was having none of that.

'How do,' Wat said brightly, as he walked up behind the man.

The fellow must have been practising his squeaking while they'd been away as he was now very good at it. 'What are you doing in there?' he nodded his head towards the moot. 'I told you you weren't allowed in.'

Wat nodded happy agreement. 'And I ignored you.'

'Well, you'll have to leave.'

'That's what I'm doing.'

'Good.'

'Following the Grand Master. The one who passed by here carried on a chair?'

'I'm not telling you that,' the man clearly thought that someone as disreputable as Wat the Weaver should not be privy to any information about Grand Masters and their chairs.

'You remember the murder monk,' Wat nodded towards

Hermitage, who smiled politely.

Table man swallowed.

'He'd like to know where the Grand Master went so he can stop him being murdered. Of course, we can always tell the guild that we were too late because some man with a table wouldn't tell us which way the victim had gone.'

'He went that way,' table man pointed off to the left in a manner that said he would like them all to leave very quickly. He also left the strong impression that he would be hanging up his table after this moot.

'Honestly,' Wat complained as they followed the directions. 'Give some men a table and the power goes completely to their heads.'

They all walked on for a hundred yards or so with no sign of any Grand Masters or chairs.

'Where are they going?' Hermitage asked. He couldn't see anything of significance in this direction. They were beyond the town walls, even moving beyond the outer hovels. What would be the point of doing anything to the Grand Master out here? There wasn't even anywhere decent to hold a hostage. The road simply led down a small incline and then rose quite sharply up towards the new castle. He looked at the new castle. 'They wouldn't be taking him to the Normans?' he gasped, thinking that anyone voluntarily going anywhere near the Normans must have some very strange ideas.

They all stopped and looked up at the construction work going on. A lot of the townsfolk had been engaged on the building for the Normans, if a Norman with a sword telling you the alternative was a quick death counts as being engaged. Earth was being moved into the great piles the invaders seemed to favour for putting their castles on top of, and huge

A Murder for Master Wat

quantities of wood were being dragged around, much of it by oxen as entire tree trunks were required.

'Why would they go anywhere near the Normans?' Cwen asked. Being the only one of them who would like to get near to the Normans, just to do something horrible to them.

Thomas was looking very thoughtful. 'Put the guild in a bad light with the new rulers?' he suggested. 'Tell the sheriff how awful the guild is in the hope that he does something about them.'

'Like kill them all?' Cwen suggested, lightly.

'It wouldn't be unusual,' Thomas admitted. 'And William Peverel has already met Grand Master Wulfstand and clearly doesn't think much of him. Mind you, he doesn't seem to think much of anyone.'

'Normans tend not to,' Hermitage explained, his wealth of experience confirming the fact.

'Are they going to threaten to hand him over to the Normans?' Hermitage offered.

'What good would that do?' Wat asked.

'Get him killed quicker?' Hermitage couldn't really think of a reason the Grey Guild would involve the Normans at all. Involving Normans was generally a very bad idea for anyone.

No one had anything more to offer, and there seemed to be a general consensus that they would carry on along the path. They would carry on a lot more slowly and carefully and if anyone remotely Norman-looking appeared, they would head back to the moot and leave the Grey Guild to do whatever they wanted.

As they rounded a thick and unkempt growth of laurel, a sight emerged that Hermitage needed a moment to take in. When he had taken it, he realised that it was quite bizarre. There was Grand Master Wulfstand, still sitting in his chair, although it was now pitched at an angle due to its missing leg. He was in a small clearing as if the Great Hall of Nottingham had been moved away, instead of the man taken out of it.

Around Wulfstand stood the members of the Grey Guild, hoods down but bent double and all panting very heavily. They hadn't noticed the new arrivals, who had been sneaking along quite quietly, as Saxons tended to do when in sight of a Norman castle.

'Bloody hell, Shuttle,' one of the guild complained. 'Have we really got to get him up that hill? Why can't the lazy bugger get out and walk?'

'We tried getting him out of the chair, didn't we?' the man who was their leader retorted. 'Bloody man won't shift. And if we did get him out, I doubt he could walk ten paces without collapsing.'

'We could set fire to the chair,' one suggested. 'I bet he'd get out of it then.'

'We are not setting fire to anything. We are following the plan. It's all gone well so far and we are not mucking it up because you lot can't be bothered to carry the Grand Master of the Weavers' Guild up a little hill.'

'It's not a little hill,' the Grey Guild's dissent went on. 'And he's a bloody big Grand Master.'

'I don't know what you think you are doing,' Wulfstand addressed them all angrily. This brought a collective sigh from the Grey Guild, and Hermitage could tell that Wulfstand had been addressing them angrily for quite some time now. Mind you, he did appear to have reasonable cause.

'You shut up,' Shuttle instructed him. 'When the Normans see what we're prepared to do to you, they'll hand over control of the guild just like that.'

'Ahem.' Wat coughed politely to get their attention.

A Murder for Master Wat

The Grey Guild all spun to face the new arrivals, and there were gasps and little mewling sounds as they realised they were discovered.

'Who are you?' Shuttle demanded when he had recovered from the surprise.

'It's that woman,' one of the guild pointed at Cwen.

'How did you escape?' Shuttle screeched.

'I asked nicely,' Cwen explained, with a smile.

'Well you're too late,' Shuttle gloated. He stepped close to Wulfstand in his chair and laid a hand on the Grand Master's head. With the other hand, he pointed a warning finger at Hermitage and the others. 'We've got him now, and if you take one step closer we'll do it right here and right now.'

Caput XXII: The Grey Guild Confesses

'All in the name of Wat the Weaver?' Cwen asked.
'Of course,' Shuttle replied.
'Have you checked with him that this is alright?'
'Wat is a symbol of our struggle.'
'Thanks very much,' Wat said.
Shuttle's hood turned in his direction. 'Who are you?'
'No one, really,' Wat shrugged. 'Just Wat the Weaver.'

A silence fell upon the clearing. One of the hoods of the Grey Guild leant over to their leader. 'Is that really him?' it asked, the words clearly audible.

'It's really me,' Wat explained. 'Ask anyone. Well, almost anyone. Anyone except the people who have set up a whole guild in my name.'

'So what if it is him?' Shuttle was defensive. 'It's not the man himself who provides our inspiration, it's his ideals.'

'The ideals of Wat the Weaver? Ha!' Cwen was dismissive of that as an idea. 'If you follow the ideals of Wat the Weaver you'll end up in a very bad way.'

'Do you mind?' Wat complained. 'I am standing here.'

Hermitage thought that if they all sat down, or went somewhere more conducive, they could have a very constructive discussion on this topic and maybe reach an amicable conclusion. One with no death in it. Wat did have a rather dubious past but was on the road to improvement. Maybe an exploration of this would better inform the Grey Guild of his situation and make them reconsider their plan.

'You've made a lot of money out of disgusting tapestries and now won't spend a penny unless it's prised from your fingers with a stick.' Cwen summed up his situation rather succinctly.

A Murder for Master Wat

Wat screwed up his face as he considered this bald and very critical statement. Then he nodded as he accepted that it was largely accurate.

'The point is,' Shuttle interrupted the denigration of their hero, 'that Wat stands separate from the guild.'

'Only because they won't have him,' Hartle explained. 'You do know he's not a master at all.'

'Good,' Shuttle was pleased. 'Another thing that just shows the pointlessness of the guild and how they have to change their ways.'

'This is all very well,' Wat spoke up. 'And naturally, I have nothing but the very deepest contempt for the Weavers' Guild in all its manifestations. I despise its rules and its instructions and most of all its people.' He nodded towards the Grand Master as if offering him a compliment. 'No, I am not a master, neither do I want to become one or care two and a half hoots about anything guild related.'

A small cheer went up from the Grey Guild.

'But you're going to get me into a lot of trouble.' Wat pleaded.

'You care not for trouble from the despised guild,' Shuttle said, proudly.

'Well, no, but it won't be just the guild, will it?'

Shuttle thought about this. 'I suppose not,' he acknowledged. 'But when we discuss the future with the Normans, we can say you're only the inspiration. You didn't have anything to do with it.'

'Yes, you could.' Wat gritted his teeth and bobbed his head about, indicating that this was not going to solve the problem. 'But for one thing, I think the Normans are going to care slightly less about the Weavers' Guild than I do. If I know anything about them, and unfortunately I do, they'll just let you get on with whatever you want as long as you don't cause trouble. Believe me, I've met King William and he's never once mentioned what he's going to do about the problem of the Weavers' Guild.'

Hermitage nodded vigorously to assure the others that this was the case.

'Still,' Shuttle tried to carry on, although he sounded somewhat disheartened by this news.

'However,' Wat pressed on. 'They do get rather excited when people get killed. Especially if they didn't do the killing.'

'Killed?' Now Shuttle sounded positively alarmed.

'Yes,' Wat tried to sound relaxed about it. 'You know, Hemling? Robert the loom maker they probably wouldn't worry about, only some Saxon trader. But the Grand Master here? Quite an important figure, mainly in his own mind of course, but probably known to the Normans. If you say you killed them all in the name of Wat the Weaver, I'll be lucky to escape with my skin.'

The silence came back to the clearing. It didn't even sound as if the Grey Guild were breathing. The only sound was Grand Master Wulfstand as he continued the struggle with his own chair.

'You'll all have had it, obviously,' Wat explained, reluctantly. 'Even though the dead were all Saxons, or will be,' he nodded acknowledgement that the Grand Master wasn't quite dead yet. 'The Normans just get irritated by people going around killing one another without permission.'

Shuttle had found his voice but it was now high and carried a great load of panic. 'Killed?' he piped.

'Yes,' Wat frowned now. He repeated the list. 'Hemling, Robert and next you kill the Grand Master.'

Shuttle threw back his hood. 'We haven't killed anyone,' he

A Murder for Master Wat

sounded truly appalled at the idea and looked very pale indeed. 'You can't go round telling people that we've killed anyone. What on earth gave you that idea?'

The other members of the guild now dropped their hoods and very young faces appeared, all of them looking as if they'd just been found in the local lord's apple orchard, a local lord who executed people for taking his apples.

'Erm, the dead people?' Wat suggested. 'Bodies, you know. Dead ones. Well, two dead ones and one soon to be.' Wulfstand was still having no luck getting out of his chair but at least he looked like he really wanted to. Wat gave him an insouciant nod of the head as if saying "pah, you wait all day for a murder and then three come along at once."

'We didn't kill them.' Shuttle's panic was taking over his body now as he hopped from foot to foot as if he really wanted to get to a privy very soon indeed.

'You've got a list,' Cwen accused them. 'Hermitage found it.'

Hermitage rummaged in his habit and came up with the small piece of parchment that had fallen from Shuttle.

'Well, yes,' Shuttle admitted. 'But that's just a list of people, it doesn't mean we're going to kill them, for goodness sake.' He looked at his accusers with rather wild eyes. 'You're all mad.'

'We're mad?' Cwen replied. 'You tied me up!'

'It is a bit of a coincidence,' Hermitage pointed out, not wanting to be diverted from the murder at hand. 'The first two people on your list are already dead and the third is here with you now. What other conclusion can we draw, other than that you plan to murder the Grand Master?'

'We're not going to murder him,' Shuttle seemed on the verge of tears now. 'Why would we murder him?'

'To make the guild change their ways.'

'By murder?' Shuttle was clearly worried by the people in front of him who thought that murder was the way to get things done.

'What were you going to do then?' Hermitage couldn't see what other possibility there was, the Grey Guild having gone to all this trouble.

Shuttle took breath. 'We were going to pour dye over him.'

That silence would do well to wait in the bushes nearby as it was being called upon quite frequently.

'Pour dye over him?' Hermitage asked, not quite able to comprehend what was being said.

'Of course. A mark of our contempt for him and the guild.'

Hermitage scowled. These people would say that they weren't going to kill Wulfstand when they'd just been caught, wouldn't they? 'What about Hemling then, and Robert?'

'Who's Robert?' Shuttle demanded, holding his arms out to add extra emphasis to the suggestion that he had not the first idea what they were talking about.

'Robert the loom maker. He was stabbed to death.'

The Grey Guild made noises like small animals.

'Not by us,' Shuttle was pleading now.

'He's on your list,' Hermitage waved the list again. Surely people couldn't ignore what was written down, how unreasonable was that? He looked at it. 'Master Hemling and then a tradesman of the moot.'

'Yes,' Shuttle agreed and went on as if explaining to an idiot. 'We cut the guy ropes on the guild's own stall.'

In fact, there was no point in the silence bothering to go back into the bushes, it might as well stay where it was wanted.

'You cut the guy ropes on a stall?' Cwen asked, sounding

quite contemptuous.

'Absolutely,' Shuttle nodded vigorously as if more nodding would make them believe him. 'That'll show the guild.'

'Cutting the guy ropes on their stall showed the guild.' Cwen shook her head at how pathetic this sounded.

'Certainly did. The canvas collapsed and everything. I bet the men there went and reported it to the guild as well.' Shuttle nodded to his companions at the audacity of this magnificent blow.

'And Hemling?' Hermitage asked. 'Master Hemling's loom was interfered with, and it killed him.'

Shuttle's mouth opened and shut several times. 'It killed him?' he breathed.

'It did.'

Shuttle's shock spilt words out of his mouth. 'How could it kill him? A simple thing like that? It happens all the time. We never meant to kill him. He must have just died. Are you sure it killed him?'

'Of course, it killed him,' Wat insisted. 'A sharpened wire warp on a loom is not going to just go "twang" is it?'

'A what the what what?' Shuttle stumbled.

'A sharpened wire warp on the loom.' Wat sounded impatient with Shuttle's denials.

'I never did anything like that.'

'Oh, really. And what did you do? You obviously did something to the loom.'

'Well, yes.' Shuttle looked at the ground as he confessed. 'I sawed halfway through his heddle.'

The looks shared between Hermitage and the others were saying that this Grey Guild really did seem largely hopeless. Of course, they could be lying. Any self-respecting murderer in this situation would lie like a liar, but Shuttle seemed genuinely bewildered and confused, and mainly terrified.

'Let me get this straight,' Cwen took up the story. 'In order to defeat the mighty Weavers' Guild and make them change their ways towards masters and apprentices, you sawed halfway through the heddle on Hemling's loom.'

Shuttle nodded eagerly, obviously hoping that Cwen saying it meant that she believed it. 'It made a great display at the opening ceremony. We heard all about it. Everyone was saying that Hemling had real trouble.' He gave his acolytes a smile at this.

'His real trouble was staying alive,' Wat said. 'What with his throat being cut and all.'

Shuttle swallowed.

'I didn't notice any sawing on the heddle,' Hartle reported. 'And we examined the loom quite closely.' He raised questioning eyebrows to Wat who nodded agreement.

'Ah,' Shuttle said, with some recovered confidence. 'We're very subtle.'

'Ha,' was Cwen's comment.

'Where was this loom you sawed through?' Wat asked, slowly.

'In Hemling's lodgings,' Shuttle explained the complexity and intelligence behind their scheme. 'We weren't going to do it while it was in the main tent, were we?' He scoffed at such idiocy.

'Big thing, was it?' Wat was nonchalant. 'Normal sort of size for a loom? Probably in the front room of the lodgings?'

'Of course,' Shuttle stood proud.

'Very well done,' Wat gave Shuttle a very slow round of applause. 'You cleverly cut through the heddle on the wrong loom. No wonder old Grum was fed up.'

Shuttle just looked from Wat to Hartle, quickly weighing

up in his mind whether this could be true. He looked to his young companions and shook his head in that way people do when they are dismissing the perfectly sound argument that has just destroyed what little credibility they had left.

Cwen gave a sigh so heavy it could have snapped a heddle all on its own. 'Then you cut through the ropes on someone's stand and finally, you were going pour dye over the Grand Master.'

Shuttle nodded again, dismissing the heddle sawing from his mind. He lifted a small pail one of the others had been carrying, dipped his finger in it and held up the tip, now bright green, for them all to see.

'And you were planning to do this in front of the Normans, thinking they'd be impressed.'

Shuttle half-smiled at his own plan.

'You're all idiots,' Cwen concluded.

Shuttle looked disappointed at this but seemed to be comfortable that being caught for idiocy was probably better than being caught for murder.

'And you couldn't even saw through the right heddle properly,' Wat scoffed.

'I said it might not be his,' one of Shuttle's acolytes hissed.

'So, Hemling's heddle didn't break because it wasn't sawed through at all.' Wat went on. 'He pulled it, snapped the wire warp that had been put there and got his throat cut.'

The Grey Guild gasped at the horror.

'In fact, if you had cut through his heddle you'd probably have saved his life.'

'What a waste of time,' Cwen complained. 'We've been chasing this lot up and down the moot and it turns out they didn't do it. They could be lying of course, but I suspect they'd get that wrong if they tried it.'

Hermitage gave some thought to what wrong lying would be. Would it be the truth, or simply another lie but not the right one? He forced his mind back to the current deaths.

Wat shook his head at the pointlessness as well. 'But if they didn't do it, who did?'

The silence sounded as if it was reminiscing wistfully about the bushes.

'Hermitage?' Wat asked.

'Hm?' Hermitage replied.

'Who did it then? Who killed Hemling and Robert?'

Hermitage felt very surprised to be asked.

'It would be interesting to know why, but who would be a good start.'

'Who?'

'That's the one. King's Investigator.'

'Aha, yes.' Hermitage came down to earth once more. He looked at the faces around him. Most of them confused, but Wat and Cwen expectant. Once more he seemed to have gathered an audience to hear his resolution of the death, and once more he didn't have a clue what that resolution was going to be. As the small crowd watched him, he paced around a bit, his hands behind his back and his most thoughtful face on the front of his head.

'Just imagine King William is here, demanding that you tell him who the killer is, or he'll burn you to the ground.'

'That's not very helpful,' Hermitage scowled.

'Worked most of the other times,' Wat observed, with a shrug.

He turned his mind to the events of the moot, everything from paying to get into the events surrounding the death of Hemling. There was one possibility that raised its head, but it seemed very unlikely. But then, he told himself, most

A Murder for Master Wat

murders turned out to be rather unlikely in the end.

His pacing continued.

'Is this how it usually works?' Grand Master Wulfstand asked, with some contempt. He appeared to have recovered what little composure he had left now that he knew he was going to be dyed and not killed. 'This investigation business? The monk wanders up and down a bit and eventually decides who did it?'

'He doesn't decide,' Wat did his own contempt. 'He works it out.'

'Pah. Whole thing seems to depend on luck to me. Lucky you have the monk near the death and then lucky if he can work it out. Not very reliable way of identifying killers, I'd have thought.'

'Luck,' Hermitage repeated.

'Yes?' Wat encouraged.

Hermitage went into his thoughtful place, the place where no sounds or people bothered him, the place where the rest of the world was not welcome and it could go its merry way unaccompanied. The place from which he occasionally emerged to find someone had tied his sandals together.

It was the place where events now threw themselves in front of him in a complete jumble but then gradually got themselves into some sort of order, seemingly without his intervention. It was as if he were watching a column of soldiers assemble itself from a camp. All the individuals came out of their tents separately, but they all knew where to go and where to stand, and before you knew it, there it was a nice neat column. And all the commander had done was shout "assemble".

A single fact was not joining in though. It still loitered out of order, or skipped around the main body and refused to take its place.

'It's the note,' he said.

'What's the note?' Cwen asked.

'Why won't the note fit?'

'What note fit where?' Grand Master Wulfstand demanded with some irritation.

'Your note.'

'Mine?'

'The one in the trunk. The one warning you about the killer coming to the moot.'

'What about it?'

'Why was it at the bottom of the trunk? If it had only just arrived and was warning you about the very moot you were in the middle of, why wasn't it at the top?'

'That's obvious,' Wulfstand snorted, clearly not thinking much of the King's Investigator.

'Is it?'

'Of course, the top of the trunk won't open. We just roll it over and take the bottom off.'

Hermitage gaped at that. 'Hartle and I got it open.'

'Not without a struggle,' Hartle reminded him.

'You did,' Wulfstand confirmed. 'And thanks for that. We hadn't been able to manage for years, the buckles all rusted up and stuck solid. Easier just to tip the thing over, stick the latest material in the bottom and then turn it back again.'

Hermitage found it hard to accept such a stupid explanation. 'But no one read the note.' He also couldn't believe that any parchment could go unread.

'People write to us all the time. If it's urgent, they'll call.'

Hermitage shook his head at this ridiculous arrangement. But it wasn't the only ridiculous thing he'd come across in this moot of weavers. At least he'd know never to go to another one.

'Well, that's it then,' he rubbed his hands, deeply satisfied in a very profound manner that all of those facts were in their proper order.

'So,' Wat urged. 'Who did it?'

'Oh,' Hermitage said, looking around. 'Where's he gone?'

Caput XXIII: What a Rotten Lot

They all looked around to see which one of them wasn't there anymore.

'Erm?' Shuttle now seemed keen to join in, as he'd been acquitted of murder so quickly.

'Thomas,' Hermitage pointed out. 'Where has Thomas gone?'

'Thomas?' The Grand Master enquired. 'Fine fellow. Helped out a lot with all this trouble.'

'And caused it in the first place,' Hermitage retorted.

'Eh, what?'

'We must find him,' Hermitage waved his arms to indicate that they had better go back down the path and hunt for Thomas.

'I say,' Grand Master Wulfstand called as they left. 'You can't leave me here.' His cry was forlorn as they left him there.

'It was Thomas?' Cwen asked as they hurried along the path.

'I think it must have been,' Hermitage explained. 'It was what the Grand Master said.'

'What he said?'

'Luck.'

'Yes,' Cwen confirmed, not seeing the point. 'He did say luck.'

'And Hartle said that it must have been a lucky hit for the metal warp to get Hemling right in the throat.'

'So?'

'So it wasn't luck at all, good or bad. Hemling never did get hit by the warp.'

'Erm,' Cwen sounded lost.

A Murder for Master Wat

'As you weavers have pointed out, a snapped warp would simply get tangled in the heddle.'

'You have been listening after all,' Hartle complimented him.

'Quite. A normal warp made of thread wouldn't have disturbed Hemling at all. As you have also told me, warps snap all the time.'

'Not if you've set your loom properly,' Hartle corrected.

Hermitage ignored the detail, which was a new experience for him. 'But a metal thread snapping and twanging would have surprised him no end. And, of course, there was always a chance that it would cause injury, in which case Thomas could step up and make it a lot worse for him. In the event the warp didn't kill him, the first person to attend him after he fell simply cut his throat.'

'Thomas,' Wat confirmed.

'The warp snapped, Hemling fell, Thomas rushed over, knocked him on the head to keep him quiet and then cut his throat while no one could see. I wondered why the lump was on the front of Hemling's head when he would have fallen backwards from the loom. Thomas then rushed out seeking aid for poor Hemling. The very same poor Hemling he had just murdered.'

'Why?' Cwen asked.

'The money,' Hermitage said with some contempt for such a base motive. 'All the money from the moot and the traders and the town. It would be a great temptation.'

'A great temptation for a master who was being kept out of the guild itself and had grown to hate them,' Hartle added.

'Oh, yes,' Hermitage smiled and nodded. 'That's a good motive. I hadn't thought that far yet.'

'The money that he has given back to the guild,' Cwen

pointed out. 'The money that's under the master's chair.'

'Is it?' Hermitage asked.

Cwen looked thoughtful. 'You mean, he lied?' she sounded quite disappointed that the killer was turning out to be dishonest as well.

'And Robert?' Wat asked.

'A loom maker?' Hermitage prompted.

'Ah, who better to fit a nice sharp metal warp with the right weight to snap?'

'Exactly.'

'So, they were in it together.'

'I believe so. Until there was some falling out and Thomas finished off Robert as well. Robert probably got too anxious about the plan to murder Hemling for the money and decided to warn the guild with his note. Thomas either killed him for betrayal or simply to keep more of the money.

'Even if the warp didn't kill Hemling, it was still a pretty suspicious thing to have on a loom,' Wat said.

'It would be, except Osbert had already written to the guild on the subject and was telling everyone about it. It could be what gave Robert and Thomas the idea. Make it look like an accident as Hemling tried out the wire, then blame Osbert for coming up with it in the first place. They could have been planning this for weeks, or months. How to kill Hemling for the moot money, but make it look like an accident with a loom?

'He even dragged me into it. Probably couldn't believe his luck, seeing a monk there just as he rushed out and announced the death. What better witness to confirm a horrible accident?'

'And if it was an accident, he could step in and carry on collecting the moot money.' Wat seemed quite impressed

A Murder for Master Wat

with this plan. 'Bit rash to just stick a knife in Robert then,' Wat suggested. 'Bound to draw attention, that sort of thing.'

'It was,' Hermitage pondered that. 'But if Robert was on the point of exposing Thomas, what else could be done? And we hear that Robert was an argumentative fellow. I gather you had dispute with him in your time.'

'I didn't do it,' Wat protested quickly. 'Don't you start on about me and murder, it's bad enough having the Grey Guild going around doing things in my name. Anyway, that was years ago, and Robert got his money.' Wat sounded despondent about this. Parting with money was always painful, even the memory of it after several years caused him to wince.

'I'm not saying you did do it,' Hermitage assured him. 'I'm just pointing out that Robert was prepared to argue over things like that.'

'He certainly was.'

'So, Thomas was not likely to have a calm discussion with Robert.'

'Hardly,' Wat accepted. 'But knowing Robert, I can't imagine him taking a knife in the chest without giving one back. Thomas must have surprised him. You know, stab first, have the discussion afterwards. That way you don't get any argument.'

While this fascinating but speculative discussion was taking place, the band of followers arrived back into the main area of the moot. Evening was now well established, the setting sun casting a rosy ambience across the place. A bit like blood, Hermitage thought, with a sigh.

He was not surprised to find that there was no sign of Thomas. He hadn't hoped that the suspected killer would be politely waiting for them, but perhaps Thomas would have slowed his pace, not wanting to be seen running through a crowd like an escaping murderer.

'He could be anywhere.' Cwen cast about.

Everyone looked hither and thither although it did seem that the members of the Grey Guild weren't entirely sure what was going on.

'He's probably halfway to Sneinton by now,' Shuttle shook his head.

No one else had any idea where that was, but it didn't sound good.

'We could ask people if they've seen him pass by,' Hermitage suggested.

'He's been here all along,' Cwen mocked the idea. 'No one would pay him any attention.'

'Perhaps the important thing is to let the guild know that none of this was anything to do with me?' Wat said. 'The Grey Guild may have been doing things in my name, but they were completely useless.' He shook his head at Shuttle. 'Which is quite embarrassing, really. If you have to have a band of desperate men calling out your name as they carry out their daring plans, you'd like there to be a bit of desperation and a touch of daring. I don't want the guild thinking that Hemling's death was anything to do that useless lot, or me. That sheriff in his castle won't care who he executes, but I'd rather it was someone else.'

'I suppose that is sensible,' Hermitage agreed.

'You suppose?' Wat sounded shocked at the lack of enthusiasm.

'No, no,' Hermitage corrected himself. 'I mean absolutely. We absolutely must go and clear all this up with the guild and the sheriff. It just seems a shame to let Thomas go like this.'

A Murder for Master Wat

'Not sure what he can do now,' Wat said. 'On the run from the moot and the guild. Hardly going to return to his workshop now he knows the King's Investigator is onto him.'

'Yes,' Hartle said, in a surprisingly sarcastic tone. 'What can poor old Thomas do with only sacks full of the moot's money to keep him company.'

Wat gave this thought. 'Perhaps we should go after him?'

'The guild,' Hermitage instructed. 'It won't take long to deal with them, not now that the Grand Master is stuck up a hill in his chair. I'll just tell them what the situation is and then we can decide what to do.'

Wat still seemed torn between saving his own life and chasing after a large sum of money. Cwen gave him a hefty shove towards the great hall and he moved along. He still looked about over the heads of the crowd to see if he could spot Thomas and the money. Or just the money.

The great hall squatted in the evening sun as if nothing was going on at all. It had doubtless seen more significant events than the odd dead weaver and so current events disturbed it not in the slightest. The people inside were still going about whatever business it was they did, and barely looked up as the troop entered.

'Well then,' Shuttle said, decisively. 'We'll, erm, leave you to it.'

Cwen snorted. 'Don't want to come and confront the wretched guild directly then? Issue your demands and insist on action?'

'We are more subtle than that,' Shuttle nodded as if containing a great secret behind his eyes.

'You go out and get on with being subtle then. The rest of us will stop taking any notice of you. Just like we were doing before.'

Shuttle ignored her and ushered his companions out of the hall once more, despite two of them issuing some rather vocal complaints about this course of action.

'I suppose that at least they're useless at everything,' Cwen said to the others. 'Weaving, resisting the guild, murder. Must be disappointing when you can't do anything right.'

Hermitage led the way back into the main room of the hall where it really did seem as if time had stood still. The chairs of the guild members were still at the far end, surrounded by the wreckage of their presence. Merchants and townsmen still talked quietly in corners. The aura of the place made Hermitage tread carefully across the floor so as not to cause a fuss.

As they drew up to the guild gathering, Hermitage noticed that the chairs had moved. Of course, with the Grand Master using his to sit halfway up the hill to the Norman castle, the others would have moved around to take up his space. It was rather like some sort of defensive rearrangement. Their lines had been breached and so they shuffled to keep out unwanted attention.

But there was also a new chair. It was off to the right and had obviously been brought in to compensate for the missing Grand Master. Hermitage was slightly surprised to find these people were capable of operating alone, without their leader to guide and issue instruction.

The new chair was similar to the others, doubtless brought up from some hall store when it was requested. It was another deep and comfortable looking construction, probably the only sort that guild men would tolerate. High sides and back rose above the head height of anyone sitting, only emphasising the impression that guild men did not like ordinary people having ready access to them.

A Murder for Master Wat

Hermitage stepped into the middle of the circled chairs and saw a face he recognised from his previous visit. He nodded his head in acknowledgement. 'We have news concerning the death of Master Hemling.'

'Harrumph,' said the guild man from the depths of his chair.

Hermitage had no idea what that meant, so just carried on. 'And we can confirm that it was nothing at all to do with Wat the Weaver.'

'That seems a rather rash conclusion,' the voice from the new chair spoke and Hermitage turned to face the speaker.

His mouth dropped open as he simply failed to comprehend what was going on.

'Thomas,' Wat said as if it was obvious all along that this would be Thomas.

Hermitage turned his open mouth to Wat.

'It's Thomas,' Wat explained.

Hermitage nodded but the mouth wouldn't shut now.

Thomas went on, ignoring the gaping monk. 'We've heard all about this terrible Grey Guild group who have been going around doing the most awful things in the name of Wat the Weaver.'

'They've been doing them awfully if that's what you mean.' Cwen had her arms folded and was trying to squeeze one of her best glares into the chair with Thomas.

'A few cut guy ropes and the wrong heddle sawed through,' Hartle explained. 'While someone else was going around killing people.' He made it quite clear, with a very hard stare, who that someone was.

'And our dear Grand Master taken,' Thomas shook his head and tutted.

'You can always go and get him,' Hartle suggested. 'You

know where he is.'

'All in good time,' Thomas replied, implying that the good time was some way off and if the Grand Master happened to come to some harm in the meantime that was just bad luck.

'Still,' Wat said, with a steely look of his own. 'At least the Grey Guild didn't kill Hemling.'

'Kill Hemling?' Thomas sounded appalled. Not genuinely appalled but he went through the motions. He sounded more smug than appalled. 'I understood that was a freak loom accident. I thought Wat the Weaver and Master Hartle confirmed the fact.'

'Until the King's Investigator worked out that Hemling had been struck on the head and had his throat cut. There was no way a metal warp could have done the job.'

'Tut, tut, tut,' Thomas shook his head. 'What awful times we live in.'

'And you were the one who rushed up to Hemling as soon as he fell.'

'Of course,' Thomas acknowledged. 'The exertion of the accident was obviously too much for him.'

'It was the exertion of you cutting his throat that was too much,' Wat said. 'And Robert the loom maker?' he made his own accusation very clear.

'Traders, eh?' Thomas sounded disappointed at the standards these people maintained. 'Probably stabbed over some dispute. It really is awful. And Hemling's accident cutting his throat like that. What bad luck.'

'I don't believe this,' Hartle looked at everyone around him. 'You killed Hemling and Robert and took the money. We all know that.'

Thomas's face became one of the utmost seriousness and threat. 'We know nothing of the sort Master Weaver.' He said "master weaver" as if it was only a very temporary appointment. 'And what money? The guild has all the money from the moot. I have no idea what you are talking about.'

Hermitage managed to shut his mouth now. He looked around the circle of very comfortable men, none of whom seemed to be showing the slightest interest in a tale of murder in their midst. 'And the note,' he said, as a new thought occurred to him. It was further speculation not supported by any evidence, but this seemed to be a day for that sort of thing. 'The note that arrived warning the guild about the killer. They didn't put it in the trunk because they never read it. They put it in the trunk because they already knew.

'They arranged all this with Thomas, who after all, does everything the guild wants. Nobody liked Hemling, that was clear. He was as difficult for the guild as for anyone else. And he was entitled to a lot of their money, according to the parchments. What better result, once the moot was well underway than for him to die? No more trouble, lots more money.' He almost gasped at his own suggestion. The best the guild men could manage was a quiet clearing of throats.

He had come across some awful people in his time. Awful killers, most of them, but there was awful killing and then there was this. The standards of behaviour on display here were too much to contemplate. Even other killers would be disappointed. But was there actually anything he could do about it?

'And Thomas comes out of it very well indeed,' Wat nodded and sounded as if this all made perfect sense. 'Helped poor Hemling in his dying moments, moments which Thomas brought with him into the tent.

'The guild have their money and he has a seat at the guild

table.' Wat even nodded acknowledgement of a game well played by Thomas. 'Except, if we were to get one of those new money-counting sorts of people,' he looked to Hermitage for the word.

'Aconter?' Hermitage said.

'Yes, one of them. If we got a counter to add up all the money, I think we'd find a lot more came in than ended up in the guild's coffers.'

Thomas waved this away with an insouciant hand.

'I expect the guild men in front of us to come out of this moot a lot richer than when they went in.' He narrowed his eyes at Thomas. 'Did they let you keep your share, or was that the price of the chair you're sitting in?' Wat nodded towards Thomas's chair, and the man shuffled comfortably in it. 'Hemling's chair,' Wat went on. 'The one that's suddenly become vacant.'

'But,' Hermitage started but didn't know where to finish. Wat looked at him to encourage the question. 'Thomas said that no one would want Hemling's job organising the moot as it was impossible to do.'

'Quite right,' Hartle confirmed. 'But there isn't going to be another moot, is there. Not for years, anyway. By that time there will be someone else in the guild who can do the job. Meanwhile, Master Thomas here sits and eats and drinks and lords it over the weaving world.'

'With purses full of money to come his way as a leader of the guild,' Wat added.

'With purses full of money,' Hartle agreed.

'And only two dead bodies in his wake,' Cwen was contemptuous.

None of this list of accusations appeared to have concerned the members of the guild in the slightest, apart from tickling their throats. In fact, one of the other men sitting in a chair was asleep once more.

Hermitage felt nothing but the most awful sadness that this seemed to be the way the world worked. Or at least how the Weavers' Guild worked. Who would have thought that a bit of weaving could be so corrupt and dangerous? Wat was right to want nothing to do with any of them. And there seemed little he could to do bring anyone to justice. Thomas was right, it could still be the case that Hemling's death was an accident, he couldn't prove anything.

'If you've finished?' Thomas asked as if this had all been an entertainment laid on by mummers. 'This Grey Guild now. That is a very serious matter.'

Hermitage really didn't think that the Grey Guild was a serious anything, particularly in the light of all the horrors that had just been revealed.

'They do seem to be a real trouble to the guild. And carrying out their wanton acts of destruction in the name of Wat the Weaver. I think this needs some serious attention.'

'You're not really going to try that?' Wat half laughed.

'The guild can't let things like that go on.' Thomas looked sorry that he was going to have to deal with them.

Hermitage felt as if he was in the presence of someone truly evil. Someone who had done wrong, the most profound wrong there was, but who seemed to have not the slightest awareness that he had so much as sneezed in polite company. Not only had this man murdered and stolen, but he was also now suggesting that he was going to do more of it. And all just to get what he wanted. This could not stand. Was there something he could do? Did he dare? In the face of Thomas, he dared do things he hadn't dreamed of. Facts were what he lived by, and investigated by, and now he didn't have any.

Facts never seemed to bother other people the way they did him. They just ploughed along, blindly confident, despite the fact they were in the wrong. He wondered how they managed to do that without stumbling to a complete standstill. Now was the time to find out.

'May I?' he said, as he wandered through the circle and sat on the top of the trunk.

Everyone looked at him with surprise, even Wat, Cwen and Hartle.

He took a breath and felt more nervous about what he was going to do than he had about anything. His friends were there with him, but if this went wrong, he was not sure there was anything they'd be able to do. 'There's just one problem with all this,' he said.

Caput XXIV: What's the Expression?

'And what would that be? Brother Monk,' Thomas asked, with some contempt.

'King's Investigator,' Hermitage corrected, politely. His nervousness and deep desire not to do what he was now doing, was tempered by the face of Thomas, who he saw as one of the most awful people he had ever come across. He needed sight of the man if he was going to carry this off.

'If you don't mind,' he asked, nicely. 'It is a troublesome title and many times have I wished that I was not burdened with it.' He gave them all a weak smile. 'But what can you do when King William himself appoints you? And summons you to attend upon murders and all sorts of awful goings-on.'

Thomas was looking a little more cautious now.

'Summons you personally,' Hermitage explained as if it was all ghastly, which it was. 'Into his presence, at his beck and call.'

'And Le Pedvin,' Wat prompted. 'Don't forget Le Pedvin.'

'Ah,' Hermitage sighed. 'Who can forget Le Pedvin? A most appalling fellow,' he confided in Thomas and the guild. 'Just seems to want to kill everyone. You know, I am sure that he will only be happy when everyone in the world is dead. And then he'll probably kill himself, just to tidy up.'

'As if it wasn't bad enough being called to deal with murder, I have to report to the king afterwards so that he can deal with it. Finish things off, as it were.' He thought that he lent the words "finish things off" a nice tone, but he didn't know if anyone else picked it up.

From the look on Thomas's face, he had picked it up very well indeed.

'Of course, the sheriff is William's representative here,' Hermitage went on. 'William Peverel already knows that there has been one death. At this very moment, he's probably wondering what a Saxon guild master is doing sitting in a chair outside his castle.'

Thomas actually shifted in his own chair. 'I'm sure we don't need to bother the sheriff,' he said, although he sounded a lot less sure of himself now.

'I'm not sure we have much choice,' Hermitage sounded as if he would really like not to go to the sheriff but his hands were tied. 'After all, he knows the King's Investigator is here and will doubtless want to know everything so that he can reassure his king.'

'And Le Pedvin,' Wat added, with a wide smile.

'And Le Pedvin,' Hermitage nodded sorry agreement. 'And the Normans just like action, generally. They seldom bother with reasoning, or argument or discussion. Straight in, burn everything to the ground, kill everyone. It's so disappointing.'

'So, erm,' Thomas sounded only vaguely engaged with the problem as if it didn't really matter. 'What do you suggest, erm, Master King's Investigator.'

'Ah, well,' Hermitage considered the ground in front of him. 'If it was up to me, which of course it isn't,' he held his hands up indicating that he was only being blown by the winds of necessity. 'If it was up to me I'd probably ask the Grey Guild to bring the Grand Master back as quickly as they could. I'd then probably have a long chat with them about what their complaints are. You know, see if masters really are treating apprentices badly? I hear that there is the most terrible fellow in erm, where was it?' he asked.

'Winchester,' Cwen said, smiling herself.

'Just so, Winchester. I can't imagine that is the sort of

person the great Weavers' Guild would want to be associated with.'

Thomas was quiet but not looking very happy at all.

'And I'm sure, when I next see King William, he will be most pleased to hear that the Weavers' Guild is putting their house in order.'

Thomas squirmed.

'Then of course there's the weregild for the deaths of Hemling and Robert.' Hermitage went on as if listing problems that were nothing to do with him.

'The what?' Thomas protested.

'Oh, I know the Normans don't believe in such things, they prefer letting the sword distribute justice, but then these were only Saxons who died. And died during the moot of the weavers' guild. I imagine you feel an enormous sense of responsibility.'

The look on Thomas's face said that he felt no such thing.

'I further imagine Hemling and Robert had family somewhere. Or the money could go to their home town? And if even that is not possible then the local churches here would welcome the donations.

'Donations?' Thomas squeaked as if he found the word deeply offensive.

'Of course. The king is a very devout fellow, always consulting priests and the Pope and such. Not that he behaves in a very Christian manner when it comes to dealing with people, but I suppose we must give him some credit.' Now Hermitage didn't even believe himself.

'Weregild?' Thomas checked.

'Now that you are a leading figure in that guild and all,' Hermitage acknowledged Thomas's new position. 'Unless, of course,' he looked questioningly at Thomas. 'You really did have something to do with the deaths?'

'Of course not,' Thomas snapped. He breathed very heavily through gritted teeth. 'Anything else?'

Hermitage considered the ceiling of the great hall and listed points with his fingers. 'Recover the master, discuss with the Grey Guild, deal with the master in Winchester, weregild for the deaths. Perhaps donations to the church as well. That would be good.'

Thomas was making some very odd noises now as if something inside him was about to do something unexpected.

'Ah, of course,' Hermitage snapped his fingers. 'Dear Wat, here,' he nodded towards Wat, who returned the bow in a very formal manner. 'No question of Wat being associated with any of the sorry goings-on here. After all, he really didn't have anything to do with it.

'And, of course, the king would probably miss him, next time we are both summoned to investigate. I can only imagine the trouble I will have. "Where's the weaver?" King William will demand. "Oh, Majesty," I will have to say, "Master Thomas of the Weavers' Guild has done something awful". "Summon Master Thomas of the weavers' guild," the king will say. He's like that, you know. Summoning people and the like.'

'And they tend to vanish after they've been summoned,' Cwen added, for completeness.

Hermitage noticed that Thomas was gripping the sides of his chair as if he could rip them off with his bare hands, and was boiling so hard with internal rage that there was a danger he would set light to it. He thought perhaps he'd better stop now. He smiled at them all.

A Murder for Master Wat

...

'Brother Hermitage, King's Investigator, I am proud of you.' Wat patted Hermitage on the back as they left the Great Moot of Nottingham behind them. Left it with a huge sense of relief as far as Hermitage was concerned. He really was going to stay in Wat's workshop and not go anywhere from now on. If he avoided the world completely, it couldn't go on killing people whenever he passed by.

The apprentices had been safely gathered in, the two new recruits, Edward and Edward, bubbling with excitement at their prospects. At least the young men of Wat's workshop seemed to have had a far more routine moot than Hermitage had experienced. They'd all got drunk, been sick and couldn't remember anything they'd done that had anything to do with weaving.

'I'm not very proud of myself,' Hermitage replied. 'What an awful way to behave. And Thomas is a killer, as we all know.'

'Know but can't prove,' Cwen pointed out. 'You could always go back and tell the sheriff that Thomas did it. I'm sure he'd deal with him if you asked. You know.' She made crude gestures that indicated someone having their head removed.

Hermitage frowned at such an awful suggestion. 'As you say, I have no proof,' he said, firmly. He thought that this fact would be enough to dissuade Cwen from such a terrible idea. Then he looked at her and saw that it had done no such thing. 'I can't condemn a man with no proof.'

'Doesn't stop the Normans,' Hartle observed.

'Still, you sorted it all out very nicely,' Wat congratulated him. 'Yes, you had no proof but you left Thomas without a place to turn and a set of instructions to do the right thing. We weavers have an expression for something like that.'

'Really?'

'Yes, it describes when you've finished a work and everything's bundled together into a nice neat parcel for sending to the customer. You know, tightly packaged so it won't come apart.'

'Oh yes, and what's the expression?'

'Stitched up,' said Wat the Weaver.

Finis

Brother Hermitage carries on with a murder all of his own:

A Murder For Brother Hermitage.

Read the first chapter below:

A Murder for Brother Hermitage

by

Howard of Warwick

Caput I: Death of a Monk

The monastery cloister collected darkness as if hoarding it for a time when it was going to come in useful. The middle of this heavily clouded night had plenty of darkness to go round and so the cloister piled it up in corners where it got quite deep.

There was a full moon up there somewhere, but it clearly wanted nothing to do with the goings-on in this cloister, on this night.

In one pool, of the particularly deep and dark variety, a monk quivered. This monk generally liked cloisters and monasteries, even though they weren't the friendliest of places. A cloister at night could be marvellous, free, as it should be, from any other monks; or priors, abbots, priests, novices and anyone else who had business being there. He tended to get on well with the buildings, not so much with the people.

It was unfair to tarnish everyone, and he was always scrupulous in his fairness. He had to admit that the abbot had welcomed him. Abbot Abbo had invited him to visit, for goodness sake. It would be a bit much for the abbot to encourage a visit and then be all difficult about it.

But Abbo had other duties, he couldn't spend all his time with his visitor; or any of his time, it seemed. The invitation in the first place, and the subsequent distance the man kept, led the monk to the conclusion that it was unlikely to be the abbot who was stalking him around the cloister in the middle of the night.

He tried to tell himself that the suggestion of stalking was completely unjustified. It was pure coincidence that someone else had entered the cloister at this late hour. Someone who

A Murder for Brother Hermitage

hadn't announced themselves, or come over to say good evening, and who seemed to be making great efforts not to be spotted.

If it was the case that some other Brother wanted to make use of the place, he only had to say so. The monk in the dark would go happily back to his cell and leave the new arrival to get up to whatever he wanted in the dark of the cloister. There might even be several of them. The monk had suspicions about what some brothers got up to in the dark of cloisters. Well, he knew it was suspicious, as it generally involved a lot of noise and a refusal to discuss the matter. What it actually was, he had not a clue. He didn't want to ask, and further suspected that he didn't want to know.

Whoever the new arrival was, he was subtle and discreet. The monk had been whiling away these quiet hours considering how many bones the prophet Ezekiel had actually seen in Chapter thirty-seven, verses one to four. Obviously, the valley in question was full of bones, and they were dry bones at that. But how big was the valley? It was the sort of topic that might make a fascinating conclave. All he had to do was find some other brothers who were as interested in resolving the question. He gave up that idea straight away.

It was then that he had noticed the first movement.

To begin with, he thought that it might be some animal of the night, scampering about the place, looking for something to eat. A simple mouse, scratching at a door or doing battle with a particularly large and obstreperous beetle. But then the noise came from another part of the cloister altogether. This would have to be a mouse with remarkably long legs; or one that had just been carried away by a giant, scuttling beetle. He told himself to calm down, as he started to worry about the beetle coming back for him.

A flicker of darkness against a background of greater darkness had convinced him that he was not the only person in the cloister this night. But that was no problem; he would simply sit still and quiet and let this new companion go about his business. As soon as the business developed into anything unnecessary, he would make his excuses. Except, of course, as soon as he had sat still for a moment he realised that he should have made himself known straight away. It was too late now to stand up and apologise for being there.

When no one else arrived to join the other presence, the monk thought that it was simply another contemplative brother who sought the peace of the cloister. He quickly concluded that this was nonsense. He'd only been here a few days but already knew that any contemplative and peaceful brothers would have been driven out of this place years ago. No, this was a monk up to something. And monks up to something were best avoided.

Doing his own version of subtle and discreet, the monk had left his seat and moved down the cloister, towards the exit and his cell. He knew he was being ridiculous, but he felt it was too awkward to make noise and pretend he hadn't noticed anyone. He felt, rather than saw the motion that cut off his escape and forced him to retreat to the pool of darkness in which he had begun his quivering.

The next rational thought was that this brother probably wanted nothing to do with him. The poor fellow doubtless thought he would have the cloister to himself and was now just as awkwardly trying to find a way out of the situation without being noticed. The silly pair could end up spending hours carefully navigating their way around one another. No, this situation simply needed him to speak up. He could pretend that he had been buried so deep in Ezekiel's bones that he hadn't noticed the other arrive.

Rational thought put carefully to one side, he cowered and did some more quivering. Soon, he became resigned to spending the entire night in his deep, dark pool while the other got on with whatever he wanted.

Ah, blessed relief, the new arrival cleared his throat. Well, that was fine then. The universal expression of embarrassed discomfort had been made and both men could now cough and bluster their way out of this place, and then spend the next day pretending that they'd never met, or ever been in a cloister at all.

But the cough was followed, and the monk wished that the deep of his dark pool would swallow him completely.

'I know you're there,' the coughing voice said with great confidence.

The monk would have stood and announced himself at this point if there hadn't been something off-putting about the voice. The words were spoken by one who had found just what he was looking for and could now get on with exactly what he'd been planning to do all along.

Whatever that plan was, it wasn't a good one; the monk was sure of that. At least the cough and the words had not been right in his ear, which would have scared the habit off the monk. It sounded as if they were away, across the cloister, but as he was crouched down with his head on his knees, it was hard to judge.

'It's no good hiding in the dark,' the voice went on.

Well, the monk would have to disagree with that proposition. Hiding in the dark seemed to be an excellent response to this situation. He had no experience of encounters with monks who were looking for you in dark cloisters but felt that one who said it was no good hiding in the dark, probably meant that it was no good for you.

'You're wanted,' the voice now explained.

Ah, that could be quite reasonable. Perhaps the abbot wanted to consult him on something at this late hour and had sent a messenger.

The urge to respond was overwhelming, but a nagging doubt controlled the urge and told it to wait a moment.

'Wanted? You're supposed to say. Wanted by whom?' The voice even changed its pitch as it took on both sides of the conversation. The monk in the dark was sure that his voice wasn't quite so high and feeble sounding.

'Wanted by whom? I say. Then you say, yes, wanted by whom? And I say, no one. You're wanted by no one, and that's why I'm here. Ha ha.'

This nonsense annoyed the monk more than anything. Being pursued by a brain-addled brother in the middle of the night really was too much. But then brain-addled monks were seldom dangerous; apart from the dangerous ones. He swallowed.

'Come on, come on,' the voice now urged. 'There's only so many corners in a cloister you know.'

The monk did know, there were four. He was hiding in one of them, so that left three. And the cloister was a simple square. If this strange brother-in-the-dark really did try to find him, they could just end up going round and round until dawn. Unless the follower could run faster than the monk, which was a strong possibility.

'Oh, enough of this,' the voice in the dark called out, impatiently. 'Where are you?'

The monk now heard quiet footsteps moving across the flagstones. As best he could tell, they were some way away, probably on the other side of the cloister courtyard. It was hard to tell as the steps were careful and cautious and the walls of the place disturbed the passage of the sound.

There was one quality to the paces that did get the monk's attention and bothered his curiosity. This feature also gave him the courage to stand from his crouched position and take his own step, back towards the exit.

'Ah, there you are,' his follower called.

With his ears now elevated above the floor, the monk was gratified to confirm that the voice was on the opposite side of the cloister.

The monk took his own careful steps towards the way out. The steps on the far side followed, caution abandoned.

If the monk hadn't been willing to speak up at first, the steps following him demanded that he say something, natural human sympathy getting in the way of common sense. 'Are you all right?' he asked, gently.

'What do you mean by that?' the voice snapped.

'Oh, nothing, nothing,' the monk replied, embarrassed. 'It's just that, well, I mean, I noticed your, erm, steps were, ah. Never mind. It's nothing.'

'You mean my limp?' The voice was all demanding anger now. 'Have you got something to say about my limp?'

'Oh, no, no. Nothing at all. Not a thing. Just that I noticed, that's all.' The monk used these moments to take quick steps forward, hoping to find the way out quite quickly.

'I've got a limp, all right.' The voice was clearly quite used to addressing this topic. 'Do you know how I got this limp?'

Well, of course, the monk didn't know how the man had got his limp. He didn't even know who the fellow was, and until he'd heard the paces had no idea that his gait was uneven. As he gave it some thought, he couldn't even recall any other brother in the monastery who had a limp. From the tone of the question, he knew that he was going to be told how the fellow got his limp, whether he wanted to know or not.

'The Battle of Hastings,' the voice said, with some pride.

'Battle of Hastings?' the monk couldn't help asking.

'When we fought off the Norman invaders.' It sounded as if the pursuer had stopped for a moment of happy reminiscence.

'Is that what they're calling it? I thought it wasn't actually at Hastings.' The monk didn't like to mention that fighting off the Normans had been spectacularly unsuccessful, in that the Normans were not, in fact, off.

The voice was heavy and insistent. 'The Battle of Hastings,' it stated, for the record.

'Ah.' The monk didn't want to engage in a debate on the nomenclature of battles; it really wasn't his area. What he really wanted was to leave, but it was so dark he was having trouble working out where he was. Being pursued in the dark by a limping, brain-addled monk didn't help his concentration.

'Took a wound defending the country, I did. Defending it from the scourge of the Normans.'

'Very good.' The monk tried to sound supportive and impressed at the same time.

'Except they tricked us,' the voice complained.

'Did they?' The monk turned his head and called over his shoulder, hoping to sound as if he wasn't moving as quickly as he could.

'We won,' the voice declared.

There was no way the monk was going to stop to contradict this blatant error. He'd let the man discuss the matter with King William or one of the Norman overlords. He was sure they'd sort it out in no time at all.

'The king withdrew from the field of victory and then the Normans said that they'd won.'

The monk felt that some reply on this point was expected. 'Outrageous,' he said.

'And what with the king being wounded and all, there wasn't anyone to stop them.'

The monk didn't like to point out that this sounded very much like a Norman victory.

'And that's where I took my wound.'

In the pause that followed, the monk could sense that his hunter was standing nodding to himself as he recalled the happy moment of getting his leg sliced by some sword or arrow.

'I bet you haven't got a wound,' the voice accused. 'Well, have you?'

'Erm,' the monk sounded as if he was thinking about this for a moment, while in fact, he was desperately looking for the door that he knew was here somewhere. 'I don't think so.'

'No, I don't think so either. Bloody monks.'

'Are you not a monk then?' This statement worried the monk more than the fact that someone was chasing him around a dark cloister.

'Me, ha!' The voice seemed to find this idea quite funny. 'They wouldn't have me.'

Now, the monk knew he was in trouble. Anyone so depraved, dangerous or insane that even the lowliest monastery wouldn't have him should be avoided at all times; let alone in a dark cloister.

He knew that most monasteries were quite selective about who they took. Moneyed younger sons of the nobility were best, but after that, it would need to be people prepared to work and follow their devotions. But there were lots of monasteries in the land. Moneyed sons of the nobility were in pretty short supply and the establishments lower down the order could get desperate and would take anyone who was capable of digging vegetables.

And then there were the truly Christian places that took the sick and the feeble.

Of course, this fellow had only said that the monasteries wouldn't have him. Perhaps he'd never asked. In which case, what was he doing in one at this time of night?

'Can't fight for the king anymore, monasteries won't have me; now I do favours for people if you know what I mean.'

The monk did know what doing a favour meant. He couldn't immediately reconcile this with the current situation.

'Someone's got a problem they need sorting out, they come to me. And pay me well.' The voice sounded quite proud of this, the contradiction of payment for favours seeming to have passed him by.

'Well done,' the monk replied, thinking that supporting this man in his efforts to improve his lot might be best in these circumstances.

'And you're the problem I'm sorting out today.'

'Me?' The monk was truly puzzled. He'd never been a problem to anyone, let alone strangers in cloisters at night.

'Made a lot of enemies, you have.'

The monk paused and gave this some serious thought. He couldn't immediately think of any.

'And they want you gone.'

'I shall go then,' the monk responded promptly, thinking that he would be quite happy to leave.

A Murder for Brother Hermitage

'Not that sort of gone. Properly gone. For good, gone.'

'Good gone?' the monk was getting lost.

'Absolutely. Glad you understand.'

The monk didn't understand immediately but soon did. 'Good God. You mean…,'

'That's it,' the voice sounded content that they both understood the situation now.

'You can't be serious.'

'I can,' the voice sounded offended at the implication of levity.

The monk really couldn't believe what he was hearing. There had to be some argument to make this whole situation go away. 'But the limp?'

'What about the limp?' The voice was angry once more.

'Oh, er, nothing really. It's just that, well, I don't have a limp, and you do.'

'Meaning?'

'Meaning that you find moving about much more of a trial than I do. Due to your courageous action, of course.'

'Your point being?'

'Well, not wanting to offend, but I can move quicker than you, I suspect. And we are in a dark cloister, which just goes round in a square.'

The expression "round in a square" would have fascinated him for days in other circumstances. He had rather more practical matters to trouble him at present.

'So?'

'So, if I move around the square you will have to come after me, but I will always be ahead.' The monk couldn't believe that he was inviting this limping, brain-addled killer to chase him around the cloister. 'And with your unfortunate injury, it is unlikely that you'll catch me.'

'Ah, I see.' The voice was content that he understood the proposal.

'Well, that's good.'

'Yes, I see your error.'

'Error?' The monk couldn't see an error, but he felt that a significant one was about to be explained.

'Yes, error. You're forgetting about the crossbow.'

'Crossbow?' The monk managed to squeak and swallow at the same time. He was in no mood to point out that he could hardly forget something he'd never been told about in the first place.

'Of course. You're quite right, there's no point a fellow with a leg that barely works trying to chase people. That would be ridiculous. No, a man in my position would have to organise a pretty fundamental advantage over their opponent.'

The monk was now very worried that the conclusion about brain-addlement may have been presumptuous.

'And in my case, it's a crossbow. Very handy Norman invention, I think. Have you ever seen one?'

'Just the once,' the monk managed to say.

'Nice, aren't they? But what with it being very dark and all, you're probably not going to get the chance to look at another one now.'

'But it is very dark,' the monk pointed out, deciding that crouching down again would be a good idea now. 'To shoot someone in the dark would be a very difficult task.'

'I agree,' the voice concurred. 'That's why I get paid so much.'

The monk heard a click.

A Murder for Brother Hermitage

The whole book is available now if you simply have to find out what's going on...

Printed in Dunstable, United Kingdom